Victoria awoke with a start and sat up in her bed. Her slumber had been disturbed by that hauntingly familiar feeling: someone was there in the darkness . . . waiting . . . whispering evil intentions.

Straining her eyes, she peered into the shadows that danced in rhythm with the wind-whipped branches outside her window. "Who's there?" she whispered. Moonlight filtered through the sheer curtains of her bedroom, casting its muted silver rays on her face. "Who are you? What do you want?"

But Victoria didn't have to ask. Deep in the recesses of her mind . . . she knew.

Gwendolynn Arden, author of *Moonlight Obsession,* is an established romance writer from the Los Angeles area. Her fans have come to expect the tender sensuality and the unique brand of humor that she brings to her novels.

From the editor's desk . . .

Dear Friend,

Captivating . . . exciting . . . heartwarming!
These are but a few of the comments we've
received from *Soaps & Serials* readers. We're
delighted. Every month the fine writers and edi-
tors at Pioneer pool all their resources to bring
you spectacular new books.

Based on actual scripts from ONE LIFE TO
LIVE, each novel is written with you in mind.
Soaps & Serials takes you back to the very beginning of the show, revealing the innocent and
infamous pasts of your favorite characters, re-
creating cherished moments from your favorite
episodes. And though each book is a complete,
satisfying read, our sensational cliffhanger ending
is just a hint of the drama that will unfold in next
month's *Soaps & Serials* book.

We hope you enjoy this special 2-books-in-1
edition of ONE LIFE TO LIVE. Look for future
volumes of this series in the coming months. If
you are interested in other *Soaps & Serials* novelizations but have been unable to find the books in
your local book source, please see the order form
inserted in this book.

For *Soaps & Serials*,

Rosalind Noonan

Rosalind Noonan
Editor-in-Chief

ONE LIFE TO LIVE

1&2

Moonlight Obsession

ONE LIFE TO LIVE™ is a trademark of American Broadcasting Companies, Inc.

PIONEER COMMUNICATIONS NETWORK, INC.

Moonlight Obsession

ONE LIFE TO LIVE ® paperback novels are published and distributed by Pioneer Communications Network, Inc.

Soaps & Serials® is a registered trademark of Pioneer Communications Network, Inc.

Cover art by Renato Aime

ISBN: 1-55726-400-7

Printed in Canada

10 9 8 7 6 5 4 3 2 1

Between the Lines

While Agnes Nixon was impressing viewers and producers with her innovative storylines on NBC's ANOTHER WORLD, the "powers that be" at ABC approached her with a tempting proposition. Could she create a new and exciting property for their network—something that had never been done before?

Tired of having her hands tied by producers who insisted on the strict soap opera formula of portraying only white, middle-class professionals in dramatic situations, Ms. Nixon jumped at the chance. She created a serial called BETWEEN HEAVEN AND HELL, which featured families from various socio-economic backgrounds. The conflicts and relationships that occurred among these diverse characters provided engrossing, realistic plots. ABC enthusiastically endorsed the concept with one important change: the name BETWEEN HEAVEN AND HELL was deemed too racy. The network finally settled on the name ONE LIFE TO LIVE . . . and the rest is history.

Moonlight Obsession

Book
One

Chapter
One

The doorknob creaked as she twisted it, causing Karen Martin to wince and cast furtive glances up and down the hospital corridor. If there was anything worse than eavesdropping, it was getting caught eavesdropping.

But the hallway was deserted, and so was the nurses' station at the far end. Between breakfast and lunch, the high points of the day, there wasn't much activity in Llanview's only hospital.

Slowly she pulled open the heavy door and tiptoed into the musty semidarkness of the stairwell. Her white rubber-soled nurse's shoes squeaked on the freshly mopped floor. But nobody heard her. Dr. Hale and Dr. Wolek had already climbed to the landing above, and their angry voices ricocheted off the cement walls around her.

"What kind of man are you? What kind of doctor?" demanded a voice that was intimately familiar to her.

"She's not my patient."

"No, but she's supposed to be the woman you love."

"Loved." The word fairly dripped with bitterness.

"If you'd really loved her, you wouldn't even consider telling her a thing like that. Think what it will do to her."

"It'll keep her from marrying you. And that's what you're worried about, isn't it, Wolek?"

There was a heavy silence that lasted only seconds, but it seemed much longer as Karen strained her ears to hear Dr. Wolek's reply. She inched along the wall, craning her neck and looking upward, hoping to catch a peek at them without being seen herself.

Then she heard footsteps below, coming toward her. It was too late to make it to the door. *Just act cool,* she thought as she tried to arrange her arms and legs in a nonchalant pose. *Just hang loose.*

"Karen, what are you doing?" Dr. Price Trainor asked as he reached the landing where she stood. His dark eyes searched her face, and she felt a guilty flush rise to her cheeks.

"Ah . . . nothing," she whispered and glanced up the staircase.

Another angry shout echoed down around them.

"If you don't care about her as a person, think about her health. This could cause a relapse."

Dr. Trainor leaned toward Karen and a conspiratorial grin lit his handsome black face. "Are you listening when you should be working, Nurse Martin? Aren't there some bedpans out there with your name on them?"

"Sh-h-h . . ." She pressed her finger to her lips. "It's Dr. Hale and Dr. Wolek. They're really having it out about something."

"Then it's *their* business . . . and their *patient's* business. It certainly isn't yours." With one hand on her forearm he propelled her toward the door.

"But—but—" she protested as another volley of angry exchanges, punctuated by profanities, drifted down the staircase.

"You're not going to do this!"

"And who's going to stop me? You?"

"I swear I'll kill you before I'll let you tell her that."

Trainor froze at the door, his hand on Karen's arm. This was no ordinary doctors' disagreement over patient care.

"Wait here," he whispered as he released her arm and started up the staircase to investigate.

Before he had taken three steps there was

a scraping of feet on the floor directly above their heads, the sounds of a scuffle, more curses, and a cry.

A second later Ted Hale tumbled head-long down the staircase toward them.

Karen screamed and plastered herself to the wall, her hand clasped over her mouth.

Trainor sprinted up the staircase, dived for the falling man—and missed.

Hale landed in a crumpled heap on the landing at Karen's feet. His body and limbs were twisted in impossible angles, a pool of blood already forming around his head.

Trainor, momentarily stunned with shock, rushed to help his fellow doctor, to go through the motions of trying to save a life hanging from a thread.

Karen looked up to the top of the stairs and saw Dr. Wolek standing there. Larry Wolek, a man she had loved, now a stranger . . . a stranger whose eyes blazed with blue fire in his ashen face. "Oh, God, Larry. You killed him!"

After a crazed shuffle during which the two doctors and the nurse scurried about in an attempt to save the life of their colleague, Hale was rushed to the emergency room.

Larry backed away as the E.R. team took over. His head was spinning, beginning to throb in confusion over the events of the past few minutes.

"Larry!" Meredith Lord rushed up to his side, her voice shaking with barely controlled hysteria. "What happened? Are you all right?"

"Merrie, what are you doing here?" Larry opened his arms and Meredith flew into his embrace, burying her ashen face against his chest. Neither of them noticed the startled expressions of Dr. Trainor and the nurses who rushed about the emergency room, working frantically to save Ted Hale's life.

"Excuse me, Larry," said Price Trainor, turning his attention from his patient for a moment, "but could you take Merrie outside? We're a bit busy in here—"

"Yes, of course."

With his arm around her waist Larry led Meredith from the emergency room and into a public waiting room.

"Oh, Larry," she breathed, clinging to him. "I thought you were dead. I was in the parking lot and I saw you through the window . . . you and somebody else. You were fighting there on the staircase and I saw you fall—or I thought it was you."

Larry glanced around the waiting room at its occupants, a teenage girl playing solitaire at a table in one corner and an elderly man reading a weekly tabloid in the other. Neither appeared to be listening. "Here, sit down, Merrie." He guided her toward a sofa covered in cracked green vinyl, speckled with round cigarette burns. Sitting beside her, he wrapped his arm around her shoulder and pulled her to his side.

"I'm so glad it wasn't you," she said, cuddling against him. "I couldn't see very well through that window, it was so dirty. Who were you quarreling with? Who fell down the stairs?"

He pressed a kiss to the top of her honey-gold hair, closed his eyes, and sighed deeply before replying. "It was Ted, Merrie."

She pulled back from him, her amber eyes wide with shock. "Ted! Oh, no! Is he the one they're working on in there now?"

Larry nodded.

"Is he going to be all right?"

"They're doing all they can," he replied evasively.

"You didn't answer my question. Is Ted going to live?"

Larry looked around the room again, noting the faded green and gold paisley wallpaper. *That damned stuff should be stripped off and something decent hung,* he thought. *Hospital waiting rooms are depressing enough without having to look at these awful walls.*

He shook his head as though trying to rearrange his jumbled thoughts. He wondered at the stupid things that ran through a person's mind at a time like this. Looking down at Merrie, he felt a rush of tenderness for this fragile woman with the brandy-colored eyes. When had he first begun loving her? He couldn't even remember.

"No, Merrie," he said gently. "I don't think Ted is going to live."

Her lower lip trembled, and she bit down hard on it. "Oh, Larry," she whispered. "What happened?"

He swallowed and felt his Adam's apple move against his collar, which seemed to be getting tighter by the moment. Silently he cursed himself for the lie he was about to tell her. "I don't know, Merrie. I don't remember."

"What do you mean, you don't remember?"

He saw the disbelief register on her pretty heart-shaped face. He had never seen disbelief and suspicion in her eyes before.

He lowered his face to hers and kissed her soft lips. As long as he was kissing her, he wouldn't have to look into her eyes.

From the hallway Karen Martin watched. Her heart burned when she saw the way he held Merrie—rich, spoiled Meredith Lord, who already had everything. She didn't need Larry, didn't love him the way Karen did.

Karen seethed as he wrapped his arms around Merrie. He had once kissed *her* that way . . . and not too long ago.

She felt a pain in her chest, a deep searing

pain, as though she were being stabbed by a rusty knife with a broken blade. She allowed the pain to have its moment—but only a short moment.

Karen Martin had never been one to wallow in hurt. Anger was much more her style.

And revenge was her antidote.

"Since when does the Llanview Police Department investigate simple accidents?" Larry Wolek asked Lieutenant Jack Neal, a gigantic black man whose size was intimidating enough without the ominous scowl that pulled his bushy eyebrows into one solid black line.

Lieutenant Neal's dark eyes scanned the waiting room, noting in one quick glance Meredith Lord's ghastly pallor, Karen Martin's self-satisfied sneer and, most of all, Dr. Larry Wolek's defensive stance.

Wolek stood nearly as tall as Neal's own six-feet-four, his body ramrod straight, his arms crossed over his chest. Lieutenant Neal had seen a lot of men with something to hide, and Larry Wolek looked guilty as sin.

"Normally I wouldn't be investigating. But I've heard allegations that this was no simple accident, Dr. Wolek." His words hung in the silence of the waiting room like a red flag of challenge.

Neal saw the contemptuous look that Wolek shot in Karen Martin's direction, and he jotted it down in his mental notebook.

Larry Wolek met Neal's gaze eye to eye. "And did this informant of yours actually witness the accident?" he asked.

"I'm here to *ask* questions, not *answer* them. I need a moment alone with you, Dr. Wolek." With a wave of his giant hand he dismissed the women. "I'd like to speak to you later, Miss Martin."

"Lieutenant Neal, may I stay with Larry?" Although Meredith's brown eyes were soft and pleading, Neal was long accustomed to denying plaintive requests.

But his tone was uncharacteristically gentle when he said, "I'm sorry, Miss Lord. I need to speak to Dr. Wolek alone. It shouldn't take long."

"It's okay, Merrie. Don't worry." Larry smoothed her gold hair with his palm and turned her toward the door. "Go have a cup of coffee in the cafeteria. I'll join you when we're finished here."

Neal wondered at Wolek's apparent concern for Meredith Lord. Obviously he was in love with her. Considering the deep trouble Wolek was in, he should have been more concerned about himself than her.

"Is Miss Lord your girlfriend?" Neal asked as soon as Meredith left the waiting room.

"I don't see how that pertains to this situation," Larry replied curtly.

Neal frowned, and his black eyes flashed briefly under drawn brows. "You're not exactly scoring points with your lousy attitude, Wolek."

When Larry didn't answer, Neal reached into the breast pocket of his blue polyester leisure suit, pulled out a pack of cigarettes, and lit one. He drew in a chestful of smoke and held it for what seemed like forever as Larry watched enviously.

"Want one?" Neal asked.

"No. I quit . . . yesterday," he added bitterly. "Great timing, huh?"

Neal replaced the cigarettes. "So, what were you and Dr. Hale fighting about just before he decided to do those double back flips down the stairs?"

"I don't remember," Larry mumbled as he watched the second hand of the clock on the wall inch past noon. He ventured a look at Neal and saw that his dark eyes were glittering with indignation.

"What kind of a fool do you take me for?" Neal growled. "It happened less than three hours ago. You don't really expect me to believe that you've forgotten that quickly, do you?"

Larry pulled at a loose thread in the seam of his brown tweed slacks. He tugged at it carefully, then snapped it off and twisted it around his forefinger. "Ted Hale is my friend," he said. "I'm still in shock from seeing him take that fall. Maybe I'll remember later . . . after the shock wears off."

"Yeah, and maybe George Wallace will beat Nixon and Humphrey this November. Or maybe your buddy, Ted, is gonna kick the bucket and you'll find yourself in jail, charged with first-degree murder. Suppose that might jar your memory a bit?"

Neal stood, tossed his cigarette onto the worn linoleum, and ground it out with the heel of his wing-tip shoe. "You'll talk to me, Wolek. One way or the other, you'll talk."

Larry rose and followed Neal as he stomped toward the door. "Wait."

The lieutenant turned at the doorway. "Yeah?"

Wolek took a deep breath. "Ted fell. I didn't push him."

"I don't believe you."

"I'm sorry, but it's true."

"Then why won't you tell me what you were arguing about before he fell?"

"I want to. But I can't. I'm really sorry."

Neal's hawklike eyes searched Wolek's face and saw no traces of deception, only incredible grief. "You know, Dr. Wolek, that's the first thing you've said that I believe."

* * *

Karen Martin was lying in wait for Lieutenant Neal at the nurses' station and pounced as he strode by. "Well, did Larry tell the truth? Did you lean on him and force a confession out of him, Lieutenant? Did you?"

Without slowing his pace Neal continued down the hall toward the Intensive Care Ward. Karen's tight miniskirted uniform made it difficult for her to match his long strides, but she scrambled along beside him, taking two steps to his one.

"Where are you going now, Lieutenant Neal? You're going to question Meredith Lord, too, aren't you? I heard her say that she saw the whole thing through the window. She's in the cafeteria. I'll go get her if you want me to. Do you want me to go get her?"

Neal stopped abruptly and Karen stumbled over her own feet. As he reached out to steady her, it occurred to Neal that he was rapidly growing tired of this nosy nurse. He felt nothing but contempt for her type, people who reveled in the misery of others and who, like vultures, seized the opportunity to pick a man's bones clean when he was down.

He wondered what Larry Wolek and Meredith Lord might have done to deserve a "friend" like Karen Martin.

"Miss Martin," he said carefully, "I appreciate your calling me and, ah, bringing

22

this matter to my attention. But now that you've been a good citizen and fulfilled your civic duty, why don't you just butt out?"

"Well!" She propped her hands on her waist and tossed back her long blond hair. "If that's the thanks I get for reporting a crime—"

Lieutenant Neal stuck his head through the doorway to the Intensive Care Ward marked NO ADMITTANCE. "Excuse me, Dr. Trainor. I need a few minutes of your time."

Trainor looked up from his patient and turned to Dr. Bill Stanton at his side. "Do you mind handling this alone for a while?"

Bill studied Ted Hale's unconscious form for a moment, then replied, "Go ahead. There's not that much we can do for him right now anyway. I'll send for you if I need you."

"My office is right here," Trainor said as he led Neal down the hall and into a dark room. He flipped open the shades, and the small office was instantly filled with bright noonday sun. "What can I do for you, Lieutenant?"

"You can tell me what happened on those stairs this morning," Neal said, settling his bulk into a wooden chair that creaked in protest.

"I saw Ted Hale take a bad fall down the

stairs. I treated him at the scene and we rushed him to the emergency ward. Then we moved him to Intensive Care."

"Is he going to pull through?"

Trainor was quiet for a moment. "His chances aren't too good," he replied softly.

"Did Hale slip on those stairs, or was he pushed?"

Trainor sat down at his desk, lifted a ballpoint pen, and began doodling on a scrap of paper. "I believe he slipped."

"Did you see him slip?"

"No. I was on the landing below when it happened."

"I see." Neal chewed his lower lip thoughtfully. "If you didn't actually witness the incident, why are you assuming that he slipped?"

"Because I know Larry Wolek. Larry wouldn't try to murder anyone."

"Did I accuse him of attempted murder?"

"No. But that's why you're here. Karen Martin told you some highly embroidered tale about what she supposedly saw and heard, and you believe her."

"Is there any reason why I shouldn't believe Nurse Martin?" he asked.

Trainor tossed the pen onto the desk with a sigh of exasperation. "Yes. Karen is a troublemaker . . . not to mention an outright liar. She was in love with Larry Wolek and he didn't return her affection. He loves Meredith Lord, and Karen can't forgive him for that. She would do anything to get even with him."

"Are you saying that she outright lied about what she heard?"

"I don't know. What did she say?"

"She says that they were arguing—shouting and swearing at each other."

"They were arguing, that's true."

"About what?"

"A patient, I believe."

"Dr. Wolek's patient?"

"I don't know."

"Dr. Hale's patient?"

"I said I don't know. A patient. Doctors frequently argue over patients' care."

"Karen Martin heard Dr. Wolek say—" Neal reached into his pocket and pulled out a small black notebook. "Let's see. . . . She heard him say, and I quote, 'I'll kill you before I'll let you tell her that.'" He flipped the notebook closed. "Did you hear Dr. Wolek say something like that?"

Price Trainor rose from his chair and walked to the window. He shoved his hands deep into his pants pockets.

"Did you hear him say that, Dr. Trainor?"

Trainor sighed and leaned his forehead against the windowpane. "Yes," he whispered.

"Exactly those words?"

"Yes. Exactly."

Meredith Lord wrung her hands as she paced the length of Larry Wolek's office. "Oh, Larry, it was dreadful. You should have heard the questions that awful lieutenant asked me. I honestly believe that he thinks you pushed Ted down those stairs. I wanted to tell him that I had seen the whole thing, but I really didn't. The window was all frosty and I couldn't see that well."

Larry leaned back in his chair and propped his feet wearily on his desk. He ran one hand over his raspy whiskers. He needed a shave, he needed a hot meal, and he sure as hell needed some sleep. "It's okay, Merrie. I didn't push Ted, so Lieutenant Neal can't prove otherwise. Please sit down. Or better yet, go on home."

He could hear the stress and the impatience in his voice, but he was almost too tired to care.

She stopped pacing and looked wounded. "Don't you want me to stay here with you?"

"I'd rather you just went back to Llanfair. You must be tired," he added, noticing her pallor. He softened his tone. "There's really nothing more you can do here, sweetheart, for me or for Ted."

"Well, if you're sure. I am a bit tired after all those blood tests this morning. They're certainly doing a lot of tests just to confirm anemia. Isn't that unusual, Larry?"

He hesitated and, before he could reply, his office door flew open. Vincent, his older brother, rushed inside.

Vince had apparently come straight from the shipping warehouse. His striped overalls bore the stains of this morning's cargo of oranges. He bounded across the room and placed his beefy hands on Larry's shoulders. Vince's ruddy, baby face was creased with worry.

"I came as soon as I heard. What's this all about? You didn't finally kill that jerk Hale, did ya?"

Larry said nothing but nodded toward Meredith, who was still standing in the corner, wringing her hands.

"Pardon me, Miss Meredith, I didn't see you standing there. I know you used to be sweet on ol' Ted . . . I mean, Dr. Hale."

"It's okay, Vincent," she replied. "I was just leaving anyway."

"Aw, you don't have to leave on my account. I'll watch my mouth if you wanna stick around."

"No. That's okay, really. Larry says he doesn't need me anymore."

Larry rose from his desk, walked over, and wrapped her cashmere sweater around her thin shoulders. "I need you, Merrie, but I don't want you to make yourself sick. And this ordeal is taking its toll on you. Go home and go to bed. I'll call you as soon as . . . anything changes."

"Promise?"

He pressed a kiss to her cheek. "Promise."

"Yeah," Vince agreed. "You oughta go home and rest. You look a bit peaked around the gills."

"Oh, okay." She squeezed Larry's arm as he walked her to the door. "Come to Llanfair tonight. We'll have some brandy in the library and try to relax."

"I don't think that's a good idea, Merrie. Your father was never too thrilled about you and me anyway, and he's going to be even less happy when he gets wind of this."

"Since when do you care how my father feels about you?"

"All right. I'll think about it," he said as he opened the door.

There, filling the doorway, was Lieutenant Jack Neal. "I just thought you'd all want to know," he said, his eyes searching each of their faces in turn, "that your buddy, Ted Hale, just checked out."

"This is exactly the kind of scandal I was expecting when I warned you about Larry Wolek." Victor Lord punctuated his statement by bringing his fist down on the leather arm of his wing-back chair. "He's nothing but a bit of low-class rabble from the wrong side of town."

Meredith cringed at the insult to her beloved, but was unable to summon enough courage to come to his defense. Lifelong habits were hard to break, and she had never stood up to her father. But she was in good company: few people in the small, tight-knit community of Llanview defied Victor Lord.

She rose from the watered-silk couch and walked over to the fireplace, where she held out her hands as though warming them. "Larry didn't kill Ted. Ted fell accidentally."

She ventured a sideways glance at her father to see how he was reacting to her difference of opinion. But Victor seemed to have tired of the argument and sat peacefully smoking his Dunhill pipe, the pungent aroma of his custom oriental blend filling the room.

She decided to press her point a bit further. "And as soon as Lieutenant Neal asks around," she said, "he'll find out what a wonderful man and doctor Larry is. Then he'll drop this stupid investigation."

"Of course he will," replied Victoria Lord, who was seated at the rolltop desk in the corner of the library. "How absurd to think that Larry would take another person's life, especially a fellow doctor."

"Don't you have some work to do, Victoria?" Lord growled. "Why do you think I made you editor of *The Banner*? So that you could sit around here, editorializing on that which doesn't concern you?"

"You made me editor, Father, because *you* are getting too *old* for the job." She smiled and mentally chalked up a point on her side of their eternal scoreboard. Victor Lord, though retired, was as virile as he had been at thirty and terribly proud of it.

"I'm not too old to demote you to paperboy if you don't watch your fresh mouth, young lady," he replied.

"Go ahead. Fire me if you like. I never wanted to be a newspaper editor anyway."

"Really?" His gray eyes narrowed as he glared at her through the cloud of smoke that floated around his silver-maned head. "And just what lofty occupation were you aspiring to when I waylaid you into the newspaper business?"

"Oh, I hadn't decided yet." She toyed with the strand of pearls around her neck. "Maybe a nuclear physicist . . . or a go-go dancer."

Meredith collapsed into giggles at the look of horror on her father's face. Victor Lord's daughter—a go-go dancer! It was nearly as preposterous as the thought of the dignified, professional Victoria wearing go-go boots and a miniskirt.

"Excuse me, Mr. Lord." A tiny Hispanic

woman in a traditional housekeeper's uniform appeared at the library door. "Dr. Stanton is here."

"Dr. Stanton?" Meredith left her place by the fireplace and returned to the sofa. "He must have gotten the results of my blood tests. Show him in, Felicia."

The housekeeper hesitated, looking uneasy. "He, uh, he asked to speak to Mr. Lord . . . privately."

"I hope it isn't bad news," Meredith said when her father had left the room. "Viki, why would he ask for Father instead of me? Something must be wrong."

Victoria left her work at the desk and sat beside her sister on the couch. She lifted Merrie's hand and found it cold, as it often was these days.

"Nothing's wrong," she said, trying to rub some warmth into the frail hand. "Father won't let anything bad happen to you, Merrie. And neither will I."

Dr. Bill Stanton waited, as the housekeeper had asked him to do, in Victor Lord's personal study. It was a man's room in every detail, from the dark oak paneling on the walls to the grizzly bearskin rug on the floor. Massive gun cabinets housed Lord's gun collection: high-caliber rifles, Civil War Enfield muskets, silver French dueling pistols. On the oak walls hung the heads of a few of

Lord's victims: a rhinoceros, a mountain lion, a Bengal tiger.

Surrounded by the opulent splendor of Llanfair, Bill Stanton, a highly successful physician, was overwhelmed. Victor Lord —self-made newspaper tycoon. Cynical and harsh as his daily headlines, he had everything that a man could want—success, money, power.

But right then, Stanton wouldn't have traded places with Lord for all the money and power in the world. Because in a few minutes, Dr. Bill Stanton was going to tell Victor Lord, multimillionaire, that his youngest daughter was dying.

Chapter
Two

"If you let my child die, I swear I'll see to it that you never practice medicine again." Victor Lord's square jaw twitched slightly as he glared down at the man who had been his personal physician for years. "I'll ruin you, Stanton, I swear I will."

Bill Stanton took a deep breath and stepped away from him. It was hard to think with Lord literally breathing down his neck. He counted to ten and tried to remind himself that this man was distraught, overwhelmed with grief. After all, he had just been told that his daughter was terminally ill. He could hardly be expected to accept the news amiably.

But as Bill stared up into those cold gray eyes, he couldn't help thinking that Lord didn't look distraught, or particularly grief-stricken. He looked irate, indignant that something might be happening within his domain that he wouldn't be able to control.

"I understand that you're upset, Mr. Lord. But threatening me isn't going to help Meredith's condition. This is a serious blood illness, and to date there's no cure. Fortunately, the disease is in remission at the moment, but we can't hope that it will remain so indefinitely."

"And what if you're wrong?" Lord demanded. "What if you botched the tests?"

"I sincerely wish that were the case, for Meredith's sake. She's a wonderful young woman. But I ran the tests three times. There's no mistake."

"I'm going to get another opinion. And another after that."

Stanton nodded graciously. "As you please, Mr. Lord. But meantime, we need to discuss Meredith's treatment."

Victor Lord walked over to his desk and sank into the diamond-tucked leather chair. "So, what do you recommend?" he asked with the first traces of resignation in his voice.

"We have a medication that she can take orally. It slows the disease's progress. That's really all we can do at this point. The most important thing right now is to see that she gets a lot of rest and that she keeps a positive frame of mind. That's why I strongly recommend that she not be told about her illness at this time."

Victor leaned back in his chair and slowly laced his fingers. Studying his manicure, he said, "And what do we tell her when she asks about the results of the tests? She'll want to know why she has to take the medication. Meredith has always been too inquisitive for her own good."

"We'll tell her that the tests showed she is anemic. We won't be lying. Anemia is a symptom of this disease. We'll say that the medication is to build up the iron in her blood."

Victor Lord sat quietly for a moment, then took a small key from the breast pocket of his satin smoking jacket and unlocked his desk. He pulled out a large, leather checkbook, scribbled a check, and handed it to Dr. Stanton.

"I want my daughter to have the best treatment. The very best. Perhaps this donation to the hospital's building fund will assure that she receives it."

When Stanton saw the multizeroed amount on the check, he was overwhelmed by conflicting emotions. With this much money the hospital could complete the cardiac unit and have funds left over.

He tried to keep the anger out of his voice . . . and the eagerness. "I appreciate the donation immensely, Mr. Lord." He laid the check on Victor's desk. "But your daughter will receive the very best care we have to offer . . . with or without your generous contribution."

Lord stood, picked up the check, and pressed it into Bill's hand. "I'm just making sure. I like to cover all bases."

Bill accepted the check gratefully. He wouldn't have looked forward to explaining to the hospital board why he had turned down such a sizable donation from Victor Lord. "Thank you, on behalf of the hospital. We can certainly put this to good use. Perhaps we can name the new cardiac wing after your daughter."

"Why would you do that?" Lord asked with a raised eyebrow. "*She* isn't the one paying for it. *I* am."

Bill Stanton studied those chilly gray eyes to see if Lord was making a joke. He should have known better. Victor Lord wasn't well known for his sense of humor. "As you wish," he said evenly.

"What I wish, Dr. Stanton, is that a certain colleague of yours, Larry Wolek, would stay the hell out of my daughter's life. I don't want her wasting what time she has in a pointless relationship with someone like him."

Bill Stanton felt his temper rising along with his blood pressure. "I don't understand your misgivings about Dr. Wolek," he said. "Larry is a fine man, and your daughter seems to be very happy when she's with him. In fact, I wouldn't be surprised if her happiness with Larry Wolek isn't one of the most important factors in her present remission. I'm quite concerned about how his current problems may affect her health."

"Don't concern yourself about Larry Wolek and my Meredith. You take care of her medical needs and I'll handle everything else in her life."

I'm sure you will, Mr. Lord, Bill Stanton thought as he left Llanfair. *You always have.*

"This is a warrant for your arrest, Dr. Wolek, for the murder of Theodore Hale. You have the right to remain silent. If you give up that right . . ."

Larry Wolek was mildly surprised at the shock that jolted his nervous system when he heard those words. It wasn't as though he hadn't been expecting to hear them. In fact, he had lain awake all last night, playing and replaying this scenario in his head.

There had been no question in his mind that the scene would be enacted. The only variables were *where* and *when*. In the middle of a counseling session with one of his depressed patients? While he was eating lunch in the cafeteria with his co-workers?"

At least Lieutenant Neal had chosen to do

the deed here in the privacy of Larry's office when none of his patients was present.

"Do you understand your rights, Dr. Wolek?" Neal was asking.

"Ah . . . yes. I do." He held out his wrists for the customary handcuffs.

Lieutenant Neal's eyes searched his face, and for a moment Larry thought he saw a flicker of self-doubt in those black depths, as though the lieutenant had entertained a fleeting thought that he might be arresting an innocent man.

"I believe we can dispense with the cuffs this time," Neal said gruffly, his professional mask slipping a bit. "You know, Dr. Wolek, I'm not happy about this at all. I've talked to a lot of people around here who know you, and from what they've said about you, I'd sooner nominate you for sainthood than arrest you for murder."

Larry bowed his head and said nothing.

"If you pitched Hale down the staircase, which I'm sure you did, you must have had a good reason. But you have to tell me what really happened on those stairs. I just can't buy that cock-and-bull story about you forgetting."

Larry continued to stare at the navy-blue wool carpeting that Merrie had chosen for him only a month before. *Ah, Merrie,* he thought and closed his eyes.

"Who were you arguing about?" Neal asked, stepping closer to Larry and putting his huge hand on the younger man's shoulder. "Who were you protecting when you pushed him down those stairs? Tell me so that I can help you."

Larry looked up at him with haunted bloodshot eyes. "I didn't push Hale," he said. "We argued, I admit that. We struggled there on the stairs. I admit that, too. But I didn't push him. He tried to shove past me, he tripped, and he fell. That's the truth, I swear."

"Okay," Neal said slowly. "And what happened before that? Who were you arguing about?"

"I'm sorry." He shook his head. "I can't say."

"Can't? You mean *won't*. Did you threaten to kill Ted Hale there on the stairs just before he fell?"

Larry hesitated before answering. "Did someone say that I did?"

"Two witnesses overheard you say, 'I'll kill you before I'll let you tell her that.' Did you say anything like that, Dr. Wolek?"

Larry took a deep breath and reached for the telephone on his desk. "Before I say anything more, I think I'd better call my attorney."

* * *

"If you take Larry Wolek's case, you'll be committing professional suicide! I won't let you do it, Dave."

"Won't *let* me? Excuse me, but I don't recall asking your permission."

David Siegal glared at his wife, Eileen, across the breakfast table. He tossed down the last swallow of black coffee and grabbed his briefcase from the chair next to him.

"Dave, don't be stupid. If you defend Larry Wolek, Victor Lord will never speak to you again. You know how he hates that guy." Eileen's green eyes flashed and her usually pale unmade-up face flushed nearly as red as her hair, which was twisted in pink and green plastic rollers.

She followed him to the door, clutching her well-worn chenille robe around her. "Just think about it first, Dave. Think about all those real-estate contracts that Mr. Lord runs through our office."

"My office," he corrected her. "My office, my practice . . . my decision. Larry Wolek is my friend, for heaven's sake. If this goes to court he'll be on trial for his life. And Larry's life and career are a bit more important to me, Eileen, than your social standing in this community."

"Larry, I want to defend you, but you aren't giving me anything to work with."

Dave Siegal tossed his pen and legal pad

onto the battered table that had forty years' worth of graffiti scratched into its surface.

The police officer standing watch outside turned and peered through the small window in the door. Reassured, he again turned his back to them.

"Maybe you don't realize how serious this is." Siegal leaned across the table to give his words emphasis. "We're talking first-degree murder here, second degree if you're lucky. We're talking about your life, Larry."

"Damn it, Dave. Don't you think I know that? Don't you think I'd tell you more if I could?"

"You don't really expect me to believe that you conveniently *forgot* what happened?"

"No. I don't. But can't you sell it to a jury? Psychological trauma and all that?"

"You're a shrink, Larry. Would you believe it if you were on the jury?"

"No."

"So, case closed."

Larry sighed and ran his fingers through his fine chestnut hair. "Okay, if it's a hopeless case, I'll just plead guilty."

"Guilty? I don't believe it! You're actually willing to go up the river on this. Larry, no one wants to see you convicted of killing Ted Hale, including Lieutenant Neal and the prosecuting attorney. They're willing to believe that he tripped and fell, the way you said, if you'll come clean about the argument. But you're lying and everybody knows it. You leave them no choice but to press charges."

"And how about you, Dave? What's your choice? Are you going to defend me or not?"

Dave Siegal was surprised at the lack of emotion in his friend's voice. Larry was an intelligent person; surely he realized the gravity of his situation. But he was acting like a man who had surrendered the war before the first battle.

"I'm going to represent you, Larry. I'll stand up with you in court and go through the motions. But I can tell you right now, you haven't given me anything at all to fight with. Right now you don't have a defense."

Victor Lord started to reach into his back pocket for his wallet but thought better of it. This Lieutenant Neal didn't look like a man who could be bought with cash, but every man had his price. Sometimes it just took a while to find what it was.

"Lieutenant, I'm sure we could bend the rules just this once. I only want five minutes of Dr. Wolek's time, and I doubt that he's terribly busy at the moment. I can make it worth your trouble."

Neal cocked one eyebrow and studied every carefully sewn stitch on Victor Lord's wool tweed lapel. That coat must have cost more than *he* made all month, including the money he earned moonlighting as a security guard at the bank. "What did you have in mind, Mr. Lord?" he asked smoothly.

Lord glanced around the busy police station and lowered his voice. "I'm a personal friend of the chief, the captain, and the mayor. I've heard that Captain Ross will be retiring soon. I'm sure that a well-placed word or two wouldn't hurt your chances at the captain's chair."

Neal thoughtfully sucked air through his front teeth before answering. "Gee, Mr. Lord, I was hoping that you'd offer something a little more concrete . . . like cash."

Lord grinned, surprised at his own misjudgment. "Really?"

"Yeah, then I could've busted you for bribery. Somebody should have years ago. Everybody knows you're carrying half of this town's politicians and law enforcement in your hip pocket, and I think it's a little crowded in there for me. You'd better run along home to your mansion on the hill and stop interfering in other people's lives. Hanging around jails isn't your cup of tea anyway, Mr. Lord. If you don't look out, you might get lice."

V. Wolek Shipping Company was the busiest and wildest enterprise on the Llanview waterfront. Semi-trucks laden with washing machines, lettuce, live turkeys, tires, and fresh halibut lined up at the docks to unload their cargos and take on goods that were manufactured in this, the industrial section of Llanview.

Vincent Wolek was intensely proud of his business, and he had the right to be. He had started as a teenage longshoreman and had worked his way up, scrimping and saving over the years, until he had enough money and experience to open a trucking company of his own.

When Vince's parents had died, he had single-handedly raised his younger sister, Anna, and his brother, Larry. Anna had grown into a fine, decent woman . . . though she hadn't found a husband yet. And Larry —Larry was Vinnie's crowning accomplishment: a doctor. A *doctor* in the *Wolek* family. Mama and Papa would have been proud.

In the center of the giant warehouse stood a tiny glass cubicle, Vince's office, from which he commanded his army of truck drivers, forklift operators, and mechanics. Usually he spent as little time there as possible, preferring to be in the thick of things, throwing around his weight, a crate or two, and the occasional employee. But today he had spent most of his time on the phone, talking to anybody who might get his little brother out of the mess he was in. He had summoned Dave Siegal, and they were seated in Vince's cubicle, exchanging pleasantries.

"What do you mean Larry ain't got a snowball's chance in Halifax? I thought you were a big-shot lawyer?"

Dave Siegal winced and tapped his foot impatiently on the oily concrete floor of the office. "I'm an adequate defense lawyer, Mr. Wolek. Better than adequate. But your brother isn't being honest with me. I was hoping you could help. Has he told you anything about why he was arguing with Ted Hale?"

"Naw. I tried to weasel it out of him, but he clammed up tighter than a miser's change purse. If you ask me, I think it was about women."

"Women?"

"Yeah. Larry's always been a bit of a lady's man, him bein' good-lookin' and a doctor to boot. Gals were always chasin' after him, and he didn't run all that fast, if you know what I mean."

Dave nodded. "He always had a date on Saturday night, huh?"

"And any other night he wanted one." Vinnie leaned back in his chair, stretched and scratched his head. "Now me, I always managed to stay ten steps ahead of them myself. I had women beggin' me to marry 'em, but I ran like a house afire. I'll bet that's Larry's problem: he didn't run fast enough."

Something unusual in the yard caught Vince's attention. "Geez-Louise, would you look at that!"

Through the open bay doors they saw that a sleek black Mercedes had pulled up to one of the loading docks. They both recognized the tall, silver-haired monarch who got out of the car and questioned one of the truckers. The trucker pointed toward the office.

As Victor Lord approached, Dave Siegal drew a deep breath. "Here comes trouble," he muttered. "He certainly didn't waste any time tracking me down."

"He better be here to see you," Vince sniffed, "'cause I got nothing to say to Mr. Victor Lord. After the way he's mistreated Larry—"

"Good afternoon, Dave." Lord nodded his regal head toward Siegal as he stepped into the office. "Wolek," he grunted in Vince's general direction.

"What are you doin' slummin' on this side of the river?" Vince asked, leaning back in his chair and crossing his brawny arms over his beer-barrel chest.

"I'm here to speak to my attorney . . . and to you," he added grudgingly.

Without standing, Vinnie used his foot to

push a rusty folding chair at Lord. "Have a sit."

Victor studied the chair with undisguised contempt and said, "No, thank you."

"Suit yourself. What do you want?" Vince asked, propping his feet on the chair.

Lord ignored him and turned to Siegal. "I came to ask you personally, David, if you truly intend to represent Larry Wolek in this murder charge."

"Yep, he sure does," Vince supplied cheerfully. "Larry deserves the best there is, and Siegal here is the best. 'Course, you know that yourself, him being your lawyer and all."

"Do you mind, Mr. Wolek?"

"Nope. Go ahead."

Dave shifted uneasily on his chair. "Yes, I am Larry Wolek's counsel in this case."

"But that could have an adverse effect on your career, David."

His meaning was clear to all except Vince, who was still mulling over the word *adverse*.

"After all, David," Lord continued, "a prominent attorney such as yourself has to be careful of the clients he accepts. I mean, taking on a hopeless case—"

"Who you callin' hopeless?" Vince jumped up off his chair, fists clenched at his sides. "You callin' my brother a hopeless case?"

Victor held both hands up before his face. "Really, Mr. Wolek, control yourself."

But Vince wasn't easily placated. "Was he sayin' that Larry's a goner?" he asked Siegal, who had quickly stood, preparing to throw himself between them if necessary. The last thing he wanted was to press assault charges against Vincent Wolek on Victor Lord's behalf.

"Tell me if that's what he meant," Vince insisted, bristling, "'cause if that's what he said, I'm gonna smack him right now."

"I think Mr. Lord was saying that it's going to be a difficult case to win, Vince. And if I don't get some help from your brother, he's right."

Victor Lord lifted his nose as he glared down at Vincent, whose face had gone from a mottled red to a livid purple. "Your brother isn't defending himself because he has no defense. He's a cold-blooded murderer, and he deserves to be locked away for the rest of his life."

"That tears it!" Vinnie yelled and rushed at Victor, his fists raised.

"Vinnie! Don't!" Dave stepped between them, but his timing was perfectly wrong. He caught the blow that was aimed for Lord and doubled over, holding his stomach in agony.

"Mr. Siegal! I didn't mean to hit you! I meant to hit that bloody—are you okay?"

Vince wrapped his arms clumsily around Dave's middle and deposited him in his chair. "Oh, Lordy, Mr. Siegal, I'm so sorry. You ain't gonna hold this against Larry, are you?"

Dave finally caught his breath and straightened up just in time to see Victor Lord strolling away with a satisfied smile curling his thin lips.

Chapter
Three

Anna Wolek untied her apron and hung it carefully on the stainless steel rod next to the dishtowels with the butterflies and daisies. Those were the "good" towels, which replaced the dingy gray ones when she and Vinnie had company for dinner.

She pulled the pot roast from the oven and glanced at her reflection in the glass door as she closed it. She would have patted her red waves into place, but it was difficult to preen with her hands full of sizzling pot roast.

As she placed the chunk of beef on her best platter and arranged the potatoes, carrots, and onions around it, she decided not to carve it in the kitchen as she usually did. If she hinted strongly enough, maybe Joe would carve it.

Joe was good at things like that. He was every bit as masculine as Vinnie, even more so, but he didn't seem to mind doing "homey" things, the way Vince did. Joe was handy to have around when there was a turkey, ham, or roast to carve. Anna was convinced that Joe Riley would be nice to have around the house almost any time.

With the butterfly dishtowel, Anna dabbed at a small grease spot on her plaid skirt and uttered a polite profanity—the only kind of profanity Anna Wolek ever uttered. She had bought this skirt especially for tonight, especially for Joe, and now it was ruined.

She sighed, picked up the platter of pot roast and carried it into the tiny apartment's living-dining area.

"Come and get it," she said, placing the roast at the end of the table, near Joe's customary spot.

"It's about time," Vinnie said, hauling himself off the faded colonial sofa. He slapped Joe Riley companionably on the back. "Come along, old man. It smells good."

"It certainly does," Joe agreed, pulling off his black leather coat and following Vince to the table. "Anna, you've outdone yourself, as usual," he said as he settled into his chair at the end across from Vincent. "You're a fantastic cook, a real treasure."

She blushed bright red beneath her freckles and placed her hand over the grease spot on her skirt. Then she realized that, as usual,

Joe wasn't looking at her. He wasn't likely to notice the spot, or the skirt, or *her* for that matter.

Anna sighed and sat down between them in the chair nearest the kitchen, ready to fulfill any request the men might make.

"You forgot the pepper, Anna," Vince said, surveying the table.

"I'll get it," Joe said, rising. "I know where it is."

"Don't be silly, sit down. You're company." Anna placed one hand on his broad shoulder and shoved him back into his seat. She left it there a millisecond longer than necessary, savoring the contact, no matter how brief. Then she disappeared into the kitchen.

"You should treat your sister better, Vinnie," Joe said reproachfully as he picked up the carving knife and fork and began to carve with a vengeance. "Slavery was outlawed, you know. And women have decided lately that they have rights, too. If you don't look out, she'll rebel and burn her bra."

"Aw, Anna would never do a thing like that. She's one of them women that likes waitin' on a man. She's a good one, my Anna. Just like Mama used to be. Mama waited on Papa hand and foot till the day she dropped dead at his feet. A fine woman."

Vince speared three potatoes from the platter, mashed them flat with the back of his fork, and ladled a cupful of gravy over each. "Yep, Anna's gonna make some man a fine wife someday. You might keep that in mind, Joseph Riley. You could do a lot worse than my little sister, Anna."

Joe said nothing, but in retaliation he carved a paper-thin slice of beef and laid it on Vinnie's plate.

"About a dozen more like that one, while you're at it," Vince said, stuffing the entire slice into his mouth. "That there Victoria Lord that you're sweet on . . . I bet she don't even know how to cook."

"No. But Victoria has a mind of her own, and she's a hell of a lot of fun to argue with," he replied.

Both men turned to see Anna standing in the doorway, pepper shaker in hand. They saw her, but neither was perceptive enough to notice the pained look in her brown eyes.

Anna didn't need to be reminded that Joe was in love with Victoria; it was something she thought about every day. And every time she thought about Victoria Lord, she felt homely and unsophisticated and downright plain. So she tried very hard not to think about Victoria at all.

"So, Vinnie, did you actually hit Victor Lord when he said that about Larry's case being hopeless?" Joe asked as he carefully placed two generous slices of roast on Anna's plate.

"Hit Victor Lord!" she gasped. "Vinnie, you didn't tell me about that. What happened?"

"Oh, nothin' much. He came gallivantin' into the warehouse today, trying to talk Dave Siegal outta takin' Larry's case. So, of course, I had to give him a piece of my mind."

"Of course," Anna replied dryly. "And I suppose you gave him a taste of your knuckles, too."

"Well, not exactly. Siegal stepped in between us, and I accidentally punched him instead."

"You hit Larry's lawyer? Mother of Mercy!" She quickly crossed herself. "Oh, Vinnie. Leave it to you to make a bad situation worse."

"Punching a lawyer isn't the best idea in the world, Vince," Joe agreed. "Is he still going to defend Larry?"

"Sure. I said I was sorry. Dave ain't one to hold a grudge."

"Lucky for you." Joe closed his eyes as he savored a bite of roast. "Heavenly, Anna, absolute heaven. Beats the heck out of TV dinners. That's what I would have had if you hadn't invited me over."

Anna ducked her head and looked up at him through her lashes. "Come over anytime, Joe. You're always welcome at our table."

"See what I mean?" Vinnie pointed at her with a forkful of carrots. "Anna's a good woman. She'd make you a fine wife, Joseph."

"Vinnie, cut it out." Anna blushed angrily. "You're always trying to get rid of me, like I was an old broken-down Ford."

"Well, you're gonna be old and broken down pretty soon, and you won't have no husband to take care of you."

"That's enough, Vinnie," Joe interjected, his handsome face creased with a scowl. "Anna's a wonderful person. She just hasn't found any man who's worthy of her yet."

She cast a triumphant sideways look at Vincent. "Thank you, Joe. How's work at *The Banner*?"

"Oh, just the usual. I've been doing some undercover work on the waterfront, trying to tie some of our local merchants here in Llanview to the Chicago syndicate."

"You mean *the mob*?" Vinnie was impressed.

"Hoodlums, gangsters, dope, racketeering, the works . . . right here in our quiet little community."

"That sounds dangerous." Anna's warm brown eyes were full of concern, but as usual, Joe didn't seem to notice.

"No, I'm careful. Besides, I've been covering Larry's case for the last two days. Mr. Lord assigned it to me, personally. I'm going to ask him tomorrow to find someone else to cover it. I'm finding it a bit difficult to remain objective, being so close to the family and all."

Anna felt an extra surge of tenderness toward Joe as she thought of the many years that he had been the Woleks' closest friend. Vince had found him, a teenager running wild on the waterfront streets, addicted to dope and heading for serious trouble with the law.

Vince had given young Joe his first job, there in his shipping company, along with his first real guidance. In the years that followed, Joe had become yet another of Vinnie's "success" stories, and the two of them had become closer than brothers.

She couldn't imagine the Wolek household without Joe Riley. And she couldn't imagine Joe Riley being objective when it came to Vince Wolek or any member of his family.

"You don't really think that they'll convict Larry of murder, do you, Joe?" she asked with tears in her voice.

For the first time, Joe seemed to really take notice of her. He reached across the table and patted her shoulder. "No. Of course not, Anna. Dave is a great lawyer, the best in the county. Larry's going to be okay. You'll see."

With Joe's strong, warm hand on her shoulder, Anna could almost believe that it was true. Almost.

"What's the matter, sugar? Tell ol' Sadie what's wrong."

Anna looked up into her neighbor's face, which was lined with age and kindly concern. She laid down her dishtowel and burst into tears.

Sadie held out her arms and gathered Anna to her plump maternal bosom. "There, there, honey pie, don't cry like that. You're worried about that baby brother of yours, aren't you?"

Anna sniffed and nodded her head.

Sadie patted Anna's auburn curls with her soft black hand. "Ah, the trials and tribulations we see on this earth because of those we love," she said as she led Anna to the table where the leftover pot roast still swam in its gravy.

Vince and Joe had left for the evening, saying something about checking out a waterfront bar for unsavory, moblike riffraff. And as usual, they hadn't invited Anna.

"The Gallopin' Corral ain't a fit place for a decent woman," Vince had said as they left. Anna strongly suspected that they were more interested in investigating the bar's quality of beer and the stature of its barmaids than in gathering information on syndicate activity.

Sadie Gray, who lived in the apartment across the hall, had heard the men leave and thought that Anna might want some company. And she had been right. Tonight of all nights, Anna needed Sadie's sympathetic ear.

Sadie settled her plumpness into the chair beside Anna. "There's nothing in life that's worse," she said, "than worrying yourself sick when those you love are in trouble. Well, there's one thing that's worse," she added with a sigh. "It's not knowing where your loved ones are or what kind of trouble they're in."

For a moment Anna forgot her own problems and wondered at Sadie's statement. In the past three years, since Anna had known Sadie, she had never once mentioned having a family. It was a subject that was simply not open for discussion.

But the pain in her dark eyes was real. And the grief on her face was almost more than Anna could bear.

"Sadie, tell me about your family," Anna gently coaxed.

Sadie shook her head as though jarred out of her reverie. "What? Oh, that. We don't need to talk about my miseries, when you've got such a mess of them yourself."

Again the tears began to roll down Anna's freckled cheeks. "Oh, Sadie. What if Larry has to go to jail for something he didn't do?"

"Now you hush that nonsense. The Lord takes care of the little sparrow, and he's watching out for Larry, too. You just gotta leave him in the Lord's care." She reached over and took Anna's hand. "Let's pray for him, and you'll feel a heap better."

Anna looked up at her in surprise. "Are you a Catholic, too?"

"No, sugar, I'm Baptist. But I don't reckon the Lord will mind."

Joe Riley dropped a dime into the pay phone and assumed that pseudo-casual pose that men have when talking on the telephone to that "special" lady. He turned his back to Vincent and his cowboy friends at the bar and plugged one ear with his finger, trying to muffle the strains of "Light My Fire" coming from the jukebox in the corner.

The phone was answered promptly on the second ring. "This is Llanfair. May I help you?" The housekeeper's voice was crisp and professional as always.

"Hello, Felicia, my dear. How are you this evening?" Joe asked in his smoothest tones.

Felicia's professional facade crumbled and she tittered like a teenybopper. "Fine, Mr. Riley. Just fine."

"And what's a lovely young woman such as yourself doing home on Friday night? Did Paul Newman stand you up again?"

"Yes," she said, "I'm afraid he did."

"Well, love, don't take it personally. I hear that he and Joanne have patched up their differences. But don't fret. Robert Redford is here at the Galloping Corral having a beer with me and Vince Wolek. I told him about those beautiful brown eyes of yours, and he's dying to meet you."

"I'd like to meet him, too," she said with just the right amount of feigned excitement.

"Great. I'll tell him to meet you in the rose garden by the gazebo for a midnight rendezvous. But Felicia . . ."

"Yes, Mr. Riley?"

"Be gentle with Bob. He's just a kid, you know. He's not accustomed to women of your . . . experience."

Felicia collapsed into helpless giggles. It had been at least twenty years since she had even kissed a man, but during these brief telephone exchanges, she remembered what it had been like to flirt with a charming rascal. And Joe Riley had far more than his share of charm.

"I'll get Miss Victoria for you, Mr. Riley," she said, resuming her professional tone.

"Thank you, Felicia."

Joe waited several minutes as Felicia summoned her mistress. He glanced around the bar to check on Vinnie and saw him locked in a life and death bout of arm-wrestling in the corner with a giant, red-haired longshoreman, who looked inch for inch as fierce as his Viking forefathers. But burly Vince could defeat anyone on the waterfront at arm-wrestling, and he liked to prove the fact as often as possible. What Vince lacked in height, he more than made up in biceps.

Joe hoped the Viking wouldn't mind losing too badly. He wasn't in the mood to join Vinnie in one of his tussles tonight. He would if he had to, but, unlike Vince, it wasn't Joe's idea of a good time.

"Good evening, Joe." Victoria's deep velvety voice washed over him, leaving him with a yearning that was becoming acutely familiar.

"Hello, boss lady."

"What did you say to Felicia? Her face was bright red and she was giggling so hard she could hardly talk."

"I told her that this was a person-to-person obscene phone call for Victoria Lord."

"You didn't!"

"No, I didn't." He leaned deeper into the phone cubicle and cupped his hand over the telephone. "By the way, what are you wearing? I didn't happen to luck out and catch you in bed, did I?" His voice was deep and husky. "I can just picture you in a black silk negligee, cut low in the front, strategically placed lace . . . tell me, am I close? Getting warm?"

There was a prolonged silence on her end, then she said, "Dream on, big boy. I just finished gardening. I'm wearing a sweaty T-shirt and faded blue jeans, and I have dirt caked under my fingernails."

"That's okay. Earthy is nice, once in a while. I like variety."

"Am I to assume that this call is personal rather than business?"

"Highly personal. I called to see if I could spend the night becoming intimately familiar with your lovely body."

"No."

"Okay, I'll settle for vaguely familiar."

"Definitely not."

"A passing acquaintance?"

"Riley!"

"All right, I give up. How about if I take you out for one quiet drink?"

"That's what you had in mind all along, isn't it? You thought if you started off with something shocking and worked your way down, I'd accept your final offer out of sheer relief."

"Have I tried this on you before?"

"Three weeks ago."

"I don't remember. . . . Did it work?"

"Yes."

"Ah-ha! I knew there was some reason why I tried it again. So, what do you say?"

"No."

He sighed and quickly switched to Device B. "Come on, Victoria. I have some important newspaper business on my mind that can't wait till Monday."

"I know *exactly* what you have on your mind tonight, Joe Riley, and it's pleasure, not business."

"You're absolutely right. And the only reason you can say no is because you have no idea how pleasurable pleasure can be."

"And you'd like to be the one to show me. . . ." she purred.

"I could probably be persuaded to."

"How generous of you."

"So, shall I pick you up in thirty minutes?"

"Not tonight, Joe, I have a headache."

"Come on, Victoria," he said with a cynical laugh. "That's a line for married folks."

"No, really, Joe. It's been a terrible day here at Llanfair with Larry being arrested and all. Merrie's taking it really hard, and Father's being difficult, as usual. I really do have a splitting headache."

He could tell she wasn't lying: he could hear the pain and tension in her voice. "I'm

63

sorry, Viki." His tone was gentle and solicitous. "Take care of yourself, and I'll give you a call tomorrow. I hope you feel better."

"Thank you. And Joe—"

"Yes?"

"I'm glad you called. Give me a rain check, okay?"

"On spending the night with me?"

"No, the one quiet drink."

Victoria hung up the gilded French telephone and glanced down at her black silk negligee with its strategically placed lace. It was uncanny, how Joe Riley knew things he shouldn't know about her . . . what she was wearing on the other end of the phone, what she was feeling when he spoke to her with that deep, gritty voice of his.

Joe knew entirely too much about people —especially women. He unnerved her . . . and excited her. Joe made her feel things that she had never felt before. The emotions he stirred in her contrasted sharply with the image she strove to maintain: cool, detached, completely in control.

She ran her hand over the satin of her nightgown and closed her eyes. For a moment she allowed herself to fantasize about Joe . . . kissing her, holding her . . .

Then she opened her eyes and tried to push the image out of her mind. If she ever allowed Joe Riley to touch her the way he wanted to, she would lose control. And control meant everything to Victoria Lord. It was the one thing she could never allow herself to lose.

The moonlight filtered through the sheer curtains of the bedroom, casting its muted silver rays on the bed where she tossed and turned. Her short blond curls, usually arranged perfectly with each wave in place, were tousled, in total disarray like the satin sheets that were twisted around her.

Her eyes were closed and her lips mumbled an incoherent reply to the nightmare voice that whispered to her subconscious.

"I know all about you, Victoria Lord," it said, this faceless voice that was all the more terrifying because of its familiarity.

"You don't fool me. I know what you're really like inside."

"No," she murmured. "No! Go away. Leave me alone."

But she could still feel it, just there, over her shoulder. She could feel its icy breath on the nape of her neck. "Your days are numbered. Count them, Victoria. There aren't many left."

"No!" she screamed and bolted upright in the bed, clutching the satin sheets to her chest. Sweat poured down her face as she struggled to breathe. She looked quickly around the room, peering into shadows that seemed pregnant with a sense of evil.

There was someone else in the room with her. She could sense another presence there, waiting in the shadows.

"Who's there?" she whispered. "Who are you? What do you want?"

But Victoria didn't have to ask. Deep in the recesses of her mind . . . she knew.

Chapter
Four

"After two weeks of exhaustive testing you haven't found anything wrong with me?"

"Would you have preferred that I had, Miss Lord?" Dr. Bill Stanton tried to filter the sarcasm out of his voice, but the bitter tone still remained. He couldn't seem to win with the Lords lately.

The heel of Victoria's Spanish calfskin pump tapped the floor as she set her face into a determined scowl.

My God, Bill thought, *she looks more like Victor every day.* Even her gray wool suit was a feminine version of her father's usual attire. The smoky-pink silk blouse did little to soften the overall effect. Victoria Lord was undoubtedly the most intimidating young woman that Bill Stanton had ever encountered.

"I would have preferred," she was saying, "that you had discovered the reason behind these headaches I've been having. I assure you that while they may be 'all in my head,' they are very real, indeed."

"I'm sure they are, Miss Lord. I'm certain that your pain is most uncomfortable—"

"Uncomfortable? Excruciating is more like it."

"Ah, yes, quite. But the fact is, there is no physiological cause. You are in perfect health, Miss Lord. Physically, that is."

She lifted one delicate eyebrow. "What are you implying?"

Dr. Stanton wriggled in his chair, trying to find a more comfortable position. But there was no graceful way out of this one. "I recommend that you see Dr. Polk. He's an excellent physician and—"

"He's a psychiatrist."

"Yes, he is. In fact, he's head of the psychiatric department here at the hospital and—"

Victoria rose from the chair, her cobalt-blue eyes flashing. "He's a *shrink.*" She spat out the last word as though she found it distasteful.

"Yes, Victoria, I think the problems you're experiencing may have something to do with the stress that your family has been under lately. What with Larry Wolek's terrible situation and with Meredith's illness."

"What about Merrie?" she asked. The anger in her eyes melted into fear. "What's wrong with my sister?"

Bill Stanton groaned inwardly. He had thought that Lord would surely have told Victoria about Meredith's condition. "I think you'd better discuss that with your father, Miss Lord."

"I did. He said that Merrie has anemia."

"That's true, she does."

Something in his eyes made her ask, "Is that all?"

"As I said, I think you should speak to Mr. Lord about that."

She picked up her purse and tucked it under her arm. "I most certainly will. But I will *not* see Dr. Polk. The last thing I need right now is someone probing my psyche."

With mixed emotions Bill watched her walk away. He didn't appreciate being told by yet another Lord that he was incompetent. He much preferred to be revered, or at least respected, by his patients. But on the other hand, he could sense Victoria's fear. Something was troubling her deeply, something that she couldn't handle, despite all of her inherited strength.

He thought of Llanfair: opulent, majestic, and as cold as a mausoleum. What had it been like, growing up in a place like that with no mother to soften the harshness of a father like Victor Lord?

Bill Stanton thought of Eugenia Lord, Victor's wife, and remembered her death. He had brought Meredith into the world that night as her mother had passed on to the next. Bill could see Eugenia every time he looked at gentle, sensitive Merrie.

But there wasn't a trace of Eugenia in her oldest child. No, Victoria was Victor's daughter, through and through.

Victoria was exhausted by the time she arrived at Llanfair that evening. She was too tired even to think of eating dinner. All she wanted was to curl up in front of the library fire with a good book and a snifter of her father's finest brandy.

As she handed her coat and gloves to Felicia in the foyer, she heard voices coming from the library.

"Do we have company, Felicia?" she asked, giving the housekeeper her purse as well.

"Yes, ma'am. Miss Meredith is entertaining Dr. Larry Wolek. He's staying for dinner."

So much for a quiet evening in the library, she thought as she debated about whether to go straight to her bedroom.

Larry's trial was beginning tomorrow morning. The least she could do was wish him well.

She walked to the door of the library, but stopped there. Inside, reclining on satin pillows beside the fireplace, were Larry and her sister. Meredith's golden hair glistened in the firelight, and Victoria couldn't help thinking how beautiful she was: delicate and as fragile as a white orchid.

Victoria felt the old protective instincts rise as she wondered about what Dr. Stanton had said. Surely there wasn't anything seriously wrong with Merrie. There couldn't be. She simply wouldn't allow it.

She watched as Larry leaned over Meredith, trailing his fingers through her hair, and heard him whisper an intimacy that had been intended for only Merrie's ears.

Victoria quickly turned and ran up the curved staircase. A chaotic wave of feelings swept over her: embarrassment at having witnessed a private moment between Merrie and her lover, but even more so, overwhelming jealousy.

She paused on the landing, her hand on the polished mahogany banister. She closed her eyes and tried to imagine herself and Joe Riley, lying there on those satin cushions. Joe would whisper those words to her as Larry had to Meredith . . . those intimate, seductive words of love. That much was easy to picture: Joe was very vocal about his desires.

Then Joe would run his fingers through her hair, except that her hair wasn't long and luxurious like Merrie's. Victoria kept hers cut short, sensible, and businesslike.

Joe would bend his head down to hers—of course he would. If she gave him the slightest encouragement, Joe would be her lover. And she knew instinctively that he would be wonderful. But would she return his kiss with the same fervor that Meredith had returned Larry's?

No.

Her sister had always been able to give and receive affection. Why couldn't she?

She sighed and continued up the stairs. Maybe, just maybe, if she ever did talk to Dr. Polk, she might ask him.

She awoke with a start and sat up in her bed. Her slumber had been disturbed by that hauntingly familiar feeling: someone was there in the darkness with her . . . waiting . . . whispering evil intentions.

Straining her eyes, she peered into the shadows that danced in rhythm with the wind-whipped branches outside her window.

"Who are you? What do you want with me?" The tremulous pleading in her voice jarred her. She hated the weakness she heard, and her anger gave her strength.

She reached over to her nightstand and flipped on the lamp.

Just as she had thought, there was no one there. The mysterious, shadowy outline was only the wrinkled clothes that she had been too tired to put away when she had undressed.

She lay back on her pillows and shuddered. This couldn't go on. She had to find out what was causing these horrible nightmares . . . even if it meant talking to a psychiatrist.

Her throat felt dry and raspy, as though she had been screaming. She got out of bed and padded across the thick oriental rug to her bathroom. Maybe a glass of water and an aspirin would help. It certainly couldn't hurt.

Victoria flicked on the bathroom light, blinking as her eyes adjusted to the glare. She filled a glass with water, lifted it to her lips—and dropped it. The glass shattered into a thousand sparkling shards across the marble floor.

But Victoria didn't notice. She didn't notice the blood that ran from her bare foot and stained the gray marble. She didn't even hear her own scream.

Her eyes were riveted to the bathroom mirror and the message that was scrawled there in red lipstick.

I hate you, Victoria Lord. I'm going to kill you.

"The prosecution would like to call its first witness, Karen Martin."

Judge Bainbridge nodded to the bailiff, who walked to the double doors in the rear of the courtroom and summoned Karen Martin from the hall.

Savoring her moment of prominence, Karen sashayed up the center aisle. Every male eye, except Larry's, was trained on the sway of her red miniskirt and the close fit of her white sweater. Knee-high patent-leather boots completed her ensemble. She had chosen these clothes carefully after the prosecution had suggested that she dress "conservatively." This was the most conservative outfit in Karen Martin's wardrobe.

Lifting her hand, she repeated the oath, then took the witness chair. This was her moment, her chance to get even with Larry Wolek and that goody-two-shoes, Meredith Lord. And she wouldn't even have to lie: the truth was damning enough.

She cast one quick look at Larry, expecting to see him angry and indignant. But he sat quietly at the defense table beside Dave Siegal, his hands folded in his lap, his head bowed.

"Will you please tell the court your occupation, Miss Martin?" Bill Kimbrough, the prosecuting attorney, stepped between her and Larry. It was just as well. For some reason she didn't want to look at Larry right now, anyway.

"What? Oh, I'm a nurse at Llanview Hospital. A licensed practical nurse."

"And what is your relationship to the defendant, Lawrence Wolek?" He moved aside and pointed toward the defense table.

Her eyes followed his direction. Larry was looking at her now, and the sad expression on his face went straight to her heart. Suddenly she didn't feel so great about this whole thing. Mostly she didn't feel so great about herself.

She searched his eyes for anger, but found none. He seemed too tired, too empty for emotion. "We were friends," she said softly, and he smiled at her.

"Could you speak up a bit, Miss Martin?" The prosecutor seemed angry with her. He stepped between her and Larry again, blocking her view.

"We were friends," she repeated, her voice echoing through the silent courtroom. "We were good friends."

It wasn't Felicia who was knocking on Victoria's bedroom door, or her father, or Meredith. She knew all of their knocks. She lifted the damp washcloth from her forehead and called, "Come in."

The door opened and there stood Joe Riley with a fistful of daisies.

"Joe. How did you get up here?"

"I bribed Felicia with the other half of this bouquet," he admitted sheepishly. "And your father is out, I believe."

"He's at *The Banner,* where, I might add, you should be right now."

He walked over to the bed where she lay and stuck the daisies into a carafe of water on the nightstand. "I'd let you smell them, but daisies stink," he said.

As he sat down on the edge of the bed, Victoria instinctively moved away from him. He pretended not to notice. "I'm not the only one who's supposed to be working. Since when does the chief editor go home sick?"

She groaned and collapsed against the pile of down pillows. "When her head is hurting so badly that she can't see straight."

"Poor baby," he murmured and leaned over her.

She looked up at him, expecting to see a mocking grin on his swarthy face. But she saw only genuine concern.

He laid one rough palm along her cheek, and she felt the effect of it through her entire body. "You don't seem to have a fever," he said, running his fingertips lightly along her cheekbone.

He leaned even closer, and she was afraid he was going to kiss her. Then she was afraid that he wasn't.

"Open up," he demanded.

"I beg your pardon?"

"Open your mouth and say ah-h-h."

She did as he told her.

"Good grief," he said with a grimace. "That's one ugly sight . . . tonsils and three fillings. Geez!"

She snapped her mouth shut and rolled over on her side, turning her back to him. "No one asked you to look, smartmouth."

She heard him laugh and felt the mattress depress with his weight as he shifted to the center of the bed. His hand moved over her shoulder and, for the first time, she realized that she was wearing her black negligee. When she had climbed into bed this afternoon, she had intended to stay there, alone, for the rest of the day.

Now she fervently wished that she had remained dressed.

"You're in my bed, Riley," she said reproachfully.

"I know. Neat how that worked out, huh?"

"What are you doing in my bed—uninvited?"

"I thought that was obvious. I'm making you feel better. You know," he said, his warm hand stroking her bare arm, "the guys at work were speculating on what you sleep in. Some said flannel granny gowns, some said cotton pajamas, but I knew that you wore lacy silky things . . . like this. But of course, I was too much of a gentleman to say so at the time."

"You discussed what I wear to bed with— with—" She sat up in the bed, sputtering and spewing. "Why you—I hate you, Joe Riley!"

She struck out at him with both fists, but he grabbed her arms and pinned them to her sides.

His good-natured laughter infuriated her all the more. "Hey, settle down. *I* wasn't discussing your nightly attire, *they* were. And for your information I told them to shut their mouths, that you were a lady and they had no business talking about you that way."

She studied him closely to see if he was only setting her up again, but he seemed sincere enough.

"Did you really come to my defense, Joe?" she asked, her voice soft and slightly breathless.

"Of course." He pushed her back onto the bed and leaned over her. His hands still encircled her wrists, and she could smell the crisp scent of his aftershave as he bent his head down to her. "So, doesn't that earn me some points?" he murmured, his lips inches from hers.

"Sure," she whispered. "I'll see to it that you get a raise."

He winced and released her arms. "That's not exactly the reward I had in mind," he said with a wry smile. "But I'll take it."

He moved several inches away from her, and she felt a curious disappointment when she realized that he had temporarily given up the seduction.

"Why did you go home early today, Viki?" he asked. "Do you really have another headache?"

"I . . . I did. But it's gone now."

"See, I told you I'd make you feel better. And you did feel great, what little bit you allowed me to feel, that is."

She grinned in spite of herself. Joe was impossible.

"What's wrong with you, Viki? Why are you getting all these headaches?"

"I don't know. I had a battery of tests done, but the doctor said there's nothing physiologically wrong."

"So, why did you run out of *The Banner* today as though someone had set your skirt afire?"

Something in his dark brown eyes—

maybe it was compassion or concern, maybe even affection—made her consider telling him. She could at least tell him part of it.

"I have a problem, Joe, a terrible problem. And I don't know what to do about it."

He reached over and covered her hand with his. "What is it?" he asked.

"Someone, I don't know who, has been threatening to kill me."

"Kill you? My God, Victoria, what are you talking about?"

She bit her lower lip and tried to stop trembling. Tears burned her eyes, threatening to spill down her face, and that would never do. She hadn't cried in years, and she wasn't about to start now, in front of Joe Riley.

He seemed to sense her inner struggle. "It's okay, sweetheart," he murmured, gathering her into his arms.

It was the first time he had actually held her, and it was wonderful. For months she had wanted to feel his arms around her, to feel him holding her close to his chest. But she had been so afraid. What would she do if she couldn't respond, and he was disappointed in her?

But there were no fears, no misgivings, as she wrapped her arms around his neck and buried her face in the hollow of his shoulder. There was nothing threatening about this embrace. And there was nothing for her to do except melt into him and accept the comfort and strength he was offering.

"Oh, Joe, I've been so frightened." She felt the sobs well up in her chest and spill over. "The other night there was this message written in red lipstick across my bathroom mirror. It said, 'I hate you, Victoria Lord. I'm going to kill you.' Then today at work the same thing was written on my desk calendar. That's why I ran out."

"There, there, don't cry," he murmured into her hair. His gentle hands stroked her back, but there was no sexual awareness in his touch. He could have been comforting a frightened child. "No wonder you've been having headaches. Have you told anyone else about this?"

"No, just you," she sniffed.

He leaned back slightly and looked down into her eyes. "Thank you for telling me. Viki, try not to worry. I'm going to find out who this is and make sure that they don't hurt you, I promise."

"Thank you, Joe," she whispered, and in that moment she believed him.

He cupped her face in his palms and wiped away her tears with his thumbs. "Viki, I—" His touch changed somehow, a subtle, sensual change. He lightly traced the outline of her lower lip with his fingertip. "I care for you," he said, "very much. I know we fight all the time, but—"

His breath was warm on her cheek as he bent his face down to hers. Her lips tingled from his touch . . . and anticipation.

Slowly his hands moved down her arms and then around her midriff. Her senses were filled with his nearness, his scent, the warmth of his body, the masculine roughness of his hand on the silk of her gown.

"Viki?" he murmured.

She heard the question in his voice and knew that he was asking for more than just a kiss.

In answer she lifted her lips to his.

"Riley!" A deep voice exploded in the room. "What the hell do you think you're doing to my daughter?"

"Well, do you think she hurt us very badly?" Larry asked Dave Siegal, who was seated next to him at the defense table.

Siegal scanned the faces of the jurors as Karen Martin stepped down from the witness stand. The men seemed to be enjoying the sight, but two older ladies were eyeing her with moral indignation.

"She didn't help us any," he replied. "Nothing's going to help us at this point, Larry, unless you come clean about that argument."

Larry avoided Dave's piercing gaze by studying his right palm. He said nothing.

Prosecuting attorney Bill Kimbrough adjusted his tortoiseshell glasses and consulted the notebook on the table before him. "The prosecution would like to call Dr. Price Trainor."

"What do you think you're doing, Riley?" Victor Lord's face was florid and his voice shook with rage.

Joe slowly moved away from Victoria on the bed. "It isn't what you think, Mr. Lord."

Viki was surprised at how calm Joe seemed to be. She wondered briefly if he had been caught in this type of predicament before.

"Victoria and I were only talking . . . about a matter that I believe should be brought to your attention immediately."

Victor cast a skeptical eye over his daughter's disheveled silk gown. "Is that true, Victoria? If this man has compromised you, say so, and I'll shoot him here and now."

Pulling the satin sheet and coverlet around her shoulders, Victoria attempted to summon her dignity. "He hardly *compromised* me, Father. And if he had, it would be none of your concern. I am well over twenty-one, you know. Besides, you aren't carrying a gun . . . are you?"

Victor didn't reply but simply stood there in the doorway staring at them both.

Finally Joe broke the silence. "Are you aware, Mr. Lord, that someone has been threatening Victoria's life?"

Not a flicker of emotion crossed those cold gray eyes. Joe began to think that he hadn't heard. "Do you understand, Mr. Lord? Victoria may be in grave danger."

"I'll thank you not to speak to me while you are still in my daughter's bed," he said through tight jaws.

Joe sighed and slid off the bed. He walked over to Victor—within striking distance. Viki was impressed.

"Mr. Lord. Someone has been leaving threatening messages for Victoria on her desk calendar at *The Banner* and on the bathroom mirror."

Still there was no response from Lord.

"This lunatic has access to your home. Doesn't that concern you a little, Mr. Lord?"

Without so much as a sideways glance at Joe, Victor walked over to Viki's bedside. "Why didn't you tell me about this, Victoria, before you confided in an employee?"

"Joe is more than an employee, Father," she said haughtily. "He is my friend, and he has offered to help me by investigating the matter."

"I have my own private investigator. Luke Myers will handle it. This family has enough scandal brewing right now because of Larry Wolek. The situation must be handled with discretion."

Joe stepped forward, his face grim, his dark eyes flashing. "I will be totally discreet in my investigation. I would never do anything that would hurt Victoria."

"You will stay out of this!" Victor shouted.

"I will do as I please on my own time," Joe returned.

The two men stood eye to eye with fists clenched at their sides.

"I'm warning you, Riley." Lord's voice was low and deadly. "Stay away from my daughter."

"Is that what you want, Victoria?" Joe asked, his eyes still locked with Victor's. "Do you want me to stay away from you?"

Victoria looked from one man to the other, carefully evaluating her words before she spoke. "Hire Luke Myers if you choose to, Father. But I want Joe to investigate on my behalf. I trust him completely."

Dave Siegal paced the oak floor before the witness stand, his footsteps the only sound in the heavy silence. He paused before the witness. "Are you quite certain, Dr. Trainor, that you heard Dr. Wolek say those exact words—'I'll kill you before I'll let you tell her that'?"

Trainor thought carefully before answering. "I'm fairly certain, yes."

"Are you certain beyond any shadow of a doubt?"

"It happened so quickly that I . . . No, I can't say I'm absolutely certain that those were his exact words."

"Dr. Trainor, have you ever known Karen Martin to lie?"

"Yes."

"On one occasion? Two occasions?"

"Many occasions."

Dave Siegal nodded and shoved his hands into his slacks pockets. "And have you ever known Dr. Wolek to lie?"

"Never."

Siegal leaned his elbows on the railing around the witness box and fixed Trainor with an unwavering stare. "Dr. Trainor, do you honestly believe that Larry Wolek pushed Ted Hale down those stairs?"

"Objection, Your Honor," Kimbrough interjected. "Calls for a conclusion on the part of the witness."

"I'll rephrase the question, Your Honor. Dr. Trainor, as a co-worker and personal friend of Larry Wolek's, do you believe him capable of murder?"

"Absolutely not. I've never known Larry Wolek to deliberately hurt anyone."

Victoria watched Meredith as she nibbled on a piece of dry toast and sipped at her jasmine tea. "Merrie, eat, for heaven's sake. You're going to need your strength this morning."

"Yes, Meredith, eat your breakfast. Did you take your medication?" Victor asked offhandedly from behind his morning edition of *The Banner*.

"Yes, I took my medicine. I wish you'd stop bugging me about it. It's only iron and vitamin supplements. I don't know what you're making such a big deal about."

Victoria peered sharply at Victor over his newspaper, but his face was inscrutable.

He folded the paper and laid it beside his linen napkin on the table. Looking at his watch, he said, "Hurry along, girls. Court convenes in one hour, and we mustn't keep the prosecutor waiting. He needs your testimony, Meredith, to put Larry Wolek behind bars where he belongs."

Meredith burst into tears, threw the bit of toast on her plate, and fled the dining room.

Victoria sat glaring at her father across the long, formal table. "You know, Father," she said, "you can really be coldhearted when you want to be."

* * *

"So, Miss Lord, you were walking through the hospital parking lot when you looked through a window and saw two men fighting there on the staircase landing. Is that right?"

"Well, they weren't exactly fighting—"

"Objection. The prosecution is leading the witness." Dave Siegal glanced anxiously at Meredith, who seemed as though she were going to start crying any minute.

"Objection sustained," Judge Bainbridge said. "You will rephrase the question."

"What were they doing there on the landing, Miss Lord, having a picnic?"

Dave Siegal rose again. "I must object, Your Honor. The prosecution is badgering this witness."

"Objection sustained." The judge scowled at Kimbrough through his wire-rimmed bifocals. "You will refrain from sarcasm, Mr. Kimbrough."

Kimbrough nodded and turned a placating smile on Meredith. "Miss Lord, did you recognize either of the men through that window?"

"Yes."

He waited for her to elaborate. "Well, who were they?"

"I only recognized one of them. He was Larry Wolek."

"The defendant?"

"Yes."

"But you didn't recognize the other man?"

"No. It was cold outside and the glass was kind of foggy."

"Did you see one man fall down the stairs?"

She twisted the tissue in her hand and cast a helpless look at the defense table. Larry caught her eye and tried to smile his support.

"Yes. I saw someone fall."

"And did you see Larry Wolek push him before he fell?"

"No. I didn't."

Kimbrough eyed her skeptically. "You could see through the glass clearly enough to recognize Dr. Wolek, but you couldn't see if Ted Hale was pushed?"

"No. No, I can't say. One minute they were standing there and the next, Dr. Hale was falling. That's all I saw."

Kimbrough sighed and shook his head in disbelief. "Miss Lord, what is your relationship with the defendant?"

"What?"

"Are you and Larry Wolek lovers?"

"Objection, Your Honor. Irrelevant."

"Objection overruled." The judge nodded at Meredith. "You will answer the question, Miss Lord."

Merrie's eyes found those of her father, seated in the rear of the courtroom. When she saw the animosity on his face, she began to tremble even more violently than before.

She glanced back at Larry, but he blinked rapidly and looked away, not meeting her eyes.

"Are you and Larry Wolek lovers?" Kimbrough repeated.

"Yes," she said, "Larry and I are lovers."

A ripple of conversation went through the court, and Merrie felt her face grow hot. Never before had she been forced to bare her private life to the public, who craved any tidbit of gossip about the high and mighty Lords.

She felt as though the room was closing in on her, as though the air was too thin to breathe. Kimbrough's face filled her vision.

"You saw what happened, but you're protecting your lover. Isn't that so, Miss Lord?"

"No, no I—"

Dave jumped up from his chair. "Objection, Your Honor."

But Kimbrough continued, ignoring the judge's gavel. "You're *lying*, Miss Lord! You saw Larry Wolek push Ted Hale down those stairs."

"No!" The room spun around her in a dizzying sea of faces: Larry's, her father's, the judge's, but mostly Bill Kimbrough's. "No, I didn't—he didn't!"

A blackness enveloped her vision, and for a moment Meredith wondered if she were dying as the sights and sounds of the court-room began to fade.

From far away she heard Larry shout, "Stop it! Can't you see what you're doing to her?"

Then she heard nothing at all.

Chapter
Five

The heavy steel door swung closed behind Dave Siegal as a uniformed police officer led him to the consultation room. Larry was already there, worried and anxious for news.

"Well, how is she? What happened?"

Dave settled wearily into a straight-backed wooden chair at the scarred table. "Dr. Stanton says that she's going to be all right. The emotional strain was too much for her. He's keeping her in the hospital for a few days."

"Is that all he said?" Larry asked breathlessly as he sat in the chair across from Siegal.

Dave studied him quizzically. "Yes. That's all. What were you expecting, Larry?"

Larry looked down at the table and ran his fingertip over a scratch in the surface.

"Nothing. I'm just worried about her. That's all."

"Yeah? Well, I got the impression that Dr. Stanton was awfully concerned about her, too. I'd like to know what's going on here, Larry. Why did you panic when she fainted on the witness stand?"

"I'm in love with her."

"I can appreciate that. But you came unglued, shouting at Bill Kimbrough like that. I thought you were going to slug him, and so did the jury. That didn't exactly help your case any."

Larry shrugged. "It doesn't matter. After Karen's and Price's testimony, I'm sunk anyway."

"I wish I could disagree, but I'm afraid you're right. She's the one, isn't she, Larry?" Dave leaned across the table, studying his client carefully. "You and Hale were fighting over Meredith Lord. You're so in love with her that you're willing to die for her."

Siegal drew a deep breath. "Did you kill for her, too, Larry?"

Victoria leaned down and kissed her sister's pale cheek. "How are you, Merrie?"

"Better," she said. "Where's Father?"

"He's . . . at home. He had some important business and—"

"He just doesn't want to see me, I know.

He suspected about Larry and me, but until today he didn't know that we've actually . . ."

Victoria sat on the edge of the bed and stroked her sister's forehead. "Father can be a real nuisance. Don't think about him now. Just rest and get better so that you can come home."

"He won't want me to come home now that he knows about Larry and me."

"Don't be silly. Of course he'll want you to come home. How else could he manipulate your life?"

Meredith smiled weakly and closed her eyes. "Viki?"

"Yes, dear?"

"What's wrong with me?"

A bolt of fear shot through Victoria. There *was* something wrong: even Merrie knew.

"What do you mean? Dr. Stanton said that you have anemia."

"But can anemia make you feel this weak?"

Victoria studied the dark circles under Merrie's eyes and the gray pallor of her once ivory skin.

"I suppose so, if it's bad enough. I'd better go, Merrie. They told me to only stay for five minutes."

"Viki"—she reached out and clutched Victoria's skirt, although the effort seemed almost too much for her—"talk to Father . . ."

She was going to add, "about Larry." But she drifted off to sleep.

"Oh, I'm going to, Merrie," Victoria said as she tucked the blanket around her sister's shoulders. "I'm going to talk to him the minute I get back to Llanfair."

Larry leaned his elbows on the table and ran his fingers through his thick chestnut hair. "So, now you see why I couldn't tell you what we were arguing about. I couldn't allow something like that to come out in open court."

Dave Siegal laid his notepad aside and shook his head. "You're a fool, Larry Wolek. You should have trusted me in the beginning and saved yourself a lot of grief."

"What do you mean?"

"I mean that if you had come forward with this information in the first place, you probably would never have been brought to trial. But maybe it's not too late."

"Wait a minute. You can't use what I've told you here today. It's privileged information between an attorney and his client. You can't repeat a word of it without my permission."

"I'm not going to, Larry. You are."

"No, I'm not. I'm not going to go into that

courtroom and announce to the world that—"

"Hold on. Nobody said anything about a courtroom. I'll call a private meeting in the judge's chambers between Judge Bainbridge, the prosecutor, you, and me. Would you be willing to tell them what you just told me, as long as it was behind closed doors?"

"And it would all be completely confidential?"

"That's right."

"Okay. I'll do it."

Victoria walked over to her father's burled oak desk and placed her hand on top of the pile of papers he was perusing. "What's the matter with Merrie?" she asked without preamble.

He lifted her hand from his papers, but he didn't pick them up again. "What are you talking about?"

She leaned against the edge of his desk with her arms crossed and a no-nonsense look in her bright blue eyes.

"There are three doctors attending her at the hospital, and Dr. Stanton is worried sick. They're running at least five tests on her at this very minute, and you can't tell me that she has a simple case of anemia."

"The problem with Meredith," he said, "is Larry Wolek. Plain and simple. She was fine until today, until she testified at his *murder* trial. She just can't face the fact that he's a cold-blooded killer."

"Larry is innocent, and if there's any justice, he'll be acquitted."

"Are you saying that you condone what he's done to your sister?" His gray eyes narrowed, and Victoria detected more than the average case of paternal envy.

"You're just jealous because he has more control over her at the moment than you do."

"I'm upset because you and your sister have suddenly forgotten every bit of morality I've taught you. I'm ashamed of you both. You're nothing but a couple of two-bit tramps."

It happened before she knew it. The sharp crack resounded through the study. Were it not for the distinctive red handprint on his cheek, she wouldn't have believed that she had slapped her father.

Victor Lord stood, holding his hand to his face. He trembled with rage as he stared down at his petite daughter, the female image of himself.

He knew that she was shocked at what she had done, but she didn't look the least bit repentant.

But she would be sorry. No one struck Victor Lord without paying a price.

He smiled down at her, his thin lips twisting into a crooked bow. "Merrie's sick," he said slowly as though savoring the words and their effect. "You wanted to know what's wrong with her . . . she has a terminal blood disease. She's dying."

"Viki, we don't have to go out tonight if you aren't up to it," Joe said as they sat at the traffic light. The engine in his Corvette idled roughly, eager to race.

She watched the red light turn to green in the reflection on the sleek black hood of the car. "It's okay. I can't stand the thought of being home alone with Victor tonight. They're keeping Merrie in the hospital for a few days."

Joe noticed that she called old man Lord "Victor" instead of "Father" as she usually did. They must have had a pretty good falling out.

Joe felt a pang of guilt, assuming that they had quarreled over him. He was big on families, and he didn't like the idea that he had interfered in one, even Victor Lord's.

"I'm really sorry about your father walking in on us like that. I'm not a bit sorry about being there with you, just about getting caught."

"It's okay, Joe. It was no big deal," she said wearily.

He chuckled. "If my ego weren't so inflated, I might be insulted. It was a pretty big deal to me. I've been fantasizing about crawling into bed with you for months now. And I almost got a kiss . . ."

"That's not what I meant. It's just that when you put everything into perspective, having Father catch us kissing doesn't seem so important after all."

He pulled the Corvette onto a side road that led down to a waterfront park. By moonlight they could see that the park was deserted. The public dock gleamed white against the dark river water that glittered with silver bits of moonbeams.

"We can go for a drink later," he said, cutting the engine. "Let's talk."

He turned in his bucket seat to face her, his black leather jacket squeaking against the upholstery. "What's wrong, Viki? Are you worrying about those threats?"

"What? Oh, no. Believe it or not, I haven't even thought about that today."

"Then what is it?" He reached out to place his hand over hers, but she quickly pulled it away. He wondered at her reaction. He'd never seen her this way before, and it frightened him. She was almost like another person. Where was his cool, levelheaded Victoria?"

"Viki, what is it, honey?" he asked again.

"Don't call me honey!" she snapped. To his dismay she began to cry. "Don't be nice to me tonight, Joe. Just let me be angry. It's all I have to keep me from crumbling apart."

He pulled away from her, astonished at her outburst. "Who are you angry with? Victor?"

"Yes, Victor—Victor Lord! Self-made millionaire. Tyrant. Bigot. Sadist." With each word she brought her fist crashing down on the padded dashboard. He could feel the fury exploding inside her. "Oh, God, Joe," she sobbed, "I despise that man!"

He watched silently as she expelled some of her frustration and hatred. Finally she was spent. She sat, crying softly, with her hands over her face.

He reached out and put his arm around her shoulder to draw her close. "Viki, sweetheart," he murmured.

"Don't!" she cried, pushing her hands between them. "Don't touch me. If you touch me now, I won't be able to say no."

"Come on, Viki. Give me a little credit here. I wasn't going to try to seduce you. I only want to comfort you. I've never seen you like this. I'm worried."

"Oh, that's right," she said bitterly. "Victoria Lord isn't ever supposed to cry or laugh in public. Or kiss a man, let alone make love to him. Or go dancing. Or march in an antiwar demonstration. God forbid that Victoria Lord would ever reveal an honest emotion."

"Hey, wait a minute. I never said anything like that. Personally, I'm relieved to see that you're human like the rest of us. Who told you all that stuff?"

She sniffed, and he handed her a crumpled napkin that had been lying on the floorboard with the remains of a fast-food lunch.

"Take a wild guess," she said, blowing her nose.

"Your beloved father, perhaps?"

"The one and only."

"So, does that have anything to do with why you're furious with him tonight?"

"Only in general."

"Viki, what did he do to you today?"

For a second he thought that she was going to answer him, but instead she opened the car door, got out, and slammed it behind her.

Quickly he stepped out and followed her as she picked her way down the moonlit path toward the riverbank. To his relief, she stopped at the water's edge.

He followed behind her. "Viki, look at me." With his hands on her shoulders she turned her to face him.

In the moon's pale light he saw her tear-ravaged face and the dark streaks of mascara on her cheeks. He'd never seen such pain on anyone's face in his life: and he'd never wanted to kiss her as badly as he did at that moment.

"What did he do to you today?" he asked. "Tell me."

"He got even with me for being with you, Joe. He called me a tramp. And then I slapped him."

Joe's face hardened with anger. "Good. If I'd been there, I would have decked him."

"But he got even with me for that, too. He always evens the score."

"What did he do?"

He felt a violent shudder run through her, and he held her tighter.

"He . . . he told me that Merrie's dying. She's going to die, Joe. My sister is going to die."

"Oh, no. Viki . . ."

She grabbed her head and bent over as though an agonizing pain had shot through her brain. Joe caught her in his arms just before she hit the ground.

"Oh, God, Joe," she sobbed. "I can't lose Merrie. I don't think I could bear it."

Chapter
Six

Felicia, the housekeeper, peeked into the library and saw Victor Lord, sitting in his favorite wing-back chair, puffing on his pipe. The firelight played on his silver hair and on the maroon satin of his smoking jacket. A blue-gray cloud of smoke circled in a lazy, swirling haze around him.

"Excuse me, Mr. Lord—"

"Yes, Felicia." His voice was curt and harsh, as it always was when he addressed those whom he considered to be "beneath" him . . . which was almost everyone. "What is it?"

"I'm worried about Miss Victoria, sir."

Lord grumbled and tapped his pipe on the marble smoking stand beside his chair. "You needn't worry about Victoria," he said. "As she has reminded me several times lately, she is an adult, fully capable of taking care of herself."

Felicia hesitated, wondering whether or not to press her point. She didn't want to risk fueling Lord's anger, but at the same time she was terribly concerned about her young mistress.

"Begging your pardon, Mr. Lord, but Miss Viki has . . . disappeared." She chose the last word carefully, hoping to at least pique his curiosity.

It worked. "Disappeared? What are you talking about, woman?"

"I took her dinner to her room earlier, because she was having another one of those awful headaches. Just now I went upstairs to get the tray, and she's gone."

"Maybe she's with—What's-His-Name. She was out with him last night until quite late."

"No, Mr. Riley called this evening and asked her to go with him to his sister's house for dinner. But she said no because of her headache." Felicia twisted her hands in her snowy apron. "Miss Viki looked really sick when I took her dinner to her, Mr. Lord. I'm worried."

Victor sighed and placed his pipe in the stand. "All right, Felicia. You check downstairs and I'll check upstairs. Then, perhaps, I can enjoy a bit of solitude."

"Thank you, Mr. Lord," she said, back-

ing out of the room with a series of curt-
sies.

"Women," he muttered as he walked up
the stairs to Victoria's room.

The first thing he noticed was the un-
touched tray of food on the nightstand. But
that was hardly unusual. Victoria hadn't
been eating much lately.

Her bed was a tumbled pile of sheets and
comforter. She had apparently occupied it
during the evening.

The clothes that she had worn that day, a
pale blue suit and a white crepe de chine
blouse, were draped over an oriental screen
in the corner of the room.

A gust of cold autumn wind blew the
bedroom window open, billowing the lace
curtains. As Victor hurried to close it, he felt
his first pangs of misgiving. It wasn't like
Victoria to leave a window unlocked on a
chilly night.

As he latched the leaded glass pane, he
noticed something white, fluttering in the
wind just outside the window. At first he
thought it was a dove; then he realized that it
was a bit of cloth.

He opened the window, reached out, and
retrieved it from where it was tangled in the
ivy-covered trellis.

Lord recognized the handkerchief instantly. It was one of a set of fine linen kerchiefs
that Victoria had bought last summer in

Dublin. She had a silly superstition about carrying one with her at all times, for "Irish Luck" as she called it.

As he fingered the delicate embroidered linen, Lord suddenly remembered the last time he had been in Victoria's room, the afternoon when he had found her and Joe Riley together.

He thought of what Riley had said about the threatening notes, and his uneasiness escalated into full-blown anger.

If some thugs had dared to kidnap his daughter . . . if they thought they were going to extort ransom money from him, they had quite another thought coming.

Victor looked back at the mussed bed and thought of Riley lying there . . . beside his daughter.

And just what part had Joe Riley played in all of this? he wondered, crumpling the handkerchief in his fist.

He intended to find out. Now.

As Lord drove his Mercedes into the Siegals' driveway, he cursed Luke Myers. Victor had hired Myers three days ago to investigate these threats against Victoria, and the man hadn't uncovered a single lead yet.

At least, Victor assumed that Myers hadn't found anything. He hadn't reported back, and Lord hadn't considered the situation serious enough to pressure him. He vowed to get on Myers's case about it to-night, as soon as he returned to Llanview.

Unless, of course, he found Victoria at the Siegals', as he expected he would. Victor surmised that his oldest daughter had accepted Joe Riley's invitation after all.

Lord pulled the collar of his raincoat up around his ears and shoved his gloved hands deep into his pockets as he walked up the sidewalk. It was an especially chilly September this year.

In a rare moment of paternal concern Lord thought of Victoria out in the cold, probably without a coat, possibly held hostage by some cold-blooded criminal.

He shook his head, banishing the thought. She was probably here with Joe Riley, safe and warm, having eaten as little as possible of Eileen Siegal's dreadful meatloaf.

He stamped his feet impatiently, waiting for someone to answer his knock. When Eileen stuck her head out the door, he was surprised to see that her red hair wasn't twisted in those awful rollers she usually wore. He had somehow thought they were surgically attached.

"Oh, Mr. Lord, how nice to see you," she gushed, ushering him into the living room. "Dave, look who's here."

Dave Siegal left his recliner and walked toward Lord with an outstretched hand. "Hello, Victor. What brings you out tonight?" His tone was cordial enough, but his face was drawn and tense with apprehension.

Victor's gray eyes quickly scanned the room, looking for Victoria. But their only visitor was Joe Riley, who sat on the sofa with a cup of steaming coffee in his hand.

Lord's eyes locked with Riley's for a brief moment before he answered Dave. "Ah . . . I was going to speak to you about some . . . business. But I see that you have company. It can wait."

"That's all right, Mr. Lord," Joe said, rising from the sofa. "I was just leaving anyway."

"No. You needn't leave on my account. It can wait until tomorrow."

Joe eyed Victor skeptically. Since when did Victor Lord apologize for disturbing anyone? It was totally out of character for him. He also seemed worried and anxious. Joe couldn't remember seeing Victor Lord ever reveal anything but total confidence and composure.

"Won't you have a cup of coffee before you leave, Mr. Lord?" Eileen asked, eager to offer hospitality to this granite pillar of Llanview society.

Victor glanced from Eileen, who looked as though she might bow down and kiss his ring at any moment, to her brother, Joseph, and he thought how different the brother and sister were. Joe was studying him carefully, reaching into his thoughts and intentions with those dark eyes of his.

Victor was uncomfortable around Riley. Joe reminded him too much of himself at that age: smart, ambitious, relentless. He made a mental note never to turn his back on Joe Riley.

"I really must be going. My business can wait until another time," he said as he hurried out the door, closing it behind him.

"Well, how do you like that?" Eileen tossed her head, sending her red curls and waves bobbing. "He didn't even wait for his coat to hit his back until he was gone again. What do you suppose he wanted?"

Dave shrugged. "I don't know. He didn't even rant and rave about me taking Larry's case. Something must be wrong."

"Something's wrong, all right." Joe grabbed his black leather jacket from the coat tree. "And I'm going to find out what it is." He threw open the door and dashed outside.

"Hey, Mr. Lord, wait a minute."

Joe caught up with the Mercedes just as Victor reached the end of the driveway. He stood panting beside the car, his breath making soft white puffs in the frosty night air. He waited as the power window silently lowered.

"Yes, Riley. What is it?"

"What's wrong?" Joe asked abruptly. He had never been good at beating around the bush.

Lord studied the dark road ahead for a moment. "Nothing. Why?"

"You didn't come here for a business discussion tonight. If you had, you would have had one. Is something wrong with Viki?"

Lord peered at him sharply in the darkness. "Why do you think something's wrong with Victoria?"

"Because I invited her to have dinner with us tonight, and she turned me down because of one of her headaches. And when you came in just now, you looked around the room and seemed disappointed that I was the only one there. My guess is that you don't know where Victoria is, and you were hoping that she'd be here with me."

"That will be a cold day in hell when I hope my daughter is with you, Riley."

"Then Viki is home, safe and sound in her bed, right?"

Victor sighed and unlocked the passenger door. "Get in," he said.

"Kidnapped?"

"It's a definite possibility. Hasn't the thought occurred to you?"

Victor silently guided the Mercedes along Llanview's dark streets. He found himself searching the shadows on either side of the road. "Yes. It has occurred to me," he admitted. "But with my reputation in this town, I would have thought that no one would be foolish enough to attempt to extort ransom from me."

"An excellent point," Joe agreed dryly. "But this person may not be aware of your reputed . . . frugality. Or they may have another motive than ransom. Like revenge."

"Revenge?" Victor sniffed, dismissing the idea. "Victoria doesn't have an enemy in this town."

"Perhaps not. But you have more than your share, I'd wager."

"Of course I do. No one rises to a prominent position like mine without making enemies along the way. But I can't believe that any of the disgruntled lot would stoop to kidnapping my daughter."

"Let's hope you're right."

Joe Riley leaned back in the plush leather seat and closed his eyes for a moment. He envisioned Viki's blue eyes, frightened, begging him for help. He thought of what Lord had told him about the open window and the handkerchief tangled in the ivy. He thought of the threatening messages scrawled across her mirror and of the many people Victor Lord had trampled on his way up the ladder.

There was a host of people in Llanview

who wanted to see Victor Lord hurt or dead. Joe hoped to God that none of them felt the same way about Lord's elder daughter.

"So, what do we do first?" Victor asked as he led Joe into the foyer of the mansion. "I suppose we should call the police, but . . ."

Joe was surprised to see the great Victor Lord at a loss. Any other time he would have been totally in command, decisive, reveling in his authority. He must have been more upset than Joe had initially suspected.

It was reassuring to Joe that Lord was capable of entertaining an emotion. Yet, it was unsettling to think that there might be cause for the older man's concern. Joe quickly pushed his own panic into the recesses of his mind before it could render him ineffectual like Victor.

"First things first," he said. "Let's check her room again. There might be something you overlooked."

They hurried up the stairs to Victoria's room. Joe paused by the door. "By the way, did that detective of yours, Luke Myers, come up with anything?" It was a legitimate question under the circumstances, but Joe couldn't keep the sarcastic tone out of his voice. He knew that Myers hadn't uncovered anything new. There was nothing to uncover: if there had been, Joe was certain that he would have found it himself.

Victor raised his head sufficiently to look down his nose at Joe. "No," he said carefully, as though the admission cost him a great deal. "Myers hasn't found anything. Have you?"

"No," he said with a sigh as he opened the bedroom door. "Not a damned thing."

Joe froze, his hand on the doorknob, his mouth open.

"What is it?" Victor asked, pushing by him. His eyes scanned the room, skidding to a halt on his daughter's bed. "Victoria!"

Vince Wolek tiptoed into his apartment and carefully closed the front door. If he woke Anna at this hour there would be hell to pay. She just loved to sock it to him for staying out late. When she propped her hands on her waist and glared at him, she looked just like Mama used to. Sometimes she forgot her place. After all, she was only a woman, and his sister at that.

Of course, Vinnie wasn't afraid of his little sister, Anna. He just didn't want to have a run-in with her tonight. He didn't want anything to drag him down from the pink cotton candy cloud he was floating on.

Vinnie was in love.

He felt his way across the dark living room and stubbed his toe on some shadowy, unidentified object. Darn that Anna, anyway. She was always rearranging the furniture on him. How was a guy supposed to sneak in at two in the morning with a sharp-edged coffee table in his path?

He stifled a curse and groped for his bedroom doorknob. Once the door was closed behind him, he threw caution aside and turned on the lamp. He pulled off his cowboy boots and tossed them on the floor beside the dirty coveralls he had taken off that afternoon.

Without bothering to undress, he lay down across the old wrought-iron bed that had been Mama and Papa's. Pulling Mama's patchwork quilt up around his shoulders, he sighed and closed his eyes. He could still see her, the girl of his dreams. Tonight was the night when Vincent Wolek had forgotten every reason why he was a bachelor.

Her eyes had been bright blue . . . and wicked when they had caught his across the bar. They had sparkled with fun-loving mischief when he had finally worked up the courage to ask her to dance.

Vinnie wasn't much for dancing: it was sissy stuff. But he had forgotten all about that, too, as he danced the night away with this beautiful redhead with the wicked blue eyes.

She had laughed at his corny jokes and complimented him on his dancing when he had gotten drunk enough to really let go. She had cheered him on when he had arm-wrestled that stranger. And when he had won, she had given him a kiss that curled his toes.

Vinnie was in love—hopelessly, blissfully, head over heels in love with Nicole Smith, a beautiful butterfly in a psychedelic mini-dress.

There was just one little thing that nagged at Vince. One little fact—an incredible coincidence.

Except for her garish clothes and colorful makeup and bright red hair, Nicole Smith looked exactly like Victoria Lord. Strange, Vinnie falling for a woman who looked just like his best friend's girl.

Oh, well, he thought as he snuggled into the warmth of the quilt and savored the scent of her perfume which lingered on his clothes. *Ah, Niki . . .*

"Victoria, where have you been!" Victor roared, throwing the door wide open.

"What?" She blinked sleepily and sat up in bed. "What is it, Father? Joe, what are you doing here?"

Joe looked questioningly at Victor. "Well?" he asked. "Did you think to check under the covers when you did your *thorough* search?"

"Don't be impudent. Of course I did. She wasn't here, I tell you." Lord crossed the room and threw back the bedcovers, revealing Victoria's white lace gown. He stared at her for a moment, then covered her.

She cast a blushing look at Joe, who was grinning lasciviously. She pulled the sheets high around her neck. "What is the matter with you two? And what are you doing in my bedroom?" she demanded.

"Looking for you, Viki," Joe replied as he walked over to her. "And I can't tell you how delighted we are to find you here in your bed."

"Speak for yourself, Riley," Victor interjected. "You may be delighted if you please, but I'm furious. This is a merry chase you've led us on this evening. Is this your idea of a prank, young lady?"

Joe watched her carefully. The surprise and confusion on her pretty face were very real. "I don't know what you're talking about, Father. What's wrong?"

When Victor said nothing but continued to stare at her, she turned to Joe. "Joe, what is it?" she asked. He could hear the panic in her voice and see the genuine fear in her blue eyes.

In spite of her father's glowering, Joe reached over and pressed Victoria's hand between his. Her palm was cold and clammy, and he could feel her trembling.

"Viki," he said gently, "earlier this evening your father and Felicia came upstairs, and you were gone. They searched the house and couldn't find you anywhere. Your father brought me back here to help search for you. We've been worried sick."

She looked to Victor for confirmation, but met only a stony glare. "But that can't be. I had a headache, and I went to bed. I've been here all night."

"I don't know where in blazes you've been tonight, Victoria," Lord said, his gray eyes narrowed with suspicion. "But you haven't been in bed. Not in *this* bed, anyway."

Joe saw the fear on her face dissolve into hurt as Victor's words found their mark. He felt his own temper flare, and he moved to stand between Victoria and her father. "That's enough, Lord," he said with deadly calm. "Why don't you go on downstairs and let me talk to Victoria alone for a few minutes."

Joe never expected Lord to do as he asked, but it was worth a try. To his surprise Victor turned on his heel and left the room, slamming the door behind him.

He turned back to Viki, who sat with her knees pulled up to her chest, her arms wrapped tightly around her legs.

Her blue eyes were moist, her long eyelashes glittering with tears. "Joe," she whispered.

In an instant he was on the bed beside her, holding her and stroking her hair. "Yes, sweetheart?"

"I'm so scared."

"I know. It's okay. Everything will be all right, I promise."

She pulled back and looked up into his eyes, which were dark with suppressed emotion. "Oh, Joe, what's happening to me?"

Chapter
Seven

Larry Wolek glanced around at the dark mahogany paneling and the bookcases filled with leather-bound law books. Judge Bainbridge's chambers reflected the dignity of the traditional barrister. On the judge's desk every pen, every paper, every file was in its place. Solid and austere—that was Judge Henry Bainbridge.

The judge sat behind his walnut desk, his fingers laced together, his forefingers steepled against his lips in a classic judicial pose.

To Larry, the walnut desk was as imposing as the fabled wall around Jericho. He would have to bring that wall tumbling down if he were to win his freedom.

His attorney, Dave Siegal, sat next to him in a straight-backed chair designed to keep its occupant uncomfortable and at attention.

Bill Kimbrough had chosen to stand, or

rather, pace from the window to the antique dictionary stand in the corner and back. His ruddy face was three shades redder than usual, and behind his tortoiseshell glasses his watery blue eyes darted between Larry, Dave, and the judge.

"Well, we're all here as you requested," he informed Siegal. "We might as well find out now what it is that you're trying to pull."

Judge Bainbridge cleared his throat with a disciplinary tone. "Kimbrough, this court has heard quite enough from you. Please curtail your sarcasm."

Kimbrough said nothing, but nodded his compliance.

"I have a full calendar, Mr. Siegal," the judge said, "If you could make your point quickly."

"Ah, yes." Dave took a deep breath and plunged in. "As we all know, the most damning evidence against my client has been his own refusal to talk about what happened on that staircase just before Ted Hale fell. But I'm happy to say that Dr. Wolek has finally related those unfortunate events to me, and he's willing to confide in you as well."

The judge leaned forward in his chair, fully attentive. Bill Kimbrough stopped his pacing as some of the scarlet coloring drained out of his face.

Dave continued, "I'm sure that when Dr. Wolek tells you what happened that day, you will understand why—being an honorable man—he was unable to reveal these facts in open court."

"Merrie, if you don't eat, how are you going to get your strength back?"

Victoria sat on the edge of her sister's hospital bed, holding a sesame cracker with a dollop of pâté under Meredith's nose.

"I don't like pâté and you know it, Viki," she said, wrinkling her nose.

"Listen, it's either this or the liver and onions they serve here at the hospital. Open up, or I'll sit on you and tickle you the way I used to when we were kids."

With a sigh of resignation Merrie opened her mouth. She grimaced and shuddered as she swallowed. "If you wanted me to eat something, why didn't you bring me a slice of Felicia's double-fudge cake? Then you wouldn't have to force me to eat."

Victoria grinned, cast a covert glance around the empty room, and pulled a plastic container from her purse. She peeled off the lid. "One generous slice of double-fudge cake for the lady," she said, presenting it with flourish. "And don't ever say that I don't take care of my little sister."

Meredith's unstable emotions teetered at

this show of affection. "Oh, Viki," she said tearfully, "I'd never say that you don't take care of me. You're a wonderful sister."

"For heaven's sake, Merrie," she said, reaching for a tissue on the nightstand. "I can't believe you'd cry over a piece of chocolate cake."

Meredith dabbed at her eyes and blew her nose. "I know, I'm so silly these days. I cry at the drop of a hat."

"I noticed," Victoria said. "What's the matter? Are you getting tired of lolling around, being waited on hand and foot, having your loved ones smuggle goodies to you?"

Meredith sniffed and nodded. "But mostly I miss Larry. I haven't seen him since . . . since that awful day in court when I fainted. He calls me from the jail when he can, but he won't tell me how the trial is going. He says I shouldn't worry about him, but I can't help it. Is he going to be all right, Viki? Is he going to go to prison?"

Victoria looked down into her sister's soft brown eyes, which demanded complete honesty.

"I don't know, Merrie. I wish I could tell you. But I really don't know."

"Ted Hale was in love with Meredith," Larry said. He stared at his hands, which were folded in his lap. "I really can't blame him for that; Merrie's a wonderful person."

He glanced over at Dave Siegal, who nodded his encouragement. "Go on," he gently prodded.

"Merrie didn't return Ted's affections. She and I . . . we've been in love for quite some time now. Ted knew that he didn't have a chance with Merrie, and he was extremely jealous of me.

"The day of the accident, Ted happened to be in Dr. Bill Stanton's office when Bill was out. Ted saw Meredith's medical records lying there on Bill's desk, and he read them. He found out then that—"

Larry's voice broke, and he sat quietly for a moment, fighting his emotions. Even Kimbrough sensed Larry's turmoil and sank quietly into a chair beside him.

Larry regained his composure and continued. "Ted found out that Merrie has an incurable blood disease. It's in remission at the moment, but a physical or psychological trauma could cause a relapse.

"That day on the stairs, he told me about her illness. I think he honestly enjoyed telling me. He had heard that Meredith and I were planning to be married, and he was determined to stop us, no matter what the cost. He said he was going to tell Merrie about her disease. That's when I said, 'I'll kill you before I'll let you tell her that.'"

"And did you? Kill him, that is?" Bill Kimbrough asked in a voice curiously void of accusation.

"No. He tried to brush by me, and I put out my arm to stop him. He shoved me away and lost his balance. I tried to catch him, but he fell. . . ."

A heavy silence filled the judge's chambers as they absorbed Larry's words.

Larry looked from the judge to Kimbrough, but their faces were inscrutable. "I can't honestly say that I'm sorry Ted died," he added. "I'm glad that Merrie didn't find out about her illness. I love her, and I would do anything to protect her. But I didn't kill Ted Hale. It was an accident."

Judge Bainbridge leaned back in his chair and studied Wolek through his wire-rimmed bifocals. "Do you realize, young man, that if you had come forward with this information, you might have spared yourself a lot of grief, not to mention saving the taxpayers the expense of your trial?"

"Yes, Your Honor, but surely you understand how devastated Meredith would have been if this had been brought out in court."

"Yes, of course. I just hope that your Miss Lord will appreciate the sacrifice you've made on her behalf, Dr. Wolek."

Larry smiled, a tired, relieved smile. "I just hope that she never knows about it."

* * *

Meredith looked up to see a delivery man holding a massive bouquet of red roses before his face. "Where do you want these, lady?" he asked in a strangely affected voice.

"Oh, they're lovely! Bring them over here so that I can smell them."

When he brought them to the side of her bed, she noticed his shoes and his brown tweed slacks. This was no florist delivery man. Her heart leaped in her chest.

"Larry!"

He peered out from behind the roses, a broad grin on his handsome face. "Hi-ya, sweet stuff. How are you?"

"How am I? How am I?" She bounded off the bed and into his arms. "I'm great! I'm—"

"Hey, wait a minute." He caught her around the waist with one arm while managing to place the roses on a nearby table with the other arm. "You shouldn't be bopping around like this. You're supposed to be in bed."

"And you're supposed to be in jail."

"They released me."

"Released you? For the day?"

"For good."

"For good? Forever?"

He smiled down at her, loving the look of pure joy on her beautiful face. "I'm free, Merrie. It's all over, and I'm free."

She burst into tears, and he caught her to him, kissing her long and luxuriously.

"Larry, I can't believe it. It's too good to be true."

"It's true."

He felt her body tremble and sag against his. "Back in the bed with you, kiddo," he said, lifting her in his arms.

He laid her down gently, but she clung to his neck. "Stay with me, Larry. Please."

"I'm not going anywhere, sweetheart," he said.

"I mean here." She patted the bed beside her.

He grinned and shook his head. "No. As tempting as that offer may be for a recently released jailbird, you really aren't up to it."

She giggled and blushed a delicate pink, her first coloring in days. "You have a dirty mind. I just want to cuddle."

"Oh, well, in that case . . . just for a minute."

He quickly dragged a chair over to the door and lodged it beneath the doorknob.

"Now we can snuggle uninterrupted," he said as he took off his shoes and slipped into bed beside her.

When he put his arms around her to draw her against him, he couldn't help noticing how thin she was, even thinner than before. He felt a sharp pang of guilt, knowing that she was sick because of worrying about him.

But that was behind them now. He was free, and he was going to take care of her.

"Why did they let you go, Larry? What happened?"

He tried to distract her with a kiss. "They just realized how ridiculous the whole thing was and dropped the charges."

She eyed him suspiciously. "Really?"

"More or less," he said, avoiding her direct gaze. "Dave Siegal is a great lawyer. He pulled some strings. You know, fancy legal footwork."

"I see," she said quietly, unconvinced.

"The important thing is that it's behind us now, and we can get on with our lives." He ran his fingertip along the lace-edged neckline of her nightgown. "We were making some important plans, Merrie, before this . . . ordeal interrupted us. Do you remember?"

"Of course I remember," she said breathlessly.

"My feelings haven't changed." He pressed the back of her hand to his lips. "Meredith, I still want to marry you. If you still want me, that is."

"If I still want you? Oh, Larry." She answered him with her hands, her lips, her embrace.

And Dr. Wolek was very glad he had put a chair against the door.

* * *

"Larry's free? Why, sugar, that's wonderful. Hallelujah! Now see there, didn't I tell you that the Lord watched out for the innocent of heart."

Sadie gave Anna a hug that left her rumpled and breathless, but feeling very loved. "I know, Sadie. It's just hard to have faith sometimes, you know?"

A look of pain crossed Sadie's face. "I know," she said. "I've had my weak moments, too, Lord knows. But your baby brother is free. He's free at last, and the angels in heaven are rejoicing."

Anna found herself listening for that celestial choir. She was always amazed at the depth of Sadie's faith. When Sadie said that the angels were singing, Anna could almost believe it.

"Well, I don't know about the angels, but I'm rejoicing, that's for sure. Vinnie is on his way home right now, and we're going to the hospital. Larry went straight there after he called us with the good news. He wanted to see Merrie right away. We're taking her some fresh fruit that came through the warehouse today. Vince says she needs to put some meat on her bones."

"That's true," Sadie admitted sadly. "She's just a mite of a thing. I've got some oatmeal cookies fresh out of the oven. Why don't you take them to her, too?"

Anna smiled and gave Sadie another hug,

just for good measure. "Why don't you come along with us and give them to her yourself?"

"So, here you are," Vince said as he walked into the golden sunlight of the hospital solarium. He was quickly followed by Anna and Sadie, each bearing a basket of fresh fruit and cookies.

Meredith was sitting in a wheelchair in a pool of sunbeams, and Larry was kneeling on one knee beside her, holding her hand.

"We looked all over the hospital for you guys," Anna said as she hurried to her brother. Larry rose and folded her into a hearty embrace.

"We were all so worried about you," she said, holding him close. "I was afraid I'd never be able to hug you like this again. I couldn't bear the thought of you being in that awful jail."

Larry squeezed her and planted a kiss on her freckled cheek. "Well, don't worry about that now. It's all over."

Anna finally released Larry, and Vinnie took his place, enveloping him in a crushing bear hug. "It's good to have you back, little brother," Vince said, looking up at the "little" brother who towered over him. Vinnie didn't seem to mind that Larry was taller, handsomer, and smarter than he. Vince could beat him at arm-wrestling any day. And that was the true test of a man.

"It's good to be back," Larry said, turning to Sadie, who stood, quietly sharing in their joy. "And Sadie, my love, how nice of you to come down. What do you have there in your basket?"

"Cookies," she said, "and they aren't for a Big Bad Wolf like you, Lawrence Wolek. They're for Little Red Riding Hood, here." She gently placed the basket in Merrie's lap and patted her knee. "There you are, sugar. Something to fatten you up a bit. I've eaten dozens of them in my day, and as you can see," she said, pointing to her ample bottom, "they do plump a body up."

"And Vinnie brought you some fresh apples and oranges from the warehouse today, Merrie," Anna said, holding out her basket.

Vince looked away in embarrassment. "No big deal," he muttered. "They were gonna go bad if somebody didn't make use of 'em."

Meredith glanced up at Vincent with a hint of surprise in her smile. This was the closest Vince had ever come to being nice to her. She had always gotten the idea that he wasn't exactly delighted about her and Larry.

At times, when he thought she wasn't looking, she had seen him eyeing her suspiciously. But then she supposed that Vincent was suspicious of anyone who was born with money, anyone who hadn't had to scramble for it the way he had.

She gazed down at the basket of fresh fruit in her lap. This produce was in no immediate danger of "going bad." Each piece had obviously been handpicked for its perfection.

"Thank you, Vinnie," she said, using his family's pet name for him. "That was very thoughtful of you."

He shrugged and walked away to stare out the window. Once again Merrie got the feeling that Vince wasn't exactly in her court.

"You're looking so pretty today, Merrie," Anna said. "This sunshine has even put some pink roses in your cheeks."

"Thank you," Meredith replied, her color deepening. "But it isn't only the sunshine . . ." She smiled up at Larry, who warmly returned it.

"Must be Larry's good news that's got her in the pink," Sadie commented.

Meredith and Larry exchanged secretive looks, and Larry cleared his throat. "My being released isn't the only good news we have."

Anna glanced uneasily over at Vince, who was still standing with his back to them, staring out the window as though he weren't listening to every word they said.

"And what good news is that?" she asked, but she already knew the answer by the way the young couple gazed at each other.

"I asked Meredith to marry me," Larry announced proudly. "And she agreed. She'll be released from the hospital this Thursday, and we'll be married on Saturday afternoon."

Anna studied Larry's face carefully. She had played the role of older sister, best friend, and mother to her younger brother, and she knew him better than anyone did. His mouth was smiling as he looked down on his beautiful fiancée, but his eyes were full of sadness. Something was wrong, but Anna couldn't imagine what it was.

"I'm very happy for you both," she said, ignoring her suspicions for the moment. "Welcome to the family, Meredith. I always wanted a sister."

"Congratulations," Sadie said, pounding Larry on the back. "That's a wonderful thing, two young people starting a new life together."

There it was again, Anna thought, that look of pain in Larry's eyes. She glanced over at Vince's back and mentally crossed herself in a silent prayer. *Please, Vinnie, don't be a mule's hind leg if you can help it.*

"Did you hear that, Vinnie?" she asked tremulously. "Larry and Meredith are going to get married. Isn't that wonderful?"

Tension filled the room as they waited for Vince's reply. Finally he turned around. His face was beet-red, an indication of his blood pressure. "Oh, yeah," he said, "that's just ducky. I can see why you want to marry her, Larry. After all, she's a real good looker, and she's filthy rich. But I just wanna know one thing: why would any daughter of Victor Lord's want to marry a poor doctor from the wrong side of the river?"

Meredith frowned into the mirror and applied more blusher to her cheeks. She dabbed a bit of foundation under her eyes in a vain attempt to hide the blue circles that seemed much darker than they had been before . . . before the trial . . . before her collapse on the witness stand.

She pushed the memory out of her mind. That was over now, and there was no reason to remember it ever again.

She was going home today: that was the only thing that mattered. And this Saturday she would become Mrs. Larry Wolek. She embraced the thought and temporarily forgot about her sallow complexion and dark circles . . . or what they might mean.

It took all of her strength to lift the small suitcase, which Viki had brought to her from Llanfair, onto the bed. Dear Viki. She had thought of everything. Tucked into the suitcase was an assortment of soft sweaters, slacks, and skirts, along with her favorite Dior lingerie.

Meredith chose a peach-colored cashmere and a matching pleated skirt. It was one of Larry's favorites, and she wanted so much to look pretty for him when he came to pick her up this afternoon.

She dressed slowly, trying to conserve her energy. She couldn't believe how much weaker she was now than before. The anemia felt as though it was getting the best of her.

Trembling with fatigue, she sat back on the bed to wait for Larry. He wouldn't be along for at least two more hours, so she could get some rest before he arrived. She didn't want to seem weak or sick. He worried about her too much as it was.

Just as she had closed her eyes and started to doze off, she heard a rap at the door. Larry was early after all.

"Come in," she called eagerly.

But it wasn't Larry who entered the room. It was Victor.

And the moment she saw his face she knew—Victoria had told him about her engagement.

"Hello, Father," she said meekly. "How nice of you to drop by."

"This is hardly a social call, and you know it," he said. His handsome face was creased with an angry scowl, the same scowl that had struck terror in Meredith's heart since child-hood. She was in trouble—big trouble.

"Why don't you sit down, Father?" she suggested, pointing to a chair.

"What I have to say, I will say standing up. Thank you for your concern." His tone was crisp with sarcasm. "I just wish that you had been concerned enough about your father to inform him of your imminent *marriage*."

He spat out the last word as though it tasted bitter on his tongue.

Meredith toyed with the pleats in her skirt, spreading them out, then folding them together. "Victoria offered to tell you for me, and I decided to let her," she said quietly.

"As usual, you were too cowardly to tell me yourself."

She winced as his words stung her pride. He was right. And that made it even worse.

"I didn't tell you because I didn't think I could bear to hear you shout at me, and glare at me, and treat me as though I were an inferior human being. The way you are right now," she added.

"And just when were you intending to tell me, your own father, that you were getting married? Five minutes before the cere-mony?"

"No," she said softly, "I was going to tell you afterward, so that you wouldn't try to stop me."

"I see." His gray eyes narrowed, and a muscle in his square jaw twitched with suppressed fury. "And that was a wise decision on your part, because I most certainly would have stopped you. And I still will, no matter what I have to do. I won't see my daughter throw her life away by marrying a piece of waterfront rabble. Little fool. Haven't you ever asked yourself *why* he wants to marry you? Haven't you once questioned his motives?"

"Now, isn't that funny," she said without humor. "Vince Wolek doesn't want us to marry for exactly the same reason. He questions *my* motives for wanting to marry *Larry*. You're both snobs, you and Vincent. You don't trust anyone who is poor, and Vince doesn't trust rich people. Money isn't the issue here. Larry and I love each other, and that's all that matters."

"Love? Ha. You've never had to live on love. I can tell you right now, it makes a pretty thin soup. With true love and a nickel you can buy a pack of gum."

"That's a bit cynical, don't you think, Father?"

"It's true."

He straightened his silk tie and crossed his arms across his chest in an authoritative stance. "Meredith, I forbid you to marry that man. I absolutely forbid it. Do you hear me?"

"I hear you." Her voice was soft, but he detected a note of defiance.

"Do you understand me? There will be no marriage Saturday afternoon."

For the first time in Meredith's life something meant more to her than her father's opinion of her. Something was finally worth risking Victor Lord's wrath. She slid off the bed and stood on shaking legs. Her brown eyes held a light of determination that Victor had never seen there before.

For a moment, one brief moment, she reminded him of his young wife, who had stood before him with that same light in her soft brown eyes. And like Meredith, she had told him that she was leaving him, walking out of his life, out of his control.

"There *will* be a wedding on Saturday, Father. If you can be happy for me and the man I love, you're welcome to attend and celebrate with us. If you can't . . . then I'll have to ask you to stay away."

The only sounds in the hospital room were those of the clock ticking on the nightstand and Victor's breathing as he fought to control his temper. He raised his hand as though to strike her, then he suddenly lowered it.

She saw the surprise on his face and the impotent rage. Then he smiled, an ugly half-smile, half-sneer. But that expression quickly vanished, too, leaving his features as blank as when he played poker with his attorney and banker.

"You can't marry him, Meredith. You mustn't . . . for his sake, if not for your own."

"But Larry wants to marry me. He wants to very much."

"Yes, but he wouldn't if he knew—"

Something in his eyes made her afraid to ask, but she had to. "If he knew what?"

That terrible smile had returned to his face. "Larry Wolek would never want you if he knew the truth about your condition," he said with chilling deliberation. "If he knew that you're dying. . . ."

Chapter
Eight

"What do you mean, she checked herself out?" Larry demanded as he leaned across the counter at the nurses' station and glared at Karen Martin, who was holding Meredith's chart.

She glanced over it, and a smug grin lifted the corners of her full lips. "Yes. She checked herself out at ten minutes after twelve." Karen glanced at her watch. "That was about half an hour ago."

"I know when it was, damn it," he growled. "What I want to know is why."

"Well, don't ask me," she replied with wide-eyed innocence as she replaced the chart in the revolving file. "I'm not Meredith's keeper. I thought that was your job."

"Let me see that." He grabbed the chart out of the file and flipped it open. "Did you see her when she left?"

"Yes. I saw her walking down the hall, suitcase in hand."

"And how did she look to you?"

Karen put her hands on her waist. "She looked skinny to me. And white as a ghost. I honestly don't know what you see in her, Larry. I know you've always had a fondness for more . . . voluptuous women."

"Oh, come on, Karen," he said. "Give it a rest. This could be serious. Meredith was expecting me to pick her up this afternoon. She was looking forward to it when I talked to her this morning. She wouldn't have left without a word unless she was . . . upset or something. Did she look upset when you saw her leaving?"

"I guess so. She looked as if she'd been crying, and she was kind of walking around like a zombie."

"And you didn't even try to stop her?"

"Look, I saw her fill out the release forms. Once she was signed out, she wasn't my problem anymore." Karen shrugged her shoulders and ran her fingers through her lush ash-blond curls. "Maybe she decided she didn't want you to take her home. Have you thought of that?"

Three of Larry's fellow doctors walked by the station, and he lowered his voice. "I wasn't going to take her to Llanfair. She was coming home with me."

"How cozy," Karen said, lifting one carefully penciled eyebrow.

"In case you haven't heard, Meredith and I are getting married Saturday afternoon."

"Really?" Karen smiled and fingered the top button on her uniform seductively. "If you're planning to get married, Dr. Wolek, you'd better find your bride."

Felicia rapped softly at Victor Lord's study door. She always knocked softly on this door because it was solid oak and she didn't want to bruise her knuckles, and because she hated to disturb Mr. Lord when he was in his study. He hated disruptions, and he readily vented his anger on the disruptee.

"What is it?" roared the deep bass voice inside.

She gingerly opened the door a crack and peeked inside.

"There's a phone call for you, Mr. Lord. It's Dr. Larry Wolek."

"Tell him to go to hell," he said without looking up from his paperwork.

"Yes, sir. As you wish, sir."

Felicia closed the door and took a deep breath as she tried to think of some compromise. She couldn't bring herself to tell Dr. Wolek, or anyone else for that matter, to go to hell. Yet, orders were orders.

Two minutes later, she appeared back at

the study door. "Excuse me, Mr. Lord. I'm terribly sorry to bother you again, but I told Dr. Wolek what you said, and he insists on speaking to you. He says it's an emergency, something about Miss Meredith."

"This had better be important, Felicia," he growled, "or you'll be on the next boat back to the old country."

"Yes, sir," she said, closing the heavy door behind her. She had no doubt that Larry Wolek's call was important. In the many months that he had been calling Llanfair, she had never heard him so worried. She hoped everything was all right with Miss Meredith.

Victor picked the telephone out of its carved box. "What do you want, Wolek?" he barked into the receiver.

There was a brief silence on the other end, then, "Is Meredith there at Llanfair with you?"

"No, why?"

"Because she checked herself out of the hospital around noon and left on her own. She was expecting me to pick her up. This isn't like her at all."

Victor smiled, self-satisfied. "Perhaps she came to her senses and abandoned the ridiculous notion of marrying you. One can always hope, can't one?"

"At the moment, I hope that's all it is, Mr. Lord," Larry replied. "I'm very concerned about her mental and physical state. She's extremely weak, and she shouldn't be wandering around on her own. When did you last see her?"

Victor hesitated before answering, "I saw her around ten-thirty or eleven this morning. We talked briefly."

"And how did she seem to you then?"

How did she seem? Victor thought of his daughter's face when he had told her the horrible truth. She had simply sat there on the bed, staring at him, her eyes round and uncomprehending. When his words had eventually filtered through to her consciousness, she had simply asked to be left alone.

Victor's respect for his youngest daughter had soared in that moment. She hadn't crumpled as he had expected her to. She had accepted the news with courage and strength that he had never seen her display before.

He hadn't enjoyed telling her. Although she had deserved to be brought down a few notches after defying him that way. It wasn't easy, telling your child that she had only a short time to live. But Lord couldn't shirk his paternal duties. He could never allow her to throw away what little time she had left on earth with a worthless nobody like Wolek. It had been his responsibility to point out to her how selfish she would be if she were to enter into a marriage in her "condition."

Victor was fairly confident that this was

the end of the fiasco. Meredith would never marry Wolek now. Nor would she tell him why, thinking that the kindest thing would be to let him down as gently as possible. Yes, as painful as it had been, Victor had remedied the situation, as always. Now all that remained was getting rid of Wolek.

"She was fine when I talked to her this morning," he said. "Perfectly fine. Don't concern yourself about my daughter, Wolek. She'll be all right—without you."

When Larry hung up the phone, he was even more convinced that something dreadfully wrong had happened to Meredith. If she had been okay when Victor saw her this morning, something terrible must have happened between then and the time she left the hospital. But what? Could she possibly have found out about her illness? Who would have told her?

He saw Karen down the hall at the nurses' station, humming contentedly as she went about her work of updating the charts.

There was only one person who hated Merrie that much, the one person, besides her father, who had seen her this morning.

Larry tried to contain his temper and his suspicions as he stomped down the hall toward the station. He had no proof, but the more he thought about his theory, the more sense it made.

"You did it, didn't you? You conniving little—"

"Did what?" Karen's blue eyes widened as she shrank back against the wall, holding a metal chart up before her defensively.

"You told her."

"Told who what? What are you talking about?"

He snatched the chart out of her hands and threw it onto the counter. "You told Merrie about her illness, didn't you?"

"What? No. I don't know what you're talking about."

He grabbed her by the shoulders, his fingertips digging into her flesh. "You just couldn't leave her alone, could you? You had to tell her that she's dying."

Her mouth fell open, gaping like a landed carp's. Her eyes were wide with shock. "What?" she said. "Meredith Lord is . . . dying?"

At his desk Victor drummed his perfectly manicured fingertips on its polished top. He looked down at his watch. Two-thirty.

It was a fifteen-minute taxi ride at most from the hospital to Llanfair. If Meredith had left the hospital at noon, where was she?

For the first time that day, Victor felt a twinge of misgiving. What if she had done something stupid? It certainly wouldn't be the first time. Meredith had always been more impulsive than the predictable Victoria.

For the first time in at least twenty years, Victor questioned a decision he had made. Perhaps he shouldn't have told her about her illness after all.

What if she couldn't face the prospect of a long, debilitating disease? What if she had done the unthinkable?

No. She was a Lord, and the Lords never took the easy way out. She was somewhere pouting, trying to worry him. She had better not be doing anything outrageous. If she embarrassed him in this community, he would never forgive her for it.

He took a small black leather book from his coat pocket and flipped through it. When he found the number he wanted, he dialed it.

"Llanview Police Department," answered a feminine voice.

"This is Victor Lord. I'd like to speak to a Lieutenant—"

"I'm Lieutenant Mason. May I help you, Mr. Lord?"

A woman lieutenant? What was the police department coming to? he wondered. He would have to speak to the chief about that.

"I'd like to speak to a particular lieutenant, Jack Neal."

"Just a moment please."

As Victor waited, he thought about his last conversation with Jack Neal, the day he had tried to bribe his way in to see Larry Wolek. He didn't like Neal, but he did respect him. There was a strength in the man that Lord related to. Besides, Victor had noticed how gentle Neal had been when he had questioned Meredith. It was as though the man had realized how vulnerable she was.

Somehow, Neal seemed like the one to call at a time like this.

"Jack Neal here." His voice was gruff and had a guarded tone to it. "How can I help you, Mr. Lord?"

"It's my daughter," Victor said, then hesitated.

"Yes?"

"She's missing."

Larry drove across the bridge which spanned the river, the river that divided the town of Llanview into halves: the haves . . . and the have nots.

Behind him on the "good" side of town were the quiet residential areas with their freshly painted houses, their perfectly edged yards, and the occasional swimming pool in the back.

Ahead of him were the factories, the docks, the shipping yards, and the dingy brick apartment houses without yards.

Larry had been raised on the have-not side of town in the small apartment where Vince and Anna had lived since before their parents' deaths. But he was at home on either side of the river. He had found that people were people. There were good ones and bad ones on both sides. And their problems were pretty much the same.

He was on his way now to have dinner with Anna and Vinnie to celebrate his release. He had hoped that Meredith would be accompanying him.

Where was she? And why had she run away?

She must have found out about her illness. But who could have told her?

He had realized too late that Karen Martin hadn't known about Merrie's disease— until he had mistakenly told her. Karen was a habitual liar. But Larry knew that she hadn't been lying today. She couldn't have faked that look of shock when he had accused her.

He had felt bad afterward for yelling at her. But his remorse had been short-lived, as he remembered her past offenses. She had had it coming, and more.

But if Karen hadn't told Meredith, who had?

Victor Lord?

He had seen her that morning at eleven o'clock, and she had run away at noon.

Why would he tell her? Surely, behind that granite facade which Lord showed to the world, there must be a father's heart.

No. Larry shook his head and buried the thought. No father would be that cruel.

Lieutenant Neal flashed his badge and watched the bank teller's pasted-on smile slip off her carefully made-up face.

"I'd just like to ask you a few questions, if you have a minute."

The teller glanced around the empty lobby for an excuse to deny him, but found none.

"Ah, sure," she said as a hundred thoughts raced through her mind. Why would the police want to question her? Had the neighbors complained about her new puppy's whining? Had someone seen her and the bank president leaving that body-painting parlor yesterday during their "long lunch"?

"How can I help you, Lieutenant?" she asked, aware of the sudden scrutiny by her fellow bank employees.

"I'd like to know if Meredith Lord was in here yesterday or today."

She let out her breath in a sustained sigh of relief. "Oh, yes, she was in yesterday. I took care of her myself."

"And about what time was that?"

"Right after lunch," she said, blushing slightly. "I took a late lunch. It must have been about two-thirty or three."

"And can you tell me whether her transaction was a deposit or a withdrawal?"

"I don't know if I should. Do you have a warrant or something?"

Neal leaned across the counter and lowered his voice intimately. "Do I really need one?"

A cold glittering in his black eyes made her think about the marijuana joint she had tucked away in the lining of her purse. She didn't really want to make an enemy of Lieutenant Neal.

"I suppose it wouldn't hurt anything," she said, pulling out a ledger and thumbing through it. "Here it is."

He tried to see over the ledger's edge, but she snapped it closed. "Miss Lord made a withdrawal yesterday from her personal savings account."

"For how much?" he asked.

"One thousand dollars."

"And how did she seem to you?"

"How did she *seem*?"

"Yeah, you know, was she happy, sad, grumpy, sleepy, dopey?"

"Oh. She was nice. Miss Lord is always nice when she comes in. Even if we've made a mistake in her account."

"Is that all?" he asked irritably. "Just nice?"

"Now that you mention it, she didn't look so great. Her eyes were swollen, like she'd been crying. And one other thing . . ."

"Yes?"

"When she said good-bye, she sounded like she really meant it."

When Larry looked up from his desk and saw Lieutenant Jack Neal standing there, his first thought was that he was going to be arrested again. Fate was going to play at least one more cruel joke on him before this whole thing was finished.

"Yes, Lieutenant?" he asked without warmth.

Without waiting to be invited, Neal sat down in one of the chairs beside Wolek's desk. "I have some news about your girlfriend, Meredith."

Larry's heart leaped into his throat, and for a moment he couldn't speak around the lump it made there. "What about Merrie? What's happened to her?"

"I don't know. But she was okay as of two-thirty Thursday afternoon." Neal propped his ankle on his knee and pulled a cigarette from his breast pocket.

"Is that all you have?"

Neal took his time lighting up, while Larry gritted his teeth with impatience.

"She was in her bank Thursday afternoon. She withdrew a thousand dollars from her savings account."

"A thousand dollars? Why would she do that?"

Neal blew two puffs of white smoke

through his nostrils. "Well, my best guess is that she took the money and left town."

"Left town?" The very thought numbed Larry's brain. They were supposed to be married by now. They should have left town together . . . on their honeymoon. He propped his elbows on his desk and buried his face in his hands. "I don't understand this," he said. "I don't understand any of it."

Neal watched him, squinting through the cigarette smoke with narrowed eyes. "Well, you never know about dames. That's why I don't get too involved with them. Love 'em and leave 'em, that's what I say."

With those words of wisdom, he flipped his cigarette stub into the wastepaper basket and sauntered toward the door. "I'll keep checking till I find her. But if I were you, I'd start looking for some greener pastures. A guy doesn't want to get caught without any hay in his manger, if you know what I mean."

Larry pulled into the driveway of his tiny Spanish bungalow, next to Vinnie's pickup. The battered old truck with v. WOLEK SHIPPING COMPANY emblazoned across the door meant that Vinnie had dropped by for a visit.

Larry groaned as he got out of the car and rubbed the back of his neck. Every muscle in his body was tight and sore from the tension of the past few weeks, especially the past three days.

He had been looking forward to a peaceful evening at home. And although Larry loved his brother dearly, Vinnie was far from peaceful. Besides, he really wasn't up to hearing Vince say "I told you so."

As Larry stepped up onto the porch, Vince rose from a lounge chair behind a potted palm on the patio. "Hi, little brother. I figured you'd be home pretty soon, so I just waited around."

"Hi, Vin," Larry said as he unlocked the door and pushed it open. "Come inside and have a beer."

"Don't mind if I do." Vince followed cheerfully, unmindful of his brother's somber mood.

"How's Anna?" Larry asked, handing him a beer and popping one for himself.

"She's fine. Oh, she's fussin' about you and Meredith. There she thought she'd got one of us married off, and bang! Everything just blew up." He stopped to take a long swig of beer. "Course, I knew that little gal was gonna give you a heartache, but I ain't gonna say I told you so."

Larry walked over to the door and scooped up the mail from the floor where it had fallen through the slot. "I appreciate that, Vinnie," he said.

"Yeah, I knew she was trouble the first

time I laid eyes on her. Could've told you then and there that she'd never marry the likes of a Wolek. But you're always sayin' that I stick my nose in your business, so I didn't say nothin' and I ain't gonna say nothin' now."

Larry fixed him with a wry smile. "I really do appreciate it, Vince. I know how hard it is for you to hold back like this."

"Yep, it's hard when you see somebody you care about making a mess of their life." He belched indelicately. "It's hard to sit back and not give 'em the benefit of your years of experience. What's the matter, Larry? You sick?"

Larry was staring at one of the letters. His face had suddenly gone as white as the envelope in his hand.

"Who's it from?" Vince asked, setting his beer aside. "The IRS? You ain't behind on your house payments again, are ya?"

"It's from Merrie," Larry said as the other letters slipped through his fingers to the floor.

He quickly tore it open. It didn't take long for him to read the letter, which was short and to the point.

"What does it say, Larry?"

"She says"—he swallowed, folded the letter, and replaced it in the envelope—"that she needs time to think about the marriage. And she asked me to forgive her."

Vincent jumped to his feet. "Why, that little—"

"Shut up, Vinnie!" Larry exploded. "Just shut your damned mouth! You don't even know Merrie. And you never gave her a chance. I'm sick of your running off at the mouth when you don't know what the hell you're talking about."

Both brothers stood, stunned. Larry had never raised his voice to Vince or been disrespectful to him in any way.

He half expected Vince to hit him. Vinnie had been known to clobber people for looking cross-eyed at him when he was in a less-than-chipper mood.

But Vince simply stood there for a long moment, saying nothing. Then he thrust his hands into his coveralls pockets and walked toward the door.

"Anna sent me over here to invite you to dinner tonight," he said quietly. Larry could see the hurt in his eyes. "She seemed to think that you'd want some company to-night, you bein' worried about Merrie and all. I'll just tell her you ain't in the mood to socialize."

Larry watched him leave in sullen silence. He supposed that he should go after him, apologize, and grovel for forgiveness. But he wasn't going to. He was too hurt and torn up inside to worry about Vinnie's injured feel-ings.

He looked down at the letter in his hand, opened it, and read the contents again. He didn't need to read it; he had already memorized those few short lines.

Dearest Larry,
I'm so sorry about leaving you like this, but I need time to be alone and think. Please forgive me. I'll always love you.

Merrie

He crumpled the letter in his fist, then quickly straightened it out over his knee, reverently smoothing the creases.

Oh, Merrie, he thought. *Where are you? And why did you leave me?*

The telephone rang, jarring his already shattered nerves.

"Yes?" he answered impatiently. Then he regretted his harsh tone. What if it was Meredith?

"Larry?" asked a feminine voice.

"Merrie?"

"No. It's Karen," replied the voice with a touch of sarcasm.

His heart sank. "Oh, hello Karen. What's up?"

"Well, I was planning to send out for pizza tonight, and I can't eat a whole pie by myself. I thought maybe you'd join me. If you aren't too busy, that is."

Her voice was soft, low, and intimate. He could hear the seductive, pleading tone. She wanted him—badly. And right now it felt good to be wanted, to be desired by anyone —even Karen.

Larry was surprised at his emotional and physical reaction. He hadn't realized just how vulnerable he was. Apparently he was worse off than he had realized, if a come-on from Karen Martin was inviting. But he wasn't that lonely or that hurt. Not quite. Not yet. "Thanks, Karen. But I'm not feeling very good tonight. I think I'm going to turn in early."

"I could come over and give you a nice back rub," she cooed.

"No, thanks. I have to go now. See you tomorrow."

On the other end Karen smiled, enormously pleased with herself. He had said no, as she had expected him to. But she had heard the hesitation in his voice. He had thought about it first, and that was more than she had dared to hope for.

"Yes, Larry. You take care of yourself, and I'll see you tomorrow at the hospital."

She hung up the phone and looked lovingly at a framed photograph which sat beside the telephone on the nightstand. It was a picture of her and Larry, taken at an air show the last Fourth of July. Larry had his arm draped companionably over her shoulder, and they both looked happy and relaxed. It had been a good day. It had been a good summer, though altogether too brief.

Karen had never fooled herself into thinking that Larry had been in love with her. They had shared some happy times and had some fun. Their relationship had been mostly physical, not emotional as his and Meredith's was. But it was the closest thing to love that Karen had ever experienced, and she had been devastated when Larry had told her that it was over.

But maybe it wasn't over after all. If Meredith would just stay away long enough for her to convince Larry that it was she, Karen, who truly loved him, who could make him happy . . .

She closed her eyes tightly and tried to send Meredith a message, wherever she might be.

I hope you're not dead, Merrie, and I hope you're not sick, she thought. *But wherever you are, stay there. Don't come back to Llanview. Don't come back to Larry.*

Chapter
Nine

Anna Wolek stood in the cafeteria line, eyeing the desserts. Just as she reached for a bowl of chocolate pudding, she thought of Victoria Lord's svelte figure and reached instead for a small salad, no dressing.

Weight control wasn't usually a priority in Anna's life, but she was feeling the effects of the extra baking she had been doing lately. Joe Riley had been over for dinner five times in the past two weeks, and each time she had baked a special dessert. Vinnie was loving it, but she could feel those cheesecakes and apple pies settling around her waist and on her hips.

It didn't do much good to lure a man with food, if one lost one's figure in the process.

Anna paid for her lunch and sat down at a table in the corner. She was disappointed to find herself eating alone. She had come to the hospital to invite Larry out to lunch at an Italian restaurant nearby. But Larry had refused, saying that he had too many patients to see this afternoon and couldn't spare the time. She had tried to talk him into having at least a bowl of clam chowder in the hospital cafeteria, but again he had refused.

Anna tried not to worry about her baby brother, but he wasn't making it easy for her. The trial had taken its toll on him, and he had never given himself time to recover. Since Meredith had run away, he had found some reason to work day and night at the hospital. Anna knew that he was desperately trying to forget. . . .

It had been so much easier years ago when all she had to worry about was whether Larry had clean clothes and lunch money for school the next day.

She glanced around the cafeteria and spotted Karen Martin smiling in her direction. Anna cursed her misfortune as she saw that Karen was heading toward her, lunch tray in hand.

She didn't like Karen and never had. Karen was just too much of a hussy for Anna to approve of her as a companion for Larry. Anna had always thought that Karen was what Vinnie would call a "feisty, fast, and friendly broad." Anna didn't mind "feisty" and "friendly." But "fast" was another matter.

"Hi, Anna, how nice to see you here. May I sit down here with you? We haven't had a good talk in a long time."

Without waiting for an invitation Karen set her tray on the table and began unloading a cheeseburger, fries, and a thick chocolate shake.

Anna looked down at her own salad and groaned. Where did Karen put it all? she wondered. She took one glance at Karen's burgeoning bustline and answered her own question. Karen put it where it counted.

"I've really been wanting to talk to you, Anna. I'm so glad I ran into you like this." She settled in the chair across from her and spread her paper napkin on her lap.

"Yes," Anna said with subdued enthusiasm, "we haven't seen much of you since the trial. We saw quite a lot of you then."

Karen squirmed uncomfortably. "Anna, I hope you and Vinnie aren't holding that against me. Larry isn't. He knows that I only told the truth on the witness stand. I was under oath and I *had* to tell the truth. I swore on the Bible and everything." Karen knew that Anna was big on the Bible. It was worth a try.

"I know," Anna said, her voice softening. "It's just that at the time it seemed like you were making things harder for Larry than you needed to."

"Oh, no. You're wrong, Anna. I was just

sick about the whole thing. I'd never hurt Larry in any way, you know that. I still feel just the same about Larry. I love him."

"You do?" Anna nearly dropped a hunk of lettuce in her lap.

"Dearly, with all my heart and soul . . . and—"

Anna held up her hand. "Okay, I get your point." At that moment it occurred to Anna that Karen would make a great actress.

"I'm so worried about Larry, Anna. Have you seen him lately? Noticed the dark circles under his eyes? He's losing weight and he's *so* cranky."

"He's upset over Merrie, Karen. He can't accept the fact that she's gone."

Karen's full bottom lip protruded in a pout. "Well, it's been nearly a month now since she left. He'd better accept it pretty soon. She's not coming back, and that's it. Good riddance, I say."

"But Larry doesn't agree with you. He loves Meredith very much."

"Oh, Larry doesn't know what's good for him," she said, dragging a french fry through a puddle of ketchup and sticking it in her mouth.

"And you do?"

"Of course. I've got what Larry needs, and the sooner he realizes that, the sooner he'll be wearing a smile on his face."

Anna's freckled cheeks blushed a delicate pink. "Larry needs more than a roll in the hay, Karen," she said, her voice tight with anger.

Karen donned an aggrieved look. "Oh, Anna, you're so mean. You take everything I say the wrong way. You never did like me. You don't think I'm good enough for your precious brother."

She stood and picked up her tray. "You're just like an old mother hen with a chick when it comes to Larry. You're a frustrated old maid, Anna, who's afraid of letting go of anyone or anything."

Anna thought about slapping her. But she was too far away, and Anna's arm wasn't long enough. She wanted to swear at her, but she couldn't remember any of Vinnie's choice words, because he didn't usually use them around her.

She thought about bursting into tears, but she wouldn't give Karen the satisfaction of knowing how badly she had hurt her.

So she did nothing. She said nothing. And it was long after Karen had left the cafeteria that Anna allowed herself to consider that there might be some truth in what Karen had said.

"Larry? Are you still here?" Karen asked, peering into the semidarkness of his office.

As her eyes adjusted to the gloom, she saw that he was lying facedown on the sofa, one arm dangling to the floor.

"Larry, you should have gone home hours ago." She closed the door behind her, blotting out the light from the corridor. She moved to turn on a lamp, then thought better of it.

Moonlight poured through the half-opened blinds, painting bars of silver and shadowy black on the carpeting, the office furniture, and Larry's prone body.

He moaned softly and shifted on the narrow sofa. His stockinged feet hung off the end, and his jacket and tie lay on the floor next to him.

"Who is it?" he mumbled, lifting his face from the cushion.

"It's me, Karen," she said as she walked over to the couch and knelt beside him.

He groaned and buried his face in the sofa.

"You poor baby," she cooed, "you must be exhausted. You haven't been home for three days. I know, I've been counting."

"Karen, please. I'm trying to get some sleep. It's been a long day . . . a long year."

"I know. You've had an awful time, so many things going wrong and—"

"Karen, I'm exhausted. I'd really like to go back to sleep if you don't mind."

"Sure, Larry, go back to sleep," she said,

trying to keep the annoyance out of her voice. "I only came up here to tell you something about Meredith."

"Meredith?"

It made her furious to see how quickly he came wide awake. Just the mention of Merrie's name and he was a changed man.

"What about Merrie?" he asked again, rising up onto one elbow.

"Well, Victor Lord was here today . . . something about a new cardiac wing that he's donating to the hospital."

"And?"

"And while he was here, Lieutenant Jack Neal came by and asked for him. I took them into the doctors' lounge so they could talk privately. And I overheard Lieutenant Neal say that he knows where Meredith is."

"Where is she?" His voice was strained, and she could feel the anxiety radiating from him. If he were only half that concerned about her . . .

"She's in San Francisco."

"San Francisco? What's she doing out there?"

"I don't know. But I heard Lieutenant Neal say that she's opened a bank account there. So he thinks she's planning to stay for a while. Probably a *long* while, Larry. I'm really sorry. I know how much you loved her."

He was silent for a few minutes. She

wished that she could see his face, but it was in shadow. Finally he laid his head back down on the sofa.

She wanted him to say something . . . anything. For a moment she regretted having told him. But no, he needed to hear it, and it was better if he heard the news from a friend, someone who truly loved him, as she did.

She reached out in the darkness and ran her hand over the back of his shirt. She could feel the knotted muscles of his back, taut with tension, just beneath the smooth cotton fabric.

He flinched slightly beneath her touch, then gradually, as her hands worked their magic on the tight, sore muscles, he began to relax.

"Let it go, Larry," she whispered, continuing to knead and caress. "Just let it all go and relax."

"It hurts, Karen," he said so softly that she hardly heard him. She knew he wasn't talking about the massage.

"I know. You gave her your heart, and she threw it back in your face. I know how much that hurts."

His hand, which was dangling to the floor, found her knee and gently squeezed it. "I'm sorry that I hurt you last summer, Karen," he said. "I never meant to do that to you."

Her hand slid down to his and covered it.

"I know you didn't, Larry. Sometimes these things just happen. Close your eyes now and go to sleep."

He did as she told him. He closed his eyes and allowed himself to melt away into a soft darkness where there was no Meredith, no confusing questions that tore at his heart, and no demanding patients.

The darkness enveloped him in its velvet warmth, pulling him into a world devoid of everything . . . except the delicious sensation of Karen's soft hands gently, tenderly stroking his body.

Victoria opened her eyes and sat up in bed. It took her several moments to realize where she was and to shake off the emotional residue from the strange dream.

She had been in a room full of people, laughing, drinking, and dancing to rock 'n' roll music. The lights had been low, and there had been someone there with her, someone special . . . a man. But his face had faded, along with the music and the euphoric feeling.

When Victoria had finally reoriented her muddled brain, she realized that she was at home in her own bed. She had gone to bed early tonight with another of her migraine headaches.

Victor had come home that afternoon from the hospital with news of Merrie's whereabouts. The thought that her sister was hundreds of miles away from her in San Francisco was nearly as disturbing to Viki as the thought that Meredith had run away without even saying good-bye. But at least they knew now that Merrie was alive and apparently fine.

Victoria knew that her father would go after Meredith. Victor couldn't bear the thought of having his daughter out of sight, out of his control.

As much as Victoria missed Merrie and wanted her back, she hoped that Victor would leave her alone long enough for her to come back on her own. But of course, that was impossible. Victor was already making plans to go to San Francisco.

Victoria rubbed her eyes with the back of her hand and wondered why they were stinging and irritated. She could smell the odor of cigarette smoke on her hands and taste nicotine on her tongue.

There was another foreign taste in her mouth: alcohol. And it wasn't her father's high-class brandy, either. This tasted remarkably like cheap beer.

She threw back the satin comforter and crawled out of bed. The floor spun for a moment, nearly knocking her off her feet. Then the room righted itself, and she stumbled to the bathroom to swish some mouthwash and get a drink of water.

As she flipped on the bathroom light switch, she remembered the night when she had found the threatening message scrawled in red lipstick across the mirror.

She was almost afraid to look, but she did. There was nothing on the polished, beveled mirror.

Relieved, she rinsed her mouth, washed her hands, and took a long drink of water. She tried not to look in the mirror. The image she saw there disturbed her. There were dark circles under her eyes that were red and bloodshot, as though she hadn't slept all night.

She turned away from the mirror and replaced the crystal glass in its holder.

A tissue lay wadded on the floor beside the wastebasket. Always one to keep things tidy, she bent down and picked it up. But before she tossed it, she felt something inside the paper.

She unwrapped it and saw, glittering against the pale pink tissue, a rhinestone earring. As she picked it up, the light caught its prisms and it sparkled like a thousand tiny rainbows.

Victoria examined the earring with wonderment. How had it gotten here? Whose was it?

It certainly wasn't hers. The thing was huge. It would hang from the wearer's ear nearly to her shoulder. She would never wear anything so gaudy. She wore diamonds, not rhinestones. And when she wore diamonds she wore only solitaires, not garish clusters.

It wasn't Meredith's. Victor would never allow a piece of costume jewelry in the mansion.

Perhaps it was Felicia's. Viki couldn't imagine Felicia wearing anything so flamboyant, but she would ask her about it tomorrow.

As she wrapped the earring carefully in its tissue, she felt an uneasiness creeping, tickling along her spine. Her strange dream. The taste of nicotine and alcohol.

Yes. She would definitely have to ask Felicia about the earring, first thing tomorrow morning.

"Good morning, Joe," Victoria said over the stack of papers on her desk. "You're late."

"Give me a break, boss lady," he groaned, sinking into a chair beside her desk. "I was on the job until three o'clock this morning."

"Were you, now? Doing what, pray tell?"

"Drinking stale beer at a sleazy waterfront dive called the Wounded Pelican. A place where I'm sure you've never been."

"Nor do I hope to be. And why were you hanging about this establishment if the beer was stale?"

"The barmaids were buxom."

Her blue eyes narrowed, and she fixed him with a baleful glare, reminiscent of Victor Lord. "And for this, I pay you a generous salary?"

"Hey, it's a tough job but—"

"Somebody has to do it."

"Right."

"And what did you find out during your sojourn into the seedy side of Llanview?"

"That my Mob connections don't hang out in the Wounded Pelican. It's too scummy even for them."

"Sounds like an evening well spent," she murmured sarcastically.

He grinned and propped his ankle on his knee. Viki's eyes traveled briefly over the faded blue denim stretched tightly over his muscular thigh. Then she glanced quickly away.

He saw the quick perusal but pretended not to. Victoria never failed to amaze him. Although she always seemed cool and collected, there was a storm brewing just below the surface. Her personality contained so many contradictory elements.

"The evening wasn't a complete loss," he said. "I ran into Vince Wolek while I was out. We had a good time shooting the breeze."

"And *The Banner*'s expense account."

He smiled, but otherwise ignored her barb. "Vinnie's in love," he said.

"How nice that someone is," she said, riffling through her papers.

Joe continued, undaunted by her lack of interest. "Yeah, ol' Vinnie met this gorgeous redhead a couple of weeks ago at the Cave, that new club down by the river. Her name's Nicole Smith, but he calls her Niki."

"That's charming." She stood and walked to a file cabinet in the corner.

Joe watched her carefully as she filed the stack of papers. "I thought you might find Niki Smith an interesting character," he said while appreciating the curve of her calves and ankles.

"Really? I can't imagine why."

Joe leaned back in the chair and crossed his brawny arms across his chest. "Well, as I said, she's a redhead. She wears these mini-dresses which Vinnie says show off her great legs and—"

Victoria turned from the filing cabinet with an impatient grimace on her face. "Is it too much to hope that this story has a point?"

"I'm getting there. Other than the fact that she has red hair, dresses very mod, and wears dangly rhinestone earrings, Vinnie says that this love-of-his-life looks exactly like you, Viki."

"Rhinestone earrings?"

Joe thought she was going to faint. He'd never seen anyone's face drained of color so quickly. "That's what he said. Long ones that hang down to her shoulder. Hey, kid, are you okay?"

"I'm fine." She sat down at her desk suddenly, as though her knees had given way beneath her. "Could you get me a glass of water, Joe? I feel one of those headaches coming on. I'd better take an aspirin."

"Sure." He hurried to the water fountain and returned to her office a moment later with a cup in hand.

But when he opened the door, he saw her sitting there at her desk, staring into the opened top drawer of her desk.

"What is it, Viki? What's wrong?" he asked, closing the door behind him.

"Joe, look . . ." Her voice was only a harsh whisper.

He walked behind her desk and stared down into the drawer. There, beside the bottle of aspirin, was a note—a bit of white paper with red writing scrawled across it.

Soon, Victoria Lord. Very soon. You'll be dead.

Chapter
Ten

"Losing your mind? That's the most ridiculous thing I've ever heard." Victor pushed his grapefruit half aside and reached for the china egg cup which held his perfectly timed, two-minute, soft-boiled egg.

Across the table sat Victoria, who stared down at her whole-wheat cereal, which she hadn't touched.

"For heaven's sake, Victoria, why would you even say such a thing?"

"Because I'm afraid it's true, Father, and I need your help. I need your support."

"Well, you aren't going to get it if you mean what I think you do. I'll never consent to your seeing a psychiatrist. They're charlatans, the lot of them. For an astronomical sum of money they put you on their couch and ask you questions about sex and feelings and rot like that. Those things are best kept in the dark, where they belong."

Victoria sighed and poked at her cereal with her spoon. "I think you're a bit out of touch with current psychiatric counseling methods," she said.

"Oh, really? And do you know so much about it? Are you eager to open your most private thoughts to a total stranger?"

"I'm not exactly eager. In fact, I'm terrified at the very thought. But I can't go on this way. I have to find out what's happening to me."

"And while you're probing your psyche, you'll be exposing this family's innermost secrets. Doesn't that bother you?"

"No. What deep dark secrets do we have, Father, that can't bear illumination?"

He scowled at her over the edge of his coffee cup. "Don't get smart with me, young lady. I simply don't relish the idea of your sitting in a shrink's office, telling him how much you've always hated your father, and how I'm responsible for your problems."

Victoria shook her head slowly in disbelief. "You really are the most self-centered, egotistic person I've ever known. You would deny me the help I need rather than risk having your name brought up during a counseling session."

"I have a reputation to protect in Llanview, and if you don't understand that—"

"You have no reputation worth protecting," she said, throwing down her spoon. "The only reputation you have in this town is that of a cold-blooded, heartless tyrant."

She stood and tossed her napkin to the table like a thrown gauntlet. "You think everyone in town is in awe of you, the great Victor Lord, sitting in his mansion on the hill and looking down his regal nose at the peasants below. But that's not the way they see you, Father. They see right through your petty hypocrisy. They hate you for your cruelty and arrogance. And those who don't hate you pity you, because they see you for what you really are: a pathetic, lonely, frightened man who is terrified of losing control of even the smallest part of his life."

She stopped, shocked at her own outburst. Victor sat, looking up at her with glacial ice glittering in his gray eyes. "Are you quite finished?" he asked, his voice low and void of emotion.

"No," she said. "I am going to make an appointment with Dr. Polk this afternoon. I would like to have your support and encouragement, but I realize that would be asking too much. And I don't need your permission."

"Victoria, wait a minute." He hurried after her as she left the dining room, and he caught her in the foyer outside the library door.

"There's nothing more for us to discuss, Father. My mind is made up." She shrugged his hand away from her arm.

"All right. You have my permission to call Dr. Polk," he said, grinding each word between clenched jaws.

"How kind of you, Father," she replied dryly.

"I only ask one thing."

"Yes?"

"Wait a few weeks. I need you to go with me to San Francisco."

"San Francisco?" She eyed him suspiciously. "I suppose you're going there to drag Merrie back home."

"That's exactly what I intend to do. Unless you go with me and persuade her to come home of her own volition."

"You don't know? What do you mean you don't know?" Vince shouted into the telephone. "How can you lose a semi-trailer full of onions?"

He slammed his beefy fist down on a stack of shipping invoices. The paper muffled the thud, taking all the satisfaction out of the gesture, so he kicked the side of the metal cabinet for added emphasis.

"Well, stick your nose in the air, stupid, and sniff around. But you'd better find those onions and make sure they're delivered to the cannery on time, or one Sicilian spaghetti sauce kingpin is gonna be rollin' the cement trucks in our direction.

"Geez, Louise!" he mumbled, hanging up the phone. Sometimes it was too much, this shipping business. If it wasn't a broken-down truck, it was labor disputes or some lamebrain misplacing his load of onions. Fortunately, the latter didn't happen every day.

He opened the small refrigerator in the corner of the office and surveyed its contents: one shriveled apple, something green that might have been a tuna sandwich in a previous life, a cola, and a beer. He thought about reaching for the beer but decided to save it to celebrate closing time. He reached for the cola instead.

Sitting back in his chair, he popped the top, drained half the can in a single swallow, and waited for the next surprise-of-the-day to hit him. He didn't have long to wait.

A series of wolf whistles echoed through the warehouse, along with catcalls and halloos of male admiration. Apparently a woman had entered this decidedly male world.

It couldn't be Anna, he thought. The guys knew that if they dared to hoot at Vince Wolek's sister they would wind up in big trouble.

In a moment he saw her, walking around a stack of crated lettuce . . . and his heart stopped. Then it raced, making up for lost time.

It was *her*—Niki.

And she was coming toward his office. He scrambled around, straightening his hair —he didn't have much, so every hair had to be in place where it counted. He grabbed a couple of nude centerfolds off the wall and stuffed them into his desk drawer. But he was used to doing that; he had to tear them down every time Anna dropped by unexpectedly.

His mouth suddenly went dry, so he downed the other half of the cola. But it went down his windpipe. He was coughing and wheezing when she stuck her flaming-red head through his office door.

"Hi, Vinnie. I thought I'd drop by. Hey, are you all right?"

"Yes," he sputtered. "Fine." Finally regaining his breath, he lost it again when he looked up at her through streaming eyes. She was just so damned pretty.

She stood there in a bright yellow turtle-neck sweater that fit her to a tee, and bell-bottoms that were orange, hot-pink, and lime-green. Nicole Smith was like a ray of multicolored sunshine in Vinnie Wolek's otherwise drab existence. She flashed him a bright smile through coral-frosted lips that looked absolutely luscious.

"May I come in?" she asked.

"Oh, sure. I'm just surprised to see you. Come right in." He grabbed a rusty folding chair, pulled a blue bandanna from his coveralls, and dusted the chair's seat. "Here, take a load off . . . I mean, it ain't a load with you, 'cause you don't weigh much, but—"

"Thanks, Vinnie."

The sparkle in her bright blue eyes unnerved him, so he looked down to avoid her unwavering gaze. To his horror, he saw the upper half of Miss December sticking out of his desk drawer. As quickly and as discreetly as possible, for a guy who seldom practiced discretion, he shoved her back into the drawer with Miss March and Miss Congeniality.

He glanced up to see if Niki had noticed. She had, but she was pretending that she hadn't. That's what he liked about Nicole: she never made him feel embarrassed or awkward. Vince had spent most of his life feeling awkward, and he didn't like it. Niki was all right.

He looked around the office for some creature comfort to offer her. "I've got a beer in the icebox. You want it?"

"Sure, that would be great."

A woman who liked beer. What more could a guy ask for?

"Vince, you don't mind me dropping by like this, do you?"

"No, of course not." He handed her the

beer and felt a shot of adrenaline race through him when his hand brushed hers. "I'm real glad to see you."

"We had fun at the Cave last night, didn't we, Vinnie," she murmured over the top of the beer can.

He thought of the kiss she had given him after a particularly cozy dance, and his blood pressure soared. "Yeah, we sure did. Are you gonna be there again tonight?"

"Oh, I don't know. I'm having these problems and—"

"Problems? What kind of problems?" Vince donned his shining armor.

"Oh, nothing I can't handle. I just need to get out of town for a while. I was wondering if you would like to go to Atlantic City with me for a week or so. We could have a really good time, Vince."

A week in Atlantic City with Niki . . . it sounded like heaven. But a whole week away from the business?

"I'd love to, Niki, but I don't see how I could get away for a whole week. Maybe next weekend."

"Oh, please, Vinnie. If I don't leave now I'm going to get stuck going with those snobby jerks and—"

The telephone rang, cutting her off. He grabbed it and barked, "Yeah, what do you want? Oh, hi, Joe. You won't believe who's here right now. Niki. That's right. The one who looks just like Victoria. Come on down, I want you to meet her."

Vince hung up and turned to Nicole. "Just wait till you meet Joe. He's been my best buddy for years now, and you won't believe it, but you look just like his girlfriend, Victoria Lord."

Nicole's eyes flashed with sudden, unexplained fury. "Victoria Lord! Don't you ever say that I look like her. I don't look a bit like that stuck-up broad. Don't ever——"

"Okay, okay!" He held up his hands in surrender. "I'm sorry. Forget I ever said it. I didn't even know you knew Victoria. Geez . . ."

"Oh, I know her, all right." Nicole's voice was hoarse with a bitterness that gave Vinnie the chills. "I know Victoria Lord better than anyone does. I despise her."

Vince looked into her hate-twisted face and wondered where the sunshine had gone. Where was the fun-loving, happy-go-lucky Niki that he was falling in love with? And who was this woman whose eyes blazed with blue hatred?

Vinnie knew one thing: whoever she was, she was stark raving mad.

"Are you sure that Anna won't mind me dropping by like this?" Joe asked as he followed Vince up the final flight of stairs to his apartment. "We should have called first or something, don't you think?"

"Naw. Anna likes company. And she especially likes you, Joe. She wouldn't mind if you threw your coat in the corner and stayed on permanently."

"Cut it out, Vinnie. Anna doesn't care about me except as a brother or a good friend."

At the end of the hall was a door with brass lettering that identified it as apartment 16H. The H dangled from one corner as it had for the past ten years. Vince hadn't fixed it, and Anna wasn't about to. She took care of the inside, and Vinnie was supposed to take care of the outside.

It grated against Joe's nerves every time he saw it. One screwdriver, two screws, and thirty seconds would set it right. He had decided once four years ago to fix it himself, but Anna had stopped him cold. She was determined that Vince would be the one to do the job, or it wouldn't be done.

So, six years later, the H still dangled on apartment 16H. And, left to Vinnie, it would probably do so for another decade.

"Come on in and make yourself at home," Vince said, ushering Joe inside. "Anna!" he shouted. "Anna, Joe's here! Get us a beer!"

Seconds later, Anna emerged from the kitchen with a broad grin on her freckled face and a beer can in each hand. She handed one to Joe, who murmured a gracious "Thank you, Anna."

"You're welcome, Joseph." She tossed the other at Vinnie, who merely grunted as he flipped the top. "You're welcome, too, Vincent," she said pointedly.

"What?" Vinnie glanced over at Joe's disapproving scowl. "Oh, yeah. Thank you very much, Anna. You're a peach."

"That's me, all right," she muttered, "a real peach. I'm glad you came by, Joe." She settled onto the couch beside him, smoothing her skirt in a self-conscious gesture.

"I told Vinnie, you must be tired of seeing my face around here," Joe replied with an affectionate warmth in his voice.

She blushed slightly and ducked her head. "That's silly, Joe. We never get tired of having you around."

Joe cast a quick look at Vinnie, who was grinning at him knowingly. "Told ya," he said.

Joe looked back at Anna, one of his dearest friends, and wondered if Vince was right. Her soft brown eyes wouldn't meet his, but she stared down at her hands, which were folded gracefully in her lap.

In an instant, Joe knew. Anna *was* in love with him. *Damn.*

He loved Anna dearly and always had. She was one of the sweetest, kindest women he had ever known, and he wouldn't hurt her for the world. But in the twenty years he had known Anna, he had never once entertained the slightest romantic notion about her. She was just Anna. Vinnie and Larry's sister. His friend. Nothing less, but certainly nothing more.

"So, what's for dinner?" Vinnie asked, riffling through the stack of bills and advertisements that made up the day's mail.

"We were going to have leftovers, but—" She glanced hesitantly at Joe.

"That's okay, Anna. I wasn't going to stay anyway. I have a report to write tonight."

"Ah, Joe, stick around," Vinnie said, frowning at the electric bill. "Anna can whip up somethin' better than leftovers. Hey! What's this? It's a postcard from Niki!" His round face lit up with delight, then flushed with embarrassment as he read it.

"Niki? You mean Nicole Smith, the woman who looks like Victoria?" Joe asked, suddenly very interested.

"Yeah." Vinnie turned it over and studied the picture on the front. "It's the Golden Gate Bridge. She's in San Francisco. I wondered why I hadn't seen her for the past two weeks."

"San Francisco?" Joe jumped up from the

sofa and reached to grab the card from Vinnie's hand.

Vince clutched it to his chest. "Hey, this here card is of a . . . personal nature."

Joe held out his hand. "Vinnie, please. This might be important. Just let me look at it, okay?"

"Okay, but don't read it out loud," he said, handing it over.

"I've already read it anyway," Anna sniffed. "I didn't think it was all that personal. That's just wishful thinking on your part, Vinnie."

One glance at the writing on the back of the postcard set Joe's pulse to pounding. He'd seen that writing before. It was a distinctive, childlike scrawl.

He'd seen it two weeks ago . . . on the life-threatening note in Victoria Lord's desk.

Larry walked out of his patient's room and stood quietly in the hall, waiting for his head to stop spinning. He often felt dizzy lately, but it wasn't any big deal. All he really needed was a good night's sleep, something he hadn't had for weeks now.

Karen Martin suddenly appeared out of nowhere. "Larry, are you all right?" she asked.

She was always there, every time he turned around, with that solicitous look on her face. It irritated the heck out of him, but it was comforting in a way to see that somebody cared.

"Yeah, fine," he said. "I want you to keep a close watch on Mrs. Tyson tonight. I really don't think that was an accidental overdose. She's been very depressed lately. I should have seen this coming."

"Larry, you can't take care of the entire world, you know. Look at you. You're dead on your feet. Why don't you go home now?"

"No. I want to stick around a couple more hours to see if she snaps out of this coma. I'll catch a couple of winks on my office sofa. Call me if she comes around."

She laid her hand on his forearm. "Larry, you can't sleep in your office. They're painting in there. Remember?"

"Oh, yeah, I forgot."

"Boy, you really are down for the count. Here, come with me."

He resisted with as much energy as he could summon, which wasn't much. "Karen, I'm okay, really."

The room began to spin again, knocking him off his axis. He swayed against her, and she caught him around the waist.

"Now don't give me a hard time, Larry. I have just the spot for you. A dark, quiet place where you can sleep as long as you want." She led him to the medicine closet at the far end of the hall. Inside, leaning against the wall, was a small cot.

"Here," she said, unfolding it. "You'll probably hang off the end, but at least you'll be off your feet."

He groaned as he stretched out and closed his eyes. "Ah, that's better. Thanks, Karen. You're a doll."

"Don't mention it," she said. She bent over and softly kissed his forehead. "Try to rest. I'll call you if Mrs. Tyson wakes up."

She turned out the light and tiptoed from the room, leaving him alone in the darkness with his jumbled, weary thoughts.

This was why he hadn't even tried to sleep. It was pointless. No matter how hard he worked, or how tired he got, he couldn't sleep. The moment his body slowed down, his brain speeded up.

Why did Meredith leave? Should he go after her or wait for her to come back to him? She had asked him for time, but how much time did she need? Did she miss him even half as much as he missed her?

Like a thousand angry demons, the thoughts assailed him from every direction, sticking their barbed pitchforks into his heart, making it bleed a few more drops.

He sat up on the cot and touched his shirt pocket. They were there, the cigarettes that he had refused ever to smoke again.

It had been over a month now since he had stopped smoking—the hardest month of his life. If he'd made it this far, why start up again?

But if he hadn't wanted to smoke again, why had he bought the cigarettes this morning?

Probably because Larry had a gut-level feeling that it was this coming month, not the last one, that was destined to be the most difficult thirty days of his life.

He reached into his pocket and pulled out the pack.

Dr. Price Trainor walked into Mrs. Tyson's room and found Karen Martin asleep in the chair next to her. The patient was thrashing restlessly in her bed, her head tossing back and forth.

He hurried to her bedside and took her hand. "Mrs. Tyson," he said, bending low over her. "Mrs. Tyson, you're all right. Settle down now. Everything's okay."

Karen stirred in her chair, then jumped to her feet. "Oh, wow! I must have dozed off. Is she awake?"

"Yes, I believe she's coming around. Aren't you, Mrs. Tyson? Come on, sweetheart, look up at me. That's a girl." He shone his ophthalmoscope into her eyes and watched the pupils dilate normally. "Yes, I believe we've got her back. Did you have a nice nap, Nurse Martin?" he asked sarcastically, not looking up from his patient.

Karen ignored him as she smoothed the wrinkles out of her skirt and ran her fingers through her long hair. "Dr. Wolek told me to wake him as soon as she came around," she said.

"Then maybe you'd better carry out the doctor's orders, Nurse Martin," he said in a voice usually reserved for very young children.

She flounced out of the room with even more wiggle in her walk than usual. Trainor chuckled softly to himself, then turned his attention back to Mrs. Tyson.

Several moments later he heard a scream that ripped through the late-night hospital quiet. He ran out of the room and saw Karen at the end of the hall. The door to the medicine room was wide open. Black smoke billowed from the room. Orange flames curled along the door frame.

"Fire!" she screamed. "Dr. Trainor! The medicine room's on fire!"

He ran to the fire extinguisher on the wall, smashed the protective glass enclosure, and yanked the fire alarm.

"No, there's no time for that!" she cried, grabbing the extinguisher out of his hand and throwing it to the floor. "Larry's in there!"

Trainor ran back to the door and peered inside, trying to shield his face from the incredible heat. He couldn't see a thing, only smoke and fire and a horrible swirling darkness.

"Are you sure?" he shouted.

"Yes!"

Without another moment's hesitation, he took off his jacket, flung it over his head and ran headlong into the furnace's blast.

Seconds later Trainor stumbled out of the room. He fell to his knees in the hall, fighting for breath. The fire had scorched his jacket. Smoke rolled from his clothes. Karen could smell his singed hair as she bent over him.

"Did you see him? Did you see Larry?" she cried.

"Yes, he's lying in the middle of the floor," he gasped, then collapsed into a horrible coughing spasm. "I couldn't get to him. I think he's dead."

"No!" she screamed, backing away from him. "Oh, God, he can't be dead! Larry!"

"Karen, don't! You'll be killed!" Trainor struggled to his feet, but he was too late. She had already disappeared in the roaring inferno.

Book
Two

Chapter
One

"Oh, God! Larry can't be dead!"

Karen stood at the threshold of hell itself. Dense black smoke and rolling flames filled the tiny room which had only moments before been a medicine room.

At her feet lay Dr. Price Trainor, overcome with smoke and fighting for breath. He had run into that fiery blast to rescue his friend, Larry Wolek, but had been forced back by the incredible heat and the choking smoke.

Karen didn't have time to stop and think. Larry was in there dying . . . burning alive.

She yanked her nurse's cap off her head and clasped it over her mouth.

"No! Karen, don't!" Trainor shouted. "You'll be killed!"

She heard his voice as though from far

away. But his warning didn't matter. Dr. Trainor didn't matter. Larry was dying.

Karen lowered her head and ran into the burning room, into the smoke and the flames.

Once inside she was completely disoriented. The smoke was so thick, a swirling black shroud hid the room . . . and Larry. She inhaled to scream, and the heat seared her lungs. The acrid smoke filled her mouth and nose, strangling her.

"Larry! Larry, where are you?"

She heard a low moan. She moved through the blackness toward the sound and nearly fell over him.

He was lying in the middle of the floor at her feet. Tiny red lines of flame danced in macabre patterns on the walls, along the floor, and, to her horror, on his shirt.

She fell to her knees beside him and beat the flames out with her hands. "Larry, it's okay," she sobbed. "I'm going to get you out of here."

She raised her head and looked around. The smoke had nearly blinded her. All she could see were flames—everywhere —closing around them. Where was the door?

She could feel her skin crawling on her face and arms, shrinking from the terrible heat that was growing hotter by the second.

Oh, God, where was the door? How was

she going to save Larry? She couldn't even save herself.

On the other side of town Larry's older brother, Vincent Wolek, sat, holding a postcard clutched against his chest.

"This is mine, Joe Riley," he told his friend, "and you don't need to be lookin' at it."

"Vinnie, don't be stupid," his sister, Anna, scolded him from across the small apartment. "Joe says it's important. Let him see it, for Pete's sake."

"I recognize the writing, Vince," Joe said, barely able to contain his excitement. "That's the same childlike scribbling that was on those threatening notes that Victoria received."

"Are you tryin' to say that *my* girl has been sendin' hate mail to *your* girl?" Vince stood, his ruddy face blushed dark red with fury. "Is that what you're gettin' at?"

"It's possible," Joe said carefully. He was treading through a mine field, and he knew it.

"That's what I thought." Vince jumped to his feet. "I'm gonna slug you, Joseph Riley. I'm gonna mop the floor with you right now for sayin' somethin' like that about my Niki."

Anna rose from the sofa and quickly placed herself between her temperamental brother and Joe. "Vinnie, shut up," she said, pushing him back into his threadbare recliner. She poked him in the chest with her forefinger to emphasize her words. "You're not gonna punch anybody, least of all Joe. You've been friends for twenty years."

"Yeah, and I've cleaned his clock when he had it comin', too," Vinnie insisted, pushing her hand away.

Joe smiled down at his friend. Vinnie was all talk. Twenty years ago Vince had inflicted minimal damage on the teenage Joe, when a younger Joe had been foolish enough to challenge the older, burly Vincent. But now that Joe was a foot taller than Vince, and Vinnie was at least a foot broader around the middle, it wouldn't be a wise move on Vince's part to challenge his old friend. It would be better to bask in past glories.

Trying to restore peace, Joe placed one quieting hand on Vince's shoulder. He could feel him still trembling with indignation. This Nicole Smith must mean a lot to him.

"Look, Vin," Joe said soothingly. "I didn't mean any disrespect to Niki. But you know I've been working day and night trying to find out who's been sending these messages to Victoria. She's trusted me with this investigation, maybe even her life, and I don't want to let her down."

Reluctantly Vince placed the postcard in Joe's hand. Joe sank onto the sofa as he carefully studied the card. He sighed and ran his fingers through his thick black hair. "It's the same, Vince. No doubt about it," he murmured, examining the writing that was scrawled in bright red ink across the back of the card.

I miss you, Vinnie. San Francisco is supposed to be a romantic town, but it's not much fun without you. Love, Niki.

"Isn't that a strange coincidence?" Anna mused, wrinkling her freckled nose. "Nicole looks just like Victoria Lord, and the two of them are in San Francisco at the same time."

"Yeah," Joe muttered. "Some coincidence. Are you thinking what I'm thinking, Vinnie?"

Vince's face clouded with suspicion. "You don't think that Victoria and Nicole are the same person, do you?"

"Think about it, Vince. Niki and Viki. You said they look just alike except for the hair, and that could be a wig. Victoria's been having those headaches and blackouts. Afterward she doesn't remember where she was or what she was doing. Maybe she's schizo."

Anna took the postcard from Joe and stared at the strange writing. "Joe, do you really think that Victoria could have a split personality, and this Niki Smith is her 'other' self?"

"It's possible."

"No it ain't," Vinnie interjected. "My Niki ain't no split part of that stuck-up Lord broad. My Niki's sweet and fun-loving; she's a laugh a minute!"

"Exactly what Victoria Lord would like to be," Joe said, "but her father keeps her under his thumb and doesn't give her room to breathe. This split personality may be Victoria's way of escaping."

Vince sniffed his disapproval. "Well, your Victoria might be loony, but my Niki ain't. And she didn't send nobody no threatening letters. She wouldn't hurt a flea even if it bit her."

"But Vince, just think—"

The telephone's loud peal cut Joe off. Anna answered it on the second ring. "Hello. Yes. Oh, no! We'll be right there."

She hung up the phone, her face turning white beneath her bright red hair. "That was the hospital. Vinnie, there's been a fire. They want us to come down right away. It's Larry . . ."

Vince charged through the swinging doors of the emergency room, closely followed by Anna and Joe.

"Where's my baby brother? Where's Larry Wolek?" he demanded of the nurse seated behind the registration desk.

"They've taken Dr. Wolek upstairs," she said. "I believe he's in Intensive Care."

Without waiting for the elevator, Vince and his entourage hurried up the stairs.

"Intensive Care?" Anna said tearfully as they opened the door onto the third floor and rushed down the hall toward the Intensive Care Ward. "Oh, Vinnie, that sounds bad."

When Vince didn't answer, Joe reached out and grasped her hand. "It'll be okay, Anna," he offered lamely.

"But a fire—"

He squeezed her hand. "I know." Joe winced at the very thought. *Fire!* A hundred terrible images flooded his mind. How could something like this happen to good people like the Woleks?

After more than ten years as a newspaper reporter, Joe had adopted the cynical attitude that most bad things happened to innocent people, not to the people who deserved them.

They were stopped at the ward door by a nurse. She held up her hand as Vincent tried to brush by her. "Excuse me, but you can't go in there."

"My little brother's in there, and I'll go in if I damn well please." He attempted to walk around her, but she effectively blocked him.

"I'm sorry, Mr. Wolek, but the doctors have their hands full in there right now with two burn patients and—"

"Oh, God." Anna collapsed against Joe,

and he caught her to him. She buried her face in the front of his sweater and began to cry.

"I really am sorry," the nurse said, her voice softening. "I'll see if one of the doctors can come out and speak with you. If you could please wait in the waiting room at the end of the hall."

For what seemed like hours they waited. Vince paced the floor, exploding every now and then with a volley of profanities.

Joe sat quietly on a sofa with his arm around a sobbing Anna, who clung to him as though he were her only source of strength.

Joe had always loved Anna. He loved her more than his own sister, Eileen, whom he had never gotten along with. Anna was the sweetest, gentlest woman Joe had ever known and one of his favorite people in the world.

He knew that she loved him, too. And though he couldn't return her romantic feelings, he respected them and tried to show her a brother's love, while not encouraging her.

"Joe," she said, wiping her eyes with his proffered handkerchief.

"Yes?" He patted her hand that lay on his knee.

"It's been such a long time. What do you think they're doing in there?"

"They're helping Larry. I'm sure they're doing everything they can for him. They'll come out in a few minutes. It hasn't really been that long."

"Well, it's been long enough to suit me," Vinnie said, stomping toward the door. "I'm gonna find out what the hell's goin' on."

"Vinnie, please don't cause trouble," Anna pleaded.

Before he could reach the door, it opened, and a doctor, whom none of them recognized, walked into the room.

He was tall and slender, a handsome man of about forty. His gentle face registered his compassion as he looked at the worried threesome.

"I'm Dr. Jim Craig," he said as he held out his hand to Vince. "I've been asked to attend your brother. I have some experience in treating burn patients."

"How is he?" Anna said, jumping up from the sofa. "Is he . . . alive?"

"Yes." Craig's pale blue eyes softened as he turned to Anna. "Dr. Wolek's condition is listed as serious, but I believe he'll make it. The most serious problem we had to address was his smoke inhalation. That's under control now, and he's breathing comfortably. He does, however, have some burns."

"Are they bad?" Vince asked with a tremor in his voice.

"Yes, they're third-degree burns. But the

major trauma is limited to a small area on his neck and shoulder. He would have been burned much worse if he hadn't been pulled to safety by—"

"Yeah, how did it happen anyhow?" Vince demanded. Now that his anxiety had been partially alleviated, his anger was on the rise again.

"We don't know all the details yet, but Dr. Wolek had fallen asleep on a cot in the medicine room, and apparently, he had been smoking."

"Smoking?" Anna was shocked. "But Larry quit smoking."

"Yes, well, as I said, we don't have all the facts yet. But somehow the room caught fire, and Dr. Wolek had to be dragged out."

"Who did it?" Vinnie demanded. "Who saved him?"

"I believe it was a nurse," Dr. Craig replied, "a nurse named Martin. Yes, Karen Martin."

"Karen? Karen saved Larry?" Anna asked, open-mouthed with astonishment.

"I don't believe it," Vince stated flatly. "That selfish little busybody never did nothin' for nobody, no time."

"Why would Karen risk her life for Larry?" Anna asked, still unable to grasp the idea of Karen dragging Larry out of a burning room.

"Is it that hard to believe?" asked a feminine voice from the doorway.

They turned and saw Karen standing there, her face and white uniform smudged with ashes and smoke. Her hands and forearms were swathed in bandages.

"Is it really that difficult to imagine me risking my life to save someone else?" she asked tearfully.

No one answered. They simply stared at her, with wonder and embarrassment on their faces.

"I'll tell you why I saved him," she said. "I risked my life for Larry because I love him. And now that I've saved his life, he'll love me, too."

"I think I should call Meredith in San Francisco," Joe said as he walked Anna to the Intensive Care Ward. "She should know about this. In spite of the fact that she ran away two days before their wedding, I'm sure that she must still love Larry."

Anna shook her head sadly. "I suppose so. I can't imagine why she left like that. And to go all the way to San Francisco . . ."

"She must have had a reason," Joe offered.

"Well, I certainly hope it was a good one. She absolutely broke Larry's heart. If he fell asleep in that medicine room while he was smoking, it was because he was exhausted. He's been working himself into the ground since she left him."

Joe could see that it would take a very long time for Anna to forgive the woman who had hurt her younger brother. Anna harbored strong maternal instincts for Larry, having raised him from an infant when their parents had died in a train accident.

Anna had been shocked and angry when Meredith Lord disappeared two days before she and Larry were to be married.

Meredith's father, Victor, and her sister, Victoria, had gone to San Francisco to bring her home to Llanview, but two weeks had passed, and they still hadn't returned.

"Are the doctors going to let you see Larry now?" Joe asked when they reached the ward.

"That nice Dr. Craig said that I can go in and see him just for a minute. Vinnie's already in there. Larry isn't conscious yet but—" Her voice broke as she was overcome with emotion.

Joe reached out and put his hands on her shoulders. "He's going to be all right, Anna. Don't you worry."

"Joe, you're so good to us," she said, very close to tears.

"That goes both ways, you know." He placed a quick kiss on her forehead beside a stray auburn curl. "I'll go call Meredith now."

She savored the short kiss long after he had turned and walked down the hall. Dear, sweet Joe. The best friend the Woleks had ever had. Anna had a big heart, and she loved Joseph Riley with every inch of it. But she was under no delusion about Joe's feelings for her. He loved her and would do anything for her, or for Larry, or Vinnie. But Joe wasn't in love with her. He was in love with Victoria Lord. Rich, gracious, beautiful Victoria.

Anna thought for a moment of the postcard that Vinnie had received from his mysterious new lady friend, Nicole Smith.

Maybe Victoria was rich and gorgeous. But if she and Niki were the same person, Victoria Lord was crazy.

Yet Anna envied Victoria, crazy or not. She simply couldn't help it. Joe was going to call Meredith to tell her about Larry, but Anna knew the other reason Joe had to call the Lords. He wanted to talk to his beloved Viki. He wanted to find out about that postcard.

In the hospital's main lobby Joe Riley waited until the one phone booth that had a door was empty. He stepped inside and carefully closed the folding door behind him.

Llanview was a small town, and the Lords were the community's most controversial and gossiped-about citizens. The last thing he wanted was to be overheard and add more grist to the already overworked mill.

First he called Llanfair, Victor Lord's mansion, and got the number of their hotel in San Francisco from Felicia, their housekeeper.

He dialed and waited, trying to organize his thoughts. What if Victor answered? Victor Lord had never bothered to conceal his disapproval of Joe Riley. He liked Joe and respected him as a man and as a newspaper reporter. But as a potential mate for Victoria? Never.

Victor's only real complaint about Joe Riley was that Joe dared to court his daughter without benefit of a seven-figure bank account. But that was reason enough for Victor to do everything in his power to keep the two of them apart. If Victor answered the phone, he would probably hang up without letting Joe speak to either of his daughters.

But it wasn't Victor who answered. It was Victoria's low, sensuously smooth voice that said, "Hello."

"Hello, yourself," he replied, sinking onto the stool in the booth. For some reason his knees had a tendency to go weak when he heard her voice. There had been plenty of other women in Joe's life, but none had affected him the way Victoria Lord did.

"How's San Francisco?" he asked. He couldn't care less about the Golden Gate Bridge or cable cars; he wanted to know about the postcard. But he knew instinctively that he'd better soft-pedal it for the time being.

"It's rainy and foggy," she said. "Rather dreary, as a matter of fact. But I'll bet you didn't call me for a weather report. What's up?"

In typical reporter style Joe answered her question with one of his own. "Is Meredith there with you?"

"No. She's lying down resting. Why?"

Joe took a deep breath. Some people reveled in delivering bad news, but he hated it. "There's been an accident here at Llanview General. Larry Wolek's been hurt."

"Larry? Oh, no. How badly?"

"He's in serious condition, but the doctor says he's going to live. He's still unconscious."

"How did it happen?"

"A fire in the medicine room. He has second- and third-degree burns on his shoulder and neck."

"That's terrible." Joe could hear the concern in her voice. Larry Wolek was very close to both of the Lord sisters, although Meredith had always been the one he loved.

"I thought that Merrie should know," Joe said quietly. "We're all still wondering why she ran away like that."

"I'm still wondering about that myself. She's very tight-lipped about the whole thing and determined not to come home."

"I'm amazed that Victor hasn't bound and gagged her and dragged her back already," Joe observed, thinking how ruthless Victor Lord was when it came to maintaining control over his daughters.

"That's what he's ready to do," Victoria replied, dropping her voice to a conspiratorial whisper. "I've been trying to talk her into returning on her own, but Father's patience is wearing thin."

"Yes, Victor isn't known for his patience."

"I'm sure that Merrie will want to come home immediately as soon as I tell her what's happened."

Joe sighed his relief. "I'm sure it would mean a lot to Larry. He's been a wreck since she left."

"Joe . . ." Her voice sounded hesitant, maybe even a bit frightened. "Have you had any luck tracing those messages I was getting before I left?"

Joe pulled the postcard from his pocket and considered his words carefully before he spoke. "No, Viki. I don't have any leads yet. I'm sorry. You haven't received any more threats lately, have you?"

"No, nothing since I've been here."

"Nothing? Not even a postcard?"

She was silent for a long time. He thought that perhaps their connection had been broken.

"No, Joe. Nothing," she said finally. "Why did you ask about a postcard?"

He stuck the card back in his pocket. "No particular reason, Viki. Just covering all bases."

"Joe, you wouldn't keep anything from me, would you?" she asked with a quiver in her voice. "I mean, if you knew something, you'd tell me . . ."

Joe wrestled with his conscience; rationalization triumphed over honesty. "Viki, don't worry," he said soothingly. "When I find out for sure who's harassing you, you'll be the first to know."

He could sense by her heavy silence that she didn't believe him. Victoria was a smart woman with finely tuned instincts. It was difficult to keep anything from her. But if Nicole Smith was who Joe thought she was, an alter ego of Victoria Lord, then Viki was fighting an equally formidable adversary —herself.

"Come home, Viki," Joe said. "Come back to Llanview as soon as you can."

"Joe Riley, if I didn't know better, I'd think that you miss me."

"Of course I miss you. Nobody else

around here uses and abuses me quite the way you do."

She laughed, and he could picture her, shaking her head in feigned disgust. "Dream on, big boy."

"I will . . . every night until you're back home."

As he hung up the phone he thought of the dreams he had been having lately about Victoria Lord. They weren't the well-worn fantasies that he had been entertaining for the past few months.

These dreams were nightmares about a beautiful blond woman who donned a red wig and a gaudy mini-dress . . . a woman who scrawled threatening messages in red lipstick on bathroom mirrors . . . a woman who called herself Nicole Smith.

Chapter
Two

"What was that all about?"

As Victoria hung up the phone she turned around to see her father entering the hotel suite with a copy of *The New York Times* under his arm and his Dunhill pipe in his hand.

"It was Joe Riley," she said, steeling herself for the argument to come.

"Riley?" He pulled the gold pocketwatch from his vest pocket, and it sprang open at his touch. "It's after midnight in Llanview. Why on earth would he call this late? Is something wrong at the paper?"

Victoria noted the genuine concern on her father's face, an expression she seldom saw on those handsome features. There was little in Victor Lord's world that he cared about. But his newspaper, *The Banner,* the cornerstone of his financial empire, was one of the few things that truly mattered to him.

"The paper is fine, Father," she replied.

"Good," he said as he settled into an easy chair and leisurely lit his pipe. Victoria felt her resentment growing as she watched him. He was undoubtedly the most self-centered person she had ever known.

"Aren't you still curious about why he called?" she said, sitting on the sofa across from him.

He carefully unfolded the newspaper and held it up between them. It seemed to Victoria that there had always been some sort of barrier between her and her father, something that kept her at a distance along with the rest of the world. No one got close to Victor Lord.

Considering the kind of person Lord was, maybe it was just as well. He would undoubtedly destroy anyone who ventured into his inner sanctum.

"No, I'm not curious," he replied dryly. "But I suppose that won't stop you from telling me."

"Larry Wolek has been in an accident," she said, carefully filtering all traces of emotion from her voice. She had learned early in life that the best way to deal with her father was on a purely intellectual plane.

Victor lowered his paper slightly and

peered over its top. "Well, is he dead?" he asked, puffing on his pipe.

"No."

He studied her face for a moment, then lifted his newspaper again. "Pity," he said. "But one can always hope."

She glared at him, her eyes burning through the paper. If he could feel her scorching gaze, he made no indication of it.

"Was it an automobile accident?" he said casually.

"No, it wasn't. It was a fire in the hospital. But why would you ask, Father? I'm sure it doesn't matter to you that your daughter's fiancé is in serious condition with second- and third-degree burns."

"You're right," he said, folding the paper and placing it in the magazine rack at his side. "It doesn't matter. But you're wrong about Wolek being Meredith's fiancé. The wedding is off. You heard Meredith say so yourself."

"Yes, I heard her. And I can't help but think that you had something to do with her decision."

"You have an overly suspicious nature, Victoria." He drew on his pipe and blew a perfect smoke ring into the air. "You really should work on that, or you'll end up a bitter, paranoid old lady someday."

"We certainly wouldn't want that, now

would we?" she said. "One bitter, paranoid old person is enough for any family."

His gray eyes narrowed as he glowered at her through the blue-gray smoke. "You'd better watch yourself, young lady. I am hardly old."

That was true, she thought as she glanced over her father's virile physique. Victor Lord was one of those men who got better, not older, year after year. His sparkling silver mane of hair gave the only clue that he had long passed his fiftieth birthday. His classically handsome face had become more rugged in the past twenty years, adding character to perfection.

Only his gray eyes gave him away. It would take most of a lifetime for a man's eyes to become so cold, so cynical. A lifetime spent in ruthless pursuit of self-interests.

"I don't think I'll wake Meredith tonight," Victoria said, looking at her watch. "She's been so weak lately, and she'll be stronger in the morning after a good night's sleep. We probably couldn't get a flight out this evening anyway. Tomorrow morning will do just as well."

"You don't mean to tell me that you are actually going to tell Meredith about this latest escapade of Larry Wolek's?"

"Of course I'm going to tell her. Meredith loves Larry, and she has the right to know that he's been seriously hurt."

Victor stood and walked over to the sofa, glaring down at his oldest daughter. "I can't believe that you would jeopardize your sister's health by telling her something like this, when you know what condition she's in. She's dying, for heaven's sake."

Victoria rose from the sofa. Victor was tall, but so was she, and in her high heels she nearly looked him eye to eye. "Lower your voice," she whispered. "Do you want her to hear you? We both agreed that she wasn't to know about her illness. Overhearing a thing like that could end her remission."

"And if you tell her about her beloved Larry, she may relapse from the shock of hearing it. Have you thought about that?"

Victoria clenched and unclenched her fists at her sides. "Yes, I've considered that possibility. But it's a chance I'm willing to take. Merrie has to be told."

He stepped closer to her until she could feel the heat of his breath on her face. "Well, I'm *not* willing to take that risk. I care about Meredith's health, even if her own sister doesn't."

Victoria's anger exploded, and she forgot to whisper. "How dare you accuse me of not considering my sister's health!" she shouted into his surprised face. "All you're concerned about is keeping her away from Larry, keeping her to yourself. You've never given a moment's thought about what's best for Meredith, or anyone else for that matter. The only one you've ever cared about is yourself."

Before she saw it coming, there was a resounding slap across her face. He had struck her.

She stumbled backward, away from him, with her hand to her cheek. Tears burned her eyes, but she fought them back. She would never again show weakness to this man.

"What's wrong, Father?" she said smoothly, her voice saturated with contempt. "You can't bear to hear the truth, can you?"

He stepped toward her with his fists raised, but she put out her arm and blocked him.

"Don't you dare," she hissed. "If you ever strike me again, I swear I'll walk away from you, and that will be the last time you see me." Her eyes flashed blue fire, and her jaw, as square and determined as his, was set in granite.

Victor lowered his fists and smiled, a sadistic smile that curled one corner of his thin lips.

"You're mine, Victoria," he said. "And I'll do with you exactly as I please. If you ever run away from me, I'll find you, and I'll drag you back. Just like I found Meredith. And I'll have my way on this issue as well. You *will not* tell Meredith about Larry Wolek. You *won't do it*. Do you understand me?"

They both heard a movement behind them. They turned to see a sleepy Meredith standing in the doorway in her flannel, rosebud-printed nightgown.

"What are you two arguing about?" she asked. "And what about Larry? What's happened to him?"

Larry woke to a world of pain and confusion. His throat and chest ached with every breath he took, and his eyes were so sore that he could hardly bear to open them. When he finally did open them and look around, he wasn't sure where he was or what had happened.

Then he remembered yesterday and the day before, when he had wakened to find Anna and Vinnie bent over him with looks of anguish on their faces. But they weren't there this time.

The face staring down at him was unfamiliar. The face of a stranger . . . a man he only vaguely remembered from yesterday. A man who had been standing behind Anna and Vinnie, wearing a white coat. A doctor.

"Who the hell are you?" he mumbled through parched lips.

The face smiled good-naturedly. "And good morning to you, too, Dr. Wolek," he said. "I'm Jim Craig, your physician of record. You've been blessed with the benefit of my expertise and, for better or worse, I'm stuck with your bad temper."

"Till death do us part?" Larry asked wryly.

"No danger of that. You've moved from the critical list to serious and on up to testy."

Larry moaned and closed his eyes. "Sorry," he said. "But I feel like Sherman's army has burned its way through my chest and throat."

He opened his eyes and looked down at the bandages that covered his left arm and shoulder. "How bad is it?" he asked.

"Second and third degree," Craig replied, pulling up a stool and sitting down. "We're going to have to do a skin graft on your neck. I think the shoulder will be okay on its own."

"Skin graft? Who's going to be doing that? Nobody here at Llanview General does grafts."

"I do," Craig said with quiet pride.

"Oh, okay. Now I know who you are. You're the new doctor from the research center. I heard you were coming next week."

"After your little marshmallow roast Dr. Polk asked me to come right away. So here I am."

"Thanks." Larry tried to lift his hand to offer it to Craig, but he grimaced from the effort and lowered it back to the bed. "Welcome to Llanview. I'm glad you're here."

"Thank you. I think I'm going to like

Llanview. It seems like a nice little town full of friendly people."

"Yes, it is. Speaking of friendly people, have I had any visitors?"

"Your brother and sister have been here night and day since the accident. They're down in the cafeteria right now having some breakfast. I'll send for them for you if you like."

"No. That's all right. Vinnie swears that he'll faint if he misses a meal. Has anybody else been by?"

"A fellow by the name of Joe Riley has been hanging around a lot. And a lady came by yesterday, but you were asleep. Her last name was Lord."

Larry smiled briefly, but even that hurt. "Meredith," he said. "I knew she'd come back when she heard."

Craig shifted awkwardly on his stool. "I'm pretty sure this lady's name wasn't Meredith. I think it was Veronica or Victoria. Yes, it was Victoria. I remember hearing Joe call her Viki. She's a friend of his, I believe."

Larry turned his face to the wall, ignoring the pain that the movement caused him.

"I'm sorry, Dr. Wolek," Jim Craig said, sensing that Victoria wasn't the visitor Larry had been hoping for. "Is there anything I can do for you? Anyone you would like me to call?"

Yes, Larry thought. *Call Meredith for me.*

Tell her that I need her now more than I've ever needed anyone. Ask her why she ran away, why she hasn't come to see me. Tell her that if she were the one who was hurt, nothing would keep me away from her. Nothing! Call Merrie and beg her for me.

"Can I get you something for the pain, Larry?" Jim Craig's voice was kind, full of compassion. It touched a sensitive, sore spot in Larry's heart. Merrie should be the one here asking him that.

"No. Just get the hell out of here and leave me alone," he said. "I don't need anything . . . or anybody."

Meredith Lord pushed the delicate lace curtains aside and stared out her bedroom window at the rose garden below. The roses were her favorite. She had always associated roses with her love for Larry. They were beautiful, delicate, rich, and full . . . bursting with promise. And thorns. The thorns were always there to prick you and make you bleed when you least expected it, just when you thought that happiness was within your grasp.

She wanted desperately to go to Larry, to take him in her arms and comfort him, as he had her so many times before. After all, that was why she had rushed back to Llanview the minute she had heard about the accident.

But on the plane back, Victor had talked to her, had forced her to face the fact that it would be terribly unfair if she were to run to Larry now. He would think that she had come back to him for good, that she was willing to pick up where they had left off. And, of course, she could never do that.

She loved Larry far too much to let him go on thinking that they had a future together. How could they, when Meredith had no future? Her illness had robbed her of even that.

She turned away from the window, unable to bear the sight of the roses and the thoughts of the many roses Larry had given her in the past. Larry had given so much of himself. What did he think of her? What was he feeling right now?

Meredith fell across the frilly eyelet bedspread and buried her face in the ruffled pillow. "Oh, Larry," she sobbed. "I do love you, and I want to be with you. But I can't. Please forgive me."

Jim Craig gathered the papers on the top of his desk and shoved them into his briefcase. He had a lot of catching up to do over the next few weeks. Familiarizing himself with over two dozen new patients wouldn't be easy, besides the personal adjustments of moving to a new home.

His teenage daughter, Cathy, was having a

difficult time making the move away from her high school and friends. But maybe a change of scene would be good for both of them. Lately she had been involved with a group of kids that gave him cause for concern. Perhaps she would choose her new set of companions more carefully. Jim certainly hoped so.

He had tried to be both father and mother to her since her mother's death. But it hadn't been easy. Jim hoped that a change in locale might ease some of the tension that had been growing between them since she had entered adolescence.

As he walked down the corridor toward the exit, he rehearsed the procedure of Larry Wolek's skin graft in his mind. He wanted to do an excellent job on Dr. Wolek. Jim Craig did his best on every patient, but he wanted to make doubly sure that the handsome Dr. Wolek remained the nice-looking young man that he was.

Besides, it occurred to Jim that Larry Wolek had already been thrown a few more of life's curve balls than he deserved. Jim wanted to get that young man on his feet, looking good, feeling great, and back at work as soon as possible.

"So, how do you like being at Llanview General?" asked the pretty nurse at the desk as he passed through the emergency ward.

"I like it just fine, but I'm calling it a day. I

can do the paperwork at home," he added, indicating his briefcase. "Good night."

As he exited the hospital he saw a long dark Cadillac pull up to the emergency entrance. A huge gorilla of a man in a pin-striped suit crawled out, dragging a tiny waif with him.

At first, Craig thought it was an unconscious child. Then he realized it was a woman—a frail bit of a woman.

The man carelessly tossed her over his broad shoulder and strode up to the entrance.

"Hey, you. Are you a doctor?" he asked Craig.

"Yes. What's the problem?"

"This gal was auditioning for a singing job at the Moonshadows. She up and passed out right in the middle of her number. The boss said I should bring her here to the hospital."

When he reached Craig, he pulled the woman from his shoulder and dropped her unceremoniously into Craig's arms.

"But . . . who is she?" Jim asked, looking down at the glossy black curls that were spread across the front of his white smock.

"Don't know," the guy said as he pushed his bulk into the Cadillac. "But if she comes around, tell her not to call us, we'll call her."

As a doctor, Jim Craig noted his patient's low blood pressure, her slow responses to stimuli, and her general condition, which was poor at best.

As a man Jim couldn't help noticing the delicate olive coloring of her skin, the shining black hair, her feminine fragility which evoked a protective male response in him.

He watched her eyes flutter open and stare up at him uncomprehendingly. They were russet brown and unbelievably large in her diminutive face.

"Where am I?" she asked.

He took her hand in a paternal gesture. "You're in a hospital. I'm Dr. Craig and I'm taking care of you. You're going to be fine."

She didn't reply, but he felt her squeeze his hand. At least she hadn't sworn at him, he thought, the way Dr. Wolek had.

"What's your name?" he asked.

"Carla. Carla Benari," she replied softly.

Italian, he thought. That explained her beautiful coloring.

"What happened to me?" she asked.

"You fainted while you were auditioning at a—"

"Auditioning! Oh, no, my job." She tried to sit up, but he gently pushed her back onto the bed.

"Hey, wait a minute. Lie back there. You aren't going anyplace until we find out why you fainted."

"But I need that job. I need the money."

"I'm sure you do. But right now you need

the rest even more. Carla, when was the last time you ate?"

Her amber eyes avoided his. "I . ah . . ."

"That's what I thought. We're going to run some tests on you, but my guess is that you haven't been taking very good care of yourself lately. Is that a possibility?"

She bit her full lower lip and pulled her hand away from his. "I'm a singer. I've been on the road for quite a while now. It's been a long time between gigs."

"I understand. But sooner or later this sort of lifestyle catches up with you. You're going to have to take some time off and build yourself up. We're going to help you, don't worry."

"Excuse me, Dr. Craig." Price Trainor pulled the privacy curtain aside. "You wanted to see me?"

"Yes, Dr. Trainor. Please come in."

Price Trainor was an impressive young black intern. Handsome, intelligent, and compassionate, he was one of Llanview General's brightest stars. In the three short days that Craig had been at the hospital, he had recognized Trainor's abilities and had determined to develop that potential.

"Carla Benari, meet Dr. Trainor," Craig said. "I have to leave now, so I'm assigning your case to him. I'm sure you'll find him most capable. I'll drop by and see how you're doing in the morning. Good night, all."

"Good night, Dr. Craig." Trainor turned his attention to his new patient. She was without a doubt one of the most beautiful women he had ever seen, though she was lamentably thin. He had never seen eyes so big, so round and luminous.

But she was more than beautiful, she was frightened. He could see the fear on her face, in her eyes. He wanted to quickly put her at ease.

"Don't worry, Miss Benari. We'll find out what's wrong with you and fix you up in no time. I'll need to examine you now . . ."

He reached out and took her arm, checking her pulse. The moment he touched her, he was acutely aware of it—a sexual magnetism that was overpowering. Trainor fought the feeling and pushed it into the recesses of his mind. He never allowed himself to entertain a sexual thought about a patient when he was examining her. It wasn't fair.

He counted the pulse in her wrist and noticed that it was getting faster by the moment. Or was it his imagination? He stole a glance at her face and saw a fleeting glimmer in her eyes that wasn't fear. Could she be feeling the same thing he was?

No. That was ridiculous. He was only taking her pulse, for heaven's sake.

He warmed his stethoscope between his

hands, not daring to look her in the eye again. "I'll need to listen to your heart now, Miss Benari." He could hear the stress in his own voice, and he wondered if she could hear it, too.

She said nothing, but obediently sat up on the bed. He carefully lowered the top edge of the hospital gown and pressed the stethoscope to her chest. He was careful to make sure that his fingers touched only the instrument and not her breast. Funny, he usually didn't give it a thought.

He listened carefully, detecting a slight murmur, but nothing that seemed extraordinary. He moved the stethoscope lower to improve his hearing, and he felt a shiver run through her. Her heartbeat was suddenly louder and faster.

"Are you about finished?" she said, her voice high and tense.

"What? Oh, almost. I need you to take a deep breath for me now . . ."

"That's enough!" she cried, suddenly pulling away from him. "I don't want you to . . . to touch me like that."

Guilt swept over him. Had his unexpected feelings for this woman betrayed him? Had he acted improperly toward her?

No. He hadn't. He couldn't help what he was feeling, but his manner had been totally professional.

"Miss Benari, I'm a doctor. I have to

touch you if I'm going to examine you. Surely you don't object to having a doctor examine you?"

"No. I don't want *you.*"

"I see. And do you mind telling me how I've managed to offend you in so short a time?"

Her eyes wouldn't meet his as she stared down at the stethoscope in his hand. "I just don't want you to touch me," she said quietly. "Tell Dr. Craig that I want another doctor."

"I see." He nodded as the realization slowly dawned on him. Only a few times in his career had Price Trainor encountered racial prejudice. Before, he had been able to shrug it off, but this time it stung deeply. Coming from this beautiful, seemingly intelligent woman, it hurt all the way through.

"I'll see what I can do, Miss Benari," he said. "Maybe there's another doctor around here who won't mind treating a bigot. Personally, I'd rather not. If there's anything that I simply can't tolerate, it's an intolerant person like you."

"She's a racist, I tell you. And she doesn't want me on her case any more than I want to be on it."

Price's dark face was flushed with anger as he stared down at Jim Craig, who was seated quietly at his desk, making notes from a medical journal.

Jim looked up from his work and put on his "patient" smile. "I'm sure you must have misunderstood, Price. I spoke with her briefly yesterday, and she seemed like a perfectly lovely person."

"Oh, I'm sure she did. A lot of bigots go around disguised as good-hearted, wouldn't-hurt-a-fly people. They don't wear buttons that say, 'Hi, my name is Carla, and I hate black people.' I'm sure she was nice to you. You're white. I've no doubt that if I were white, she'd be *lovely* to me, too."

"Price, there's no one else available right now to take her case."

"How about you? You're the one who thinks she's great."

Jim pointed to the mountain of patient files on his desk. "Do I look to you like a guy who has time on his hands?"

"No. I'm sorry. It's just that—"

"I know. I sympathize with your situation. But I would consider it a personal favor if you would see this one through. I want that young lady to have excellent care, and I believe you are the one most capable of providing that care."

Price shook his head slowly, realizing that he had lost the battle. How could he say no to a request like that? "Okay. I'll run the

231

tests on her. But if she stabs me with a needle, my blood will be on your hands."

"I'll take that risk," Jim said, already engrossed in his journal.

"That's big of you," Price mumbled as he left the room and headed for the lab.

"Make a fist, please, Miss Benari." Price realized what a foolhardy request that was to make of a person who was sitting there, glaring up at him with baleful brown eyes.

"Thank you," he said when she complied with his request. "Now, if you'll be very still, I'll get this blood sample before you know it."

He leaned over her and expertly plunged the needle into her arm, neatly piercing the vein the first time.

With a grimace on her pretty face, Carla stared up at a spot on the ceiling and bore the operation with stoic silence.

"There," he said, withdrawing the needle. "That wasn't so bad, was it?"

"No, I guess not."

"Well, try not to sound so surprised. Any first-year med student can take blood."

He had meant it as a joke, but she didn't seem to be in a joking mood.

She reached up and wiped the fine mist of perspiration from her upper lip. He noticed that her rich olive coloring was several shades lighter than before and had a slight greenish cast to it.

He walked over to the refrigerator in the corner of the lab and poured a small glass of orange juice.

When he offered it to her, she took it and muttered an unenthusiastic "Thanks."

"Don't mention it. I only did it because it's National Be-Nice-to-a-Bigot Week."

Her brown eyes flashed with anger. "Will you stop calling me . . . that?"

"If you stop treating me as though I've done you wrong. You don't even know me, lady, but you hate me. What else do you expect me to think?"

He pulled open a drawer, grabbed a small adhesive bandage, and slammed the drawer closed. With more vigor than necessary, he ripped off the bandage's protective covering.

"What makes you think that I hate you?" she asked guardedly as he applied the bandage to the needle prick on her inner arm.

"Oh, maybe the way you cringe every time I touch you. Like you just did."

Her eyes narrowed, and she blinked rapidly several times.

"Or maybe the way you're always glaring at me," he added. "If looks could kill, they'd be measuring me for a coffin right now."

"I'm sorry," she said through gritted teeth. Perfect white teeth, he noticed in spite of himself.

"Yeah, you look all broken up with remorse."

She heaved a sigh and, just for a moment, he thought that she did look sorry.

"If you won't accept my apology, there's really nothing else I can do, Dr. Trainor." She stood on shaky legs. "May I go back to my room now?"

He was busy labeling the blood sample. "Yes, but wait a minute. I'll wheel you back up myself." He placed the specimen in its appropriate tray along with his list of instructions.

"That's okay. I'd rather walk."

She had taken three paces when her knees buckled beneath her. He caught her just before she hit the floor.

"Whoa, take it easy," he breathed, holding her against his chest. "Apparently, you didn't have any blood to spare."

Before he knew it was coming, a physical awareness of her flooded over him—a sexual attraction that was stronger than he had felt for any woman, black or white. And once again, it took him completely off guard.

He expected her to push away, but she didn't. She leaned against him, as though seeking the strength and solidity he offered. Of their own accord his arms tightened around her, pressing her closer until he could feel her warmth, her softness. He could smell the delicate scent of her hair.

He looked down into her eyes, and instead of seeing hostility burning there, he saw another fire smoldering in those amber depths.

Her hands moved slowly up his chest to his collar, where they circled around to the nape of his neck. For one crazy moment, he considered kissing her. And in that wonderfully insane second, he knew that if he did, she would kiss him back.

"Ah, excuse me," said a voice from the door behind them.

They jumped apart like guilty children caught playing doctor. Turning, they saw Jim Craig, who stood in the doorway with a look of puzzlement on his face. "Does this mean that the two of you have settled your differences?" he asked.

Chapter
Three

Meredith nervously shifted the potted plant from one hand to the other as she stepped out of the elevator and walked down the hospital corridor toward his room. Larry loved growing, living things as much as she did, and this robust philodendron seemed just the sort of gift to perk him up.

Better yet, it might show him that she was thinking of him, that she still cared about him.

No matter how hard she tried, she couldn't stay away. She couldn't bear the thought of him lying there in pain, wondering if she had forgotten him. Somehow, she would let him know that she loved him . . . as a friend. And for his sake she would hide her other feelings and not encourage him to think that they had a future.

But as she neared his room at the end of

the hall, her heart pounded feebly against her ribs. The weakness that had plagued her lately swept over her, leaving her shaken and cold.

She stopped, leaned against the wall, and took three deep breaths. The philodendron in her trembling hand quivered as she gripped it and held it tightly against her chest.

Someone opened Larry's door, and Meredith jumped, her taut nerves jarred by the unexpected sound.

Karen Martin stepped out of the room. She was wearing street clothes instead of her nurse's uniform, a tight blue sweater dress that fit her every curve to perfection. The skirt was too short and was now out of style, except for those women who were long of leg and short of modesty.

Meredith instantly felt like a Pollyanna in her delicate daisy-spangled cotton dress. She always felt a bit naive and unworldly around the voluptuous Karen Martin.

Karen's blue eyes widened perceptibly at seeing Meredith. She glanced down at the plant and smiled a tense, tight-lipped smile.

"Merrie, how nice to see you!" she said in a hushed tone. "What are you doing here?"

"I've . . . I've come to see Larry."

Several expressions played across Karen's face, all of them negative. She reached out and firmly grasped Meredith's elbow. "I think we should talk about that first," she said, propelling Meredith into the empty room across the hall.

Karen quietly shut the door behind them, then whirled on Meredith. "How dare you show your face around here after what you did!"

Meredith recoiled from the attack. "What? What are you talking about?"

"You know exactly what I'm talking about. Do you think you can come waltzing in here as though nothing has happened after what you did to Larry?"

"What did I do?"

"You ran out on him. You deserted him after you said you loved him. You broke his heart."

Merrie fought back the tears that sprang to her eyes. She wanted to scream at Karen, to tell her that she was wrong, but she couldn't. Everything Karen was saying was true.

"It's your fault that he's lying in there burned. He worked until he made himself sick, trying to forget you. He was so tired that he fell asleep with a lit cigarette in his hand. It's all your fault, Meredith Lord. And he hates you for it."

Meredith shook her head. "No. Larry would never hate me."

"He does. He told me so himself."

"I don't believe you."

"Oh, yeah? Well, go ask him yourself. Let him tell you to your face how much he despises you for what you've done to him."

"You're lying. You want him for yourself. That's why you're saying all of this."

Tears filled Karen's eyes and spilled down her rouged cheeks. "Yes, I want him. I love Larry. I was the one who pulled him out of that fire and saved his life. I'm the one who's nursing him back to health. Where were you when he needed you, Meredith? If I hadn't been there for Larry, he'd be dead right now. You think about that, Meredith, before you try to force yourself back into his life."

Meredith couldn't hold back her tears any longer. She turned her back to Karen and set the plant on a table nearby.

Karen was right. She was absolutely right. Karen had been there for Larry when he had needed someone most. He had every reason to despise the woman who had run out on him and left his life in shambles.

She couldn't go to him now. She couldn't risk it. The one thing that she couldn't stand was to hear Larry tell her that he no longer loved her, that he hated her. It was better hearing it from Karen.

Merrie turned and walked past Karen without raising her eyes. She paused at the door, her hand on the knob. "Take care of him," she said softly. "Make sure that he gets well."

"I will," Karen replied as Meredith closed the door behind her. "I most certainly will."

"Peekaboo. It's me again." Karen poked her head through the half-open door.

"Oh, hi, Karen." Larry shifted, trying to find a less miserable position on his bed. "I thought you went home for the day," he grumbled.

"I was going to. But I decided to pop in and check on you once more."

"So, you checked. I'm still here," he said. "I'm not planning on going out this evening."

She ignored his sarcasm. "Is there anything else I can do for you?" she asked. "Anything at all?"

A light of interest glimmered briefly in his eyes. "Yes, there is one thing . . ."

She hurried into the room, eager to fulfill any request. "What is it, Larry?"

"Could you find out if anyone has heard anything from Merrie? If anyone has seen her or Victoria?"

Karen's blue eyes suddenly went frosty. "I asked around this morning, Larry," she said, "and I heard that Meredith is still in San Francisco."

"Oh. Okay, thanks." He leaned back on his pillow. The gleam in his eyes flickered, then died.

"I'm sorry that you haven't heard from

her, Larry," she said. "I know how much it hurts you to know that she doesn't care anymore."

"Thanks, Karen," he said dryly. "I really appreciate your concern for my welfare."

"Larry . . . I bought you a little something to cheer you up," she said, revealing the gift that she had hidden behind her back.

"Why, Karen, a philodendron, my favorite. How thoughtful of you."

"Meredith? Merrie, why have you returned so soon? I thought you went to the hospital to see What's-His-Name."

Her father's voice reached out to snare her as she tried to tiptoe past the open door of his study.

She knew that he had deliberately left it open and had been watching for her to return. He always watched for her and demanded to know every move she had made while not in his presence. It had been irritating at the age of twelve. It was unforgivable now that she was a full-grown woman.

She paused only briefly before the door. "I *did* go to the hospital. I *didn't* see Larry. I hope you're satisfied."

He looked up from the French dueling pistol that he was cleaning and smiled at her knowingly. "I told you he wouldn't see you, that you would be wasting your time."

"Well, it's my time, isn't it, Father? I'll

squander it on whomever I choose. And for your information, Larry didn't refuse to see me. I decided not to see him."

Victor went back to cleaning the pistol. "My, my, there may be hope for you yet."

To escape his smug satisfaction she crossed the marble-tiled foyer to the library. The quiet, secluded library had always been her refuge. She loved the solitude she found there, the musty smell of old books and the scent of the pine logs that blazed in the fireplace. As a child Merrie had spent her happiest hours curled in the old leather wing-back chair in the corner, with a book and a McIntosh apple.

She needed that solitude now, that comforting, familiar escape. But as she neared the library door, she heard voices, Victoria's and Joe Riley's.

"But, Joe," she heard Viki say, "if you've uncovered something, you must tell me what it is."

"Victoria, I just don't think it's best to—" Joe halted mid-sentence when he saw Meredith at the door.

"Merrie, you're back from the hospital so soon?" Victoria rose from her chair by the fire and walked over to greet her sister.

Meredith sensed a certain uneasiness in the room. She could tell that they had been discussing something important, something they obviously didn't want to discuss in her presence.

"Yes, I didn't stay long," she replied.

"How was Larry? Was he glad to see you?"

"I didn't see Larry," she admitted for the second time in five minutes. She wished they wouldn't ask so many questions.

"But why not?"

"I just didn't. Okay?" she snapped. Merrie saw the hurt on Victoria's face and regretted her brusque tone. She seemed to be regretting everything she did these days.

"I'm sorry, Viki. I'm very tired. I think I'll go lie down until dinner."

From the library door Victoria watched her sister walk away and noticed how slowly she climbed the stairs. Where was the bouncy Meredith that she remembered? Her heart turned over to think that Merrie might actually be losing the battle with her disease.

"Is she all right?" Joe asked, his voice heavy with concern.

"What? Oh, yes, I suppose so," she said, walking back into the room. "I just wish she could get back together with Larry. When she's with him she's always so happy, so strong. This ordeal is sapping what little energy she has left."

Victoria sighed deeply and sat on the watered-silk couch beside Joe. He moved closer to her and considered putting his arm around her, but thought better of it.

"I think this whole business with her and Larry is taking its toll on you, too," he said.

"Oh, that's ridiculous. I'm fine," she replied, brushing the idea away as though it had no substance whatsoever. Like her father, Victoria Lord considered herself indestructible.

"I think you're more vulnerable than you know right now, Viki," Joe said gently. Her hand rested on the sofa between them; he covered it with his own.

"And just what is that supposed to mean?" she asked.

"Nothing."

She jerked her hand away from his. "It did, too, mean something. Joe Riley, you're hiding something from me, and I want to know what it is."

"Do you? I wonder," he said.

"Of course I do. Out with it."

"All right. But first I have to ask you some questions. Do you know a woman by the name of Nicole Smith?"

He watched her face turn nearly as pale as her blond hair. "No, I don't. Am I supposed to know her?"

Joe shrugged. "I'm not sure. But she knows you. She and Vince Wolek had a conversation about you, and she seems to have some pretty strong feelings on the subject of Victoria Lord. Negative feelings."

"Vince Wolek? What does he have to do with this?"

"He's in love with Nicole Smith."

Joe studied her carefully, using his sharply honed skills as a newspaperman. He could have sworn that he detected a flash of guilt in her blue eyes. She glanced away uneasily, afraid to face his steady gaze.

"What is this Nicole Smith like?" she asked.

He recaptured her hand, and he could feel it trembling beneath his. "Other than the fact that she has red hair and dresses in gaudy, hip clothes . . . she looks exactly like you, Viki."

A shiver ran through her body, and Joe knew that she wasn't cold. The room was toasty warm from the fire that blazed in the fireplace.

He moved to put his arm around her shoulders, but she quickly stood and walked to the window.

With her back to him she asked, "Have you seen Niki Smith yourself?"

"No, I haven't." He rose and walked over to stand behind her. Carefully he placed his hands on her shoulders and turned her to face him. He had to see her face when he asked the question. "Viki, how did you know that Nicole Smith's nickname is Niki?"

She stared at him uncomprehendingly for a moment. "But you just said so—you just—"

"No, I didn't. I only told you that her name was Nicole Smith, not Niki. How did you know that?"

"Niki, Nicole, why does it matter? What's the big deal?"

"The big deal is . . . I believe that Niki is the one who's been sending you the threatening notes."

She tried to shrug his hands away, but he held her tightly. "That's silly. Why would some woman that I've never even met want to hurt me?"

"I'm afraid that Niki's the only one who knows the answer to that," he said.

Her eyes narrowed suspiciously. "This is all your fault, Joe Riley," she said in a low ominous whisper.

"My fault? How the hell can it be my fault?"

"Nicole Smith is probably one of your old girlfriends who's jealous of me now."

"That's stupid, Viki," he said with a dry chuckle. "You're really grasping at straws."

"Oh, so now you think I'm stupid?"

"No. I said that your idea was stupid. Why would any of my old girlfriends be jealous of us?" he asked, glancing over her businesslike gray suit and the high-necked crepe blouse. He thought of all the times when he had fantasized about what lay beneath those perfectly tailored clothes, beneath her perfectly maintained facade.

"To the best of my knowledge," he added, "we haven't done anything for anybody to be jealous of."

"And I suppose that's *my* fault?"

"Well, God knows it's not *my* fault. I've done everything I can to remedy the situation. Everything short of clubbing you over the head and dragging you off to my lair."

"And I suppose you'd like to do that?"

"At times like this, the thought intrigues me. Especially the clubbing part."

"Take your hands off me, Joseph Riley, and get out of here."

"Okay." He removed his hands slowly, allowing them to trail down her arms first. "I'll go, but not before I've shown you something that I'm afraid you need to see."

She backed away from him, suspicious of the light in his dark eyes.

He reached into the pocket of his leather coat. "I should have shown you this the day you returned from San Francisco, Viki, but I was afraid you weren't ready. I'm still not sure if you are or not, but here goes."

He pulled Vinnie's postcard from his pocket.

"What's that?" she asked. He could hear the fear in her voice.

"It's a postcard from Nicole Smith to Vince Wolek. He received it several weeks ago, right after you and your father went to San Francisco to get Merrie."

He held it out to her, but she looked away. "I don't want to see it."

"I'm not surprised," he said. "But I want you to see it." He shoved it under her nose. "It's from San Francisco. Look at the handwriting, Viki. Do you recognize it?"

He heard her breath leave her in a single gasp as she stared down at the card.

"I thought you'd remember it, Viki. It's the same as the message that was scrawled in lipstick across your bathroom mirror. It's the same writing that was on your desk calendar at work, isn't it?"

"Damn you, Joe—you know it is," she said, bursting into tears.

She grabbed the card out of his hand. "All right. You've done your detective work, now get out of here." Before he could stop her, she tore the card into tiny pieces and threw it into the fire.

"Viki, please," he pleaded. "Let me help you. I care about you. I want to help you through this."

"Get out!" she screamed. He tried to take her in his arms, but she pushed him away and backed against the wall. "I said get out and leave me alone!"

"Okay. I'm going. Viki, I'm really sorry that I—" He couldn't stay to finish his statement. He left the room only a split second before a heavy oriental vase crashed against the wall.

"Niki! I was beginnin' to think you were gonna stand me up." Vince moved over in the booth to allow the pretty redhead to slide in beside him.

"Ah, Vinnie." Her hand moved across the seat to fondle his knee. "I wouldn't stand you up, sweetheart. I just had a little trouble getting away, that's all."

"Trouble with your family?" he asked cautiously. Anytime he asked about her relatives or other friends she clammed up.

"Ah, yes . . . my family. Are you going to buy me a drink or not?"

"Oh, sure." He snapped his fingers and summoned the waitress. "A beer for the lady and another one for me."

He grinned down at her, thinking how lucky he was to be out with somebody as pretty and sexy as Nicole Smith.

Before meeting Niki, Vince had always figured that any woman who wore miniskirts and lots of blue eye makeup was a loose broad—especially if she drank beer. Everyone knew that real ladies only drank white wine or Shirley Temples . . . or maybe pink champagne on New Year's Eve.

But Nicole was different. She might dress sexy and say a bad word once in a while, but she was a lady through and through. You could just tell by the graceful way she moved and the big words she used. Nobody walked and talked like that unless they were from good stock.

And no matter what Joe Riley said, she wasn't Victoria Lord dressed up like somebody else. She was just plain Niki, *his* Niki. Joe was just jealous.

Vince glanced around the bar and noted with satisfaction that at least five of his cronies were casting furtive glances in his and Nicole's direction. Their faces were green with envy, except for Barney's—his was green because he'd had too much to drink.

In a fit of daring Vinnie reached over and pulled Niki closer to him. He planted a big kiss right on her lips . . . a good, long kiss. If the guys were gonna gawk, he might as well give them something to gawk at.

"Hey, Vince," she said, catching her breath. "You're feeling frisky this evening."

"I missed you a bunch," he admitted shyly. "I'm glad you're back in town."

"So am I. But if you missed me, you had only yourself to blame. Remember, I tried to get you to go away to Atlantic City with me before I left, but you wouldn't."

"I had to work, Niki. I can't just leave my business like that. I've worked like the dickens my whole life building that shipping company. I can't just up and leave on a lark. Not even for a gal as pretty as you."

"I know. I understand."

Her bottom lip protruded in a pout, which he found absolutely irresistible. So he kissed it away.

She smiled up at him and ran her fingertip along the fancy stitching on the cuff of his western shirt. He felt the touch all through his body.

"Niki, maybe . . . maybe we could go to Atlantic City this weekend," he suggested. "I don't mean nothin' improper. We could have separate hotel rooms and—"

She pressed her finger to his lips. "You're a perfect gentleman, Vincent. And I know you wouldn't breach propriety."

Vince mulled that over for a minute. He wasn't sure if he would breach propriety or not, since he didn't know what it meant. But it sounded like it might be fun if you did it right. And Niki seemed like just the person he would like to do it with. "So, do you wanna go to Atlantic City with me this weekend?" he asked again.

She drained the last sip of her beer and motioned to the waitress for another.

"That's what I wanted to talk to you about tonight. I'm afraid that we're going to have to maintain a low profile for a while."

Maintain a low profile? He wondered if that was anything like breaching propriety. "What do you mean? You ain't giving me the ol' heave-ho, are you?"

"No, of course not, Vince." She squeezed his hand reassuringly. "It's just that certain people have been sniffing around and—"

"Sniffing around? You mean some other guy's been makin' passes at you?"

"Lots of guys," she said mischievously. "But I don't pay any attention to them," she added when she saw his temper rising. "You're the only man I'm interested in at the moment, Vince."

He looked into her eyes and saw a smoldering interest that surprised him. She was so pretty and so sexy—and quite a bit younger than he was.

"Why do you like me, Niki?" he asked, his vulnerability showing through his machismo. "Why would a pretty gal like you hang around with an old broken-down truck driver like me?"

She leaned over and placed a kiss on his cheek. "You aren't old, Vince. And you aren't a truck driver. You're a successful, self-made businessman, the owner of V. Wolek Shipping Company. You're ambitious and hardworking, not to mention sweet and generous."

Vince glanced over at the covey of his drinking buddies in the far corner of the bar. "Sh-h-h. Don't say that 'sweet' stuff too loud in a joint like this. Somebody might hear you. I got a reputation to uphold, you know."

"Good evening. May I join you?"

Vince nearly jumped out of his seat when Joe Riley slid into the booth beside him. He had to admit that he wasn't especially happy to see his friend. "Hey, Joe. What are you doin' in here?"

Joe cast a covert glance around the bar. "Doing a bit of undercover work," he whispered.

"Yeah, I bet." Vinnie had the sneaking suspicion that if Joe was there to investigate anybody, it was Niki.

"Aren't you going to introduce me to your lovely companion?" Joe asked, nodding in Nicole's direction.

"This here's Niki. Niki, this here's Joe Riley." With the social amenities attended to, Vince crossed his arms over his chest, leaned back in the booth, and pouted.

Nicole extended a delicate hand adorned with four garish rings across the table to Joe. Vinnie could have sworn that Joe shook it a lot longer than was necessary. He kept holding on to her and looking her square in the eye.

"You can let her hand loose now, Joe, unless you're figurin' on taking it home with you," Vinnie snapped.

"What type of undercover work are you doing, Joe?" Nicole asked. "Are you a policeman?"

Joe gave her a funny look, as though he were playing a game with her. "No. I'm a newspaper reporter. I work for *The Banner*. I'm sure you've read *The Banner*. It's the only paper in town."

She fumbled with the cocktail napkin under her beer mug. "Yes, of course. I read *The Banner* every day."

"I'm sure you do," he said smoothly.

Vinnie didn't like the way this conversation was going. Joe was out to cause trouble; Vinnie was sure of it. He watched uneasily as Joe looked Niki up and down. Vinnie could tell that Joe was studying her, scrutinizing her red hair, her big floppy earrings, the bright swirls of color in her low-cut dress.

Vince decided that Joe was probably wishing that Victoria wore stuff like that. Victoria might be a good-looking woman, but you couldn't really tell what was under all those fancy clothes she wore. Niki wasn't ashamed to show off her sensational build.

"I understand that we have a mutual

friend," Joe was saying. "I believe you know my boss, Victoria Lord."

That ripped it. Joe was asking for trouble now, and Vince was more than ready to give it to him. "You cut that out, Joseph Riley. You're just tryin' to stir things up. Why don't you take a walk, a *long* walk?"

"That's okay, Vince," Niki said. "He can stay." She reached into her purse and pulled out a pack of cigarettes. Her hand shook as she lifted one to her lips. Vince was there on cue, match in hand.

"I thought you quit smoking," Joe said with a baiting tone to his voice.

"*Victoria* stopped smoking," she snapped. "*I* didn't."

Joe studied her through narrowed eyes as she inhaled deeply from the cigarette. "Victoria went to San Francisco this past month. I understand you did, too."

"So?"

"Joe, knock it off before I wallop you," Vinnie warned, aware that Niki's patience was wearing thin.

But Joe ignored him and leaned across the table toward Nicole. "Why do you hate Victoria Lord?" he demanded with his usual lack of finesse. "Why are you sending her those threatening messages?"

"I'm not," she said, her tolerance finally giving way to a fiery temper. "And I'm in no mood to sit here while you play twenty questions!" She stood, crushed out her cigarette, and strode toward the door, leaving the two men sitting there with their mouths open.

As Vinnie watched her brightly colored miniskirt swish out of sight, he turned to Joe. "Well, I reckon you know now that she ain't your precious Victoria. Victoria Lord ain't never had that kind of fire!"

Chapter
Four

"You look fantastic this evening, Carla." Jim Craig beamed down at his date and caught his breath when she flashed him a bewitching smile.

Her perfect white teeth gleamed against her tanned skin, and the strapless red satin dress she wore set off her dark coloring beautifully.

Jim was glad that he had worn his best black suit instead of his old gray one.

Carla slipped her arm companionably through his as they entered the brightly decorated cafeteria.

Anna Wolek and a host of volunteers had transformed the meeting room into a Christmas fantasy. Sparkling snowflakes and silver sleigh bells hung from evergreen bowers spangled with red and gold ribbons. In the center of the room was a glittering Christmas tree with a white dove of peace nestled in its top.

Like all American cities, the small community of Llanview had suffered its share of losses to the war in Vietnam. Now, during the holidays, the prayer for peace was even more fervent than ever.

"Isn't it lovely?" Carla said, breathing in the mingled scent of the pine cuttings and the aroma of the freshly baked goodies on the refreshment table. "And doesn't everyone look elegant?"

"They do, indeed." Jim glanced around the room at his new friends and colleagues, who were decked out in their finest attire for this, the most auspicious occasion of the year. "It's especially nice to see Larry Wolek up and about," he commented with satisfaction.

Larry sat in one of the folding chairs that lined the wall on the far side of the room. Next to him sat his sister, Anna, looking uncharacteristically glamorous in a green velvet dress. Her short red curls had been forced into a formal upsweep and a fall of matching ringlets cascaded down her back.

Only two hours before, Jim had come down to the cafeteria for a cup of coffee and had seen her teetering on a chair as she hung decorations. She had been wearing ragged jeans and a blue kerchief around her head. He marveled at how she could have pulled off such a transformation without benefit of a fairy godmother.

"Larry looks tired," Carla remarked.

"I'm sure he is. This is his first time out of bed, for all practical purposes, since the accident. He wasn't too keen on coming, but I insisted. I thought it might do him some good. He's been very depressed lately."

"It looks like somebody is trying to offer him some . . . ah . . . Christmas cheer," she said.

They watched as Karen Martin pulled Larry out of his chair and led him beneath a sprig of mistletoe. The kiss she gave him lasted so long that, one by one, every head in the room turned in their direction. Finally, Larry ended the embrace by pushing away, his face flushed with embarrassment.

"The gentleman seems a bit reluctant," Carla observed. "But I'm not sure why," she added, noting Karen's low-cut blue taffeta dress. The black lace stockings emphasized her long slender legs, and her blond hair spilled over her shoulders in a tumble of softness.

Jim cleared his throat. "I believe that the gentleman is in love with another lady and would prefer not to be pursued quite so hotly by this one."

"I see. And which of these lovelies is pursuing you, Dr. Craig?" she asked playfully.

"None that I've noticed . . . and I usually notice those things."

"That's difficult to believe. I'd think that the handsome new Dr. Craig would be the hottest catch in town."

He looked down into her russet eyes and wondered if she meant what she was saying or if this was her usual dating chatter. There was only one woman who interested Jim Craig, and he was lucky enough to be holding her hand.

Carla's delicate beauty and her vulnerability had captured his heart from the first moment that she had been literally dropped into his arms. He had been intrigued by the aura of mystery surrounding her. Who was this exotic beauty with olive skin and bewitching dark eyes?

"What are you thinking?" she asked, smiling quizzically up at him.

"That I'd like to be your friend," he said. He wanted to be much more than that, but instinct told him that if he moved too quickly she would bolt like a frightened deer.

"You *are* my friend," she said. "Only a friend would have taken such an interest in my welfare. I happen to know that you're responsible for me getting that singing job at the Seven Winds. And don't look so innocent. I got my information from a very good source."

He shrugged. "I didn't do that much. Just one little word in the right ear . . ."

"Was all it took," she supplied. "Thank you, Jim. I don't know how I can repay you."

"Well, as a matter of fact you can repay me right now." He pointed to the old battered piano in the corner. "You could sing us a song or two. This party could use some livening up."

"Are you sure? I don't know these people and—"

"Get them to sing some Christmas carols. It's the best way I know to break the ice."

He walked her to the piano, where she took a seat and immediately began a medley of holiday favorites.

Jim stepped back to watch her, but he was anything but detached. When she sang of "chestnuts roasting on an open fire," visions flooded his mind of a romantic evening before a roaring fireplace with her at his side. Her low alto voice was deeply sensuous, stirring feelings that had long been dormant in him.

Since his wife's death, Jim had buried himself in his work, seldom coming up for air. But this evening was different somehow. For once he wasn't Dr. James Craig, healer and counselor of the afflicted. He wasn't

Daddy, father of a teenage girl. He was just Jim, a man, who was enjoying the company of a beautiful woman. It felt good, and he vowed to do this kind of thing more often.

Before long the piano was surrounded with carolers. Some could carry a tune; some couldn't. But all were caught up in the yuletide spirit.

"She's something else, isn't she?"

Jim turned to find Price Trainor standing behind him. He shook his proffered hand. "She certainly is. Is this the first time you've heard her sing?"

Price's jaw tensed slightly, but Jim was too busy watching Carla to notice. "Yes, she sings . . . very well."

"You should hear her rendition of 'Stormy Weather.' It'll have you taking cold showers for a week."

"I don't doubt it," Price muttered. "She's looking great. Whatever you've been doing with her seems to be working."

There was a question in Trainor's statement, but Jim didn't catch it. "She's got a job now, a 'gig,' as she calls it. She's been getting some rest, and she's eating regular meals. That seems to have done the trick. Have you gotten the results from her tests?"

"Yes. There's nothing of any consequence. Just a matter of being run down, that's all."

"I really appreciate your taking her case

for me, Price," he said. "I wanted her to have the best care possible."

The humble gratitude in Craig's voice pricked Trainor's conscience. Every time he thought of how he had caught her in his arms there in the laboratory, hot and cold chills ran through his body. Would Craig be so grateful if he knew how many nights Price had lain awake, reliving that moment and embroidering on the fantasy of what might have happened if Jim hadn't walked in on them?

"No problem," Trainor mumbled, "any time." *Any time you have a beautiful, under-fed, Italian singer,* he added to himself. *And preferably if she isn't prejudiced against blacks.*

From out of the throng of merrymakers walked Dr. Polk, the gray-haired patriarch of Llanview General Hospital. From the concerned look on his face as he hurried toward them, they knew that he wasn't going to wish them a Merry Christmas.

"I'm sorry to spoil your evening, Jim," he said, "but we've just had a four-year-old boy brought into Emergency. He pulled a pot of boiling water down on himself, and his burns are severe. Could you come up and—"

"Of course, I'll be right there." Jim followed after him, then paused and turned back to Trainor. "Price, this will probably take a while. Would you please apologize to Carla for me? And would you mind giving her a ride home?" Without waiting for an answer, he disappeared into the ever-thickening crowd.

Trainor glanced over at Carla, who was fast becoming the life of the party. He slowly perused her delicate figure—delicate, but decidedly female. The bronzed skin of her shoulders glistened like the satin of her dress. And it was probably just as soft . . .

Great, he thought. *That's just great.*

"Look, lady. I don't like this any more than you do. So why don't we both try to make the best of a rotten situation?"

Carla plastered herself against the door of Price's Mustang, putting as much space as possible between them.

"I could have walked home," she said. "It isn't all that far."

"If you don't improve your attitude, you may be walking yet," he threatened, casting her a withering look across the darkness of the car's interior.

"Just pull over to the curb," she said. "Pull over and let me out right now. I don't have to tolerate this—"

"Yes, you do. I promised Jim Craig that I would deliver you home safe and sound.

And I'm going to do just that. For his sake, not yours."

That wasn't totally true, he admitted to himself. He hadn't promised Jim anything. But it sounded good, so he stuck by it and continued his speech.

"Jim Craig seems to think that you're about the finest person he's met in a long time, though I can't imagine why. I suppose he's seen a different side of you—the side you show to your own kind."

"And what *kind* is that?" she snapped.

"WASP."

She stared at him silently for a moment before replying. "I hardly qualify as white, anglo, or Protestant."

"WASP, Italian, it's all the same. You aren't black."

"And is that why you think I don't like you, Dr. Trainor? Because you're black?"

He pulled into the parking lot of the apartment building where she lived. He shut off the engine and turned out the headlights, leaving them in almost total darkness.

"In the first place," he said, "I think you *do* like me, far more than you'll admit. And in the second place, I think that you're denying the feelings you have for me because of the fact that I'm black."

He heard her gasp softly. "Oh, you do? Well, you're wrong on both counts, Dr.

Trainor. I think you are possibly the most arrogant, ill-tempered man I have ever met. And I wouldn't like you if you were white, green, or purple." She opened the car door, climbed out, and slammed it behind her.

He quickly followed her out of the car and up the walkway to her apartment. "You just hold on a minute, there!" he shouted after her.

She stopped in front of her door, key in hand. "Why are you following me, Dr. Trainor? What do you want? Surely you don't expect to be invited inside?"

"I wouldn't come in if you begged me," he said, knowing that he was lying. "I'm escorting you to your door, safe and sound."

"Aren't you carrying this gentleman thing a bit too far?"

"Considering whom I'm seeing home, yes, I would say so."

She stood there, glaring up at him. The muted light from the streetlamp shone in her luminous eyes, and her body trembled with anger.

He wished that he hadn't noticed that fact, but he had. He wasn't sure what he was going to do about this overwhelming physical awareness of her.

He moved a step closer to her. "You do like me, you know, Carla," he said, his voice low and intimate. "And whether you'll admit it or not, there's nothing you'd like better right now than to have me kiss you good night."

She said nothing, but in an unconscious movement, she moistened her lower lip with the tip of her tongue.

Or *was* it unconscious? he wondered. There was only one way to find out. He stepped still closer to her and put his hands on her shoulders, gently easing back the lacy shawl from her skin.

His hands covered her bare shoulders, and he realized he had been right; her skin was softer, much softer than satin.

When he whispered her name, she tilted her head back and closed her eyes. It was all the invitation he needed.

At first his lips were tentative as they tasted hers, then he became more bold as he felt her melting against him, her arms encircling his neck.

For long moments they lingered in the golden lamplight, their lips belying the harsh words they had just spoken.

Finally he broke the kiss, and his lips traveled across her cheek to her ear. "Admit it, Carla. Tell me that you want me. I want to hear you say it."

His lips found a sensitive spot on her neck and then on her shoulder. He felt a shudder run through her and heard her moan softly.

His hands moved up to cup her face. He gazed down at her with triumph shining in his dark eyes.

"Say it, Carla," he said, forcing her to look up at him. "Admit that you want me, even if I *am* black. Maybe even *because* I'm black."

She uttered a harsh, angry cry and slapped him hard across the face.

He moved away from her, holding his hand to his cheek. Even in the darkness his eyes blazed with fury.

"That's what you wanted, isn't it, Miss Benari?" he said bitterly. "You wanted me to kiss you, and I did. You wanted to enjoy that kiss, and you certainly did. And you slapped me so that you wouldn't have to admit to yourself that you wanted me. You, Carla Benari, wanted to kiss a black man, and you can't stand the thought of that."

He reached out and pulled her shawl back over her shoulders in a mockingly tender gesture. "Well, don't worry, Miss Benari. You can delude yourself into thinking that I forced that kiss on you, if you like. But we both know better. Just like we both know that it's going to happen again . . . and again."

Trainor, you're an idiot, he told himself for the hundredth time that night as he tossed and turned in his bed.

Kissing a white woman . . .

Twenty years ago your forefathers were hung for less.

But times are changing.

They aren't changing that fast.

His mind whirled on a carousel of confusion and anger. How could he feel this way about someone who hated him and his people? Why had he allowed himself to do such a stupid thing?

And of course, there was Jim Craig, a man who had tried to befriend him in every way possible, a good man who trusted him. He knew that Jim was interested in Carla —more than interested. He was probably in love with her.

Am I in love with her? he asked himself. *No, not love, lust. I'm in lust with her. That's all it could be.*

But as he drifted off to sleep, Price kept seeing her beautiful face, her round eyes and the gentle way she had looked at him just before he had kissed her. She had been so wonderfully soft and warm in his arms. And she had smelled so nice.

If it was only lust he felt for her, why had it hurt so badly when she had slapped him? And why was he willing to risk the terrible pain of rejection for the chance to hold her in his arms again?

"Now, why would you want to do a thing like that?" Jim asked the young doctor who stood before him. The expression on Price Trainor's dark face clearly revealed the anguish he was feeling.

Jim walked around his desk and placed his hand on the younger man's broad shoulder. "Llanview is your home, Price. You're nearly finished with your internship, and you have a solid position here at the hospital. Why would you want to leave town now?"

Price walked away from him and sat in a chair beside Jim's desk. He leaned forward, put his elbows on his knees, and buried his face in his hands. "I just need a change of scenery for a while, that's all," he said, shaking his head wearily.

Jim could hear the fatigue in Trainor's voice and wondered if he had gotten any sleep the night before. "Have you thought this through, Price?" he said. "I'd hate to see you make a rash decision about your career. I can't help but wonder why you're doing this, and why you haven't mentioned it before now."

"It's . . . personal," Price said.

"I see." Jim didn't really see, but it was obvious that Trainor wasn't going to divulge his reasons. "Okay," he said with resignation. "I'll talk to Dr. Polk, and we'll start looking for a replacement for you. But I have to tell you, it won't be easy. You're a great asset to this hospital."

"Thank you." Price rose from his chair and shook Jim's hand. "You've been very kind to me, Dr. Craig, and I want you to know that I really appreciate your confidence in me."

Jim studied the young man's face carefully. If he didn't know better, he would think that he saw some guilt in those dark eyes. But what would Price Trainor have to feel guilty about? He seemed just fine last night at the Christmas party . . . last night when he had asked him to take Carla home. . . .

"Just one more thing, Price," he said, blocking the younger man's path to the door. "I want to ask you one question, and I'd like an honest answer."

Trainor's demeanor was as evasive as his tone. "Okay."

Jim's blue eyes narrowed with suspicion. "I'd like to know if your decision to leave has anything to do with Carla Benari."

"May I sit here with you?"

"Yes, of course." Carla moved her lunch tray aside to make room for Anna's salad bowl.

"You're Anna Wolek, aren't you? I saw you last night at the party."

"Yes, I am. And I want to thank you for the wonderful contribution you made to the festivities. Everyone enjoyed your singing so much. You're very good."

"Oh, thank you," Carla said with a self-conscious shrug of her thin shoulders.

Anna was surprised to see that Carla seemed actually shy about her talent. She had appeared so confident and at ease the night before.

But today she looked tired and worried. Anna recognized a troubled person when she saw one, and, as usual, she was quick to offer a friendly shoulder to cry on. "Is everything okay?" she asked, reluctant to pry into the affairs of a woman whom she had just met.

"Sure, I'm fine," Carla replied. Then she reconsidered. "No, I'm not really."

"It must be hard, being in a new town and not having very many friends," Anna observed.

"Yes, it is. I met a lot of nice people last night but . . ." Her voice faded away. She quickly lifted her soft drink and sipped at it, masking her emotions.

"But acquaintances aren't the same as friends," Anna said.

Carla nodded in silent agreement.

As she watched Carla struggle with her feelings, Anna was reminded that beauty wasn't always a buffer against loneliness.

"I thought that you and Dr. Craig were good friends," Anna said. "You seemed to like each other."

"Oh, we do. I mean, he's a nice man, and he's been very kind to me, but—"

"But?"

"But it's not as though I'm in love with him, or anything like that."

Instantly Anna felt a twinge of pity for Dr. Craig. It had been obvious to everyone at the party that he was captivated by Carla. It was unfortunate that she didn't feel the same way about him.

"Are you involved with anyone, Anna?" Carla asked shyly.

Anna immediately thought of Joe Riley; then she remembered Victoria Lord. "No. Not really," she said. "Why?"

"I was just wondering if you were ever attracted to someone whom you couldn't stand."

"I beg your pardon?"

"It sounds silly, I know. But I'm attracted to this man, and all we do is fight when we're together. I just don't understand it."

Anna didn't have to ask who the man was. She had seen Carla leaving the party with Price Trainor, and she had sensed the tension between them from all the way across the room.

"Do you and this man have anything in common?" she asked carefully.

The question seemed to upset Carla. "Only an overpowering, physical attraction. And we both seem to be fighting it."

"Maybe it's just the idea of being together that you're fighting."

Carla nodded as she considered Anna's suggestion. "You may have a point there. But what can we do about our feelings for each other?"

"I'm probably not the person to ask about that. I haven't exactly had a lot of experience in the romance department," Anna admitted.

The look of disappointment on Carla's pretty face went straight to Anna's heart. Carla truly needed a friend who could give her some good advice. But Anna didn't feel at all qualified to give it, especially on such short notice. She needed some time to think about this.

"Why don't you come over to my house for dinner?" she suggested. "My brother, Vince, is going out for a night on the town with his buddies, and it'll just be the two of us. Then we can talk about this problem all you want."

"Really?"

"Sure. I'll make us a turkey dinner with all the trimmings."

"That would be great. I haven't had a home-cooked meal since . . ." She suddenly looked very sad. "Not for a long time. I'd love to come to your home, Anna. Thank you."

"Well, I hope this new friend of yours isn't on a diet," Sadie Gray commented as she surveyed Anna's kitchen. The counter was laden with pecan and pumpkin pies, home-made rolls, fresh salad greens, and the ingredients for stuffing. The aroma of roasting turkey filled the tiny apartment, putting Sadie's tastebuds on alert.

Anna scowled as she ran her finger over the row of labels in her spice rack. "Calories are no problem for this guest," she said. "Carla Benari is one of those few people who don't have to count their calories. All she has to worry about is being blown away by a strong draft."

"Lucky her," Sadie commented as she eased her plump body into one of Anna's kitchen chairs. She picked up one of the rolls from the table, slathered it with butter, and popped it into her mouth. Her round black face lit up with rapturous delight as she savored the mouthful. "Um-m-m, good," she murmured in appreciation.

"Don't envy Carla too much," Anna said, rummaging in her cupboard, looking through her supply of infrequently used spices. "I think the reason why Carla's so skinny is that she hasn't had enough money to buy food lately. And that's a rough way to diet."

"That's true." Sadie shook her head sadly. "It's a crying shame that folks go to bed hungry in a land of plenty. It's a fine thing you're doing, Anna, inviting her over for dinner like this. If this spread doesn't fatten her up, nothing will," she said, helping herself to yet another roll.

"The food isn't the only reason why I invited Carla over," Anna said, crawling up onto the counter so that she could see those spices in the back of her cupboard, the ones with the dusty lids. "I think she needs to talk to somebody about a rather unique problem that she has. We discussed it a little bit this morning in the hospital cafeteria, but I don't have any answers for her. I've never been in her situation."

"And what situation is that?" Sadie asked. She enjoyed the vicarious excitement that gossip lent to her own sedate life. "If you don't mind telling me, that is," she added diplomatically.

Anna crawled off the counter, shaking her head with dismay that she hadn't found what she was looking for. "Actually, you might have an opinion on this matter," she said.

"And what matter is that?"

"Interracial relationships."

It was as if a curtain quickly fell over Sadie's usually open face; her black eyes lost some of their luster. "I think interracial friendships are fine . . ." she said guardedly. "I think you and I are proof of that."

"Of course we are, Sadie. But I'm not talking about friendships. I mean *romantic* relationships. Carla is attracted to a black man."

"And she's white?"

"Well, yes, she's Italian."

Sadie nodded. "It's the same thing. What's black is black, and what ain't is white. There's no middle ground these days."

Anna sat down at the table beside Sadie and helped herself to a roll, minus the butter. "But I can understand Carla's attraction to this man, Sadie. He's a fine person, a doctor, and he's very handsome."

"I'm sure he is," she said. "But it doesn't matter. It won't work."

She seemed so adamant that Anna was taken aback. "Sadie, I have to say that I'm surprised. I never realized that you were prejudiced."

"I like to think that I'm not, though it's hard to be sure in a day and age like this," she said. "But whether I am or not has nothing to do with it."

"What do you mean?"

Sadie took a deep breath and settled back in her chair. "Marriage is difficult at best, Anna. Even when a couple has everything going for them, it's hard. But when society itself condemns your union . . ."

"I understand," Anna said.

"No, you don't. You can try to understand, and you can think that you do, but you don't. Nobody does unless they've been there." Sadie shook her head and closed her eyes as though blotting out some internal pain. "You can't imagine what it's like," she said. "Even a simple trip to the grocery store is an ordeal. People stare at you, letting you know in their own silent way that they hate you and everything your marriage stands for.

"Then there are the relatives. Neither family, yours or his, really accepts your marriage, though they pretend to. Not to mention the added problems when the babies come along."

She opened her eyes, and Anna was struck by the intensity and hurt registered there. "It takes a heap of loving to get through that, Anna," she said. "To be able to absorb all that hate and keep on loving. A few can do it, but most can't."

As Anna listened to her friend, she couldn't help wondering where all the pain was coming from . . . the anguish that she heard in Sadie's voice, the despair that she saw in her dark eyes.

Could anyone feel so intensely about a situation unless they, themselves, had lived it? Was this why, in all the time Anna had known Sadie, she had never once talked about her family, except to say that she had "lost" them years ago?

Anna reached across the table and placed

her hand over Sadie's plump brown one. She squeezed it lovingly, trying to express her sympathy for her friend's unspoken heartache.

"I'm sorry, Sadie. I shouldn't have asked you about it. I should never have brought up the subject. Forgive me."

"There's nothing to forgive. We're friends. We can talk about anything."

No, Sadie, Anna thought. *Not everything.*

Carla took those final stairs two at a time, surprising herself. It had been a long time since she had felt as energetic as this. But then, it had been a long time since she had been invited to a friend's home for dinner.

It had been years since she had stayed in one town long enough to make a girlfriend. And even though she had just met Anna Wolek, she had the feeling that they would be close friends in no time at all.

Anna was one of those rare people who opened her heart and folded you inside without asking too many questions, without prying into what made you tick.

Nosy friends were exactly what Carla didn't need. The last thing she wanted right now was someone delving into her private life . . . or her past. She had too many things that she had kept hidden from the world for too long for her to welcome anyone's scrutiny.

She walked down the narrow hallway, looking for apartment number 16H, the number she had hastily scribbled on a napkin in the hospital cafeteria.

Standing in the hall outside the door, she could smell the aroma of turkey. It had been years since she had eaten a homemade turkey dinner, more years than she cared to remember.

Carla pushed the thought of home from her mind. That was the one thing she couldn't allow herself to think about: home . . . all the people she had left behind.

It had been too many years ago. The road between here and there had been too long, and far too crooked. *You can't go home,* she told herself as she cursed the turkey, along with it's wonderful aroma and the memories it had evoked. *You can never go home.*

She knocked on the door and waited for a minute or two, then knocked again, harder this time.

She reached into her purse, took out the napkin, and compared the apartment number with the one she had written. Yes, it was the right one. Glancing down at her watch, she saw that she was fifteen minutes early. Maybe Anna had stepped out for something.

"Excuse me, Miss Benari?" said a kind voice behind her. "Anna had to run to the corner market to get some sage. You can wait for her over here if you like."

Carla turned to face the friendly voice.

Both women gasped as they stared into each other's shocked faces.

Sadie was the first to speak. "Clara?"

Carla finally found her voice, but it was only a hoarse whisper. "Mama?"

Chapter
Five

"Well, don't just stand there with your mouth gaping, unless you're trying to catch flies." Sadie opened her apartment door wider and stepped back, motioning Carla inside. "Come on in."

Carla wondered for a moment if her legs would support her; they seemed suddenly drained of all feeling. But they carried her into the apartment with only the slightest wobble.

Sadie closed the door quietly and turned to face her daughter. In that brief instant Carla felt the overwhelming urge to rush into her mother's arms, to bury her face against Sadie's warm shoulder, and tell her how happy she was to see her. But she didn't. And then the moment had passed, leaving them standing there in awkward silence.

Sadie walked over to a wooden rocking chair and sat down, carefully arranging a patchwork pillow at the small of her back. Without meeting Carla's eyes, she waved her hand toward the sofa. "You might as well have a seat. If you want to, that is. If you have the time to spare," she added bitterly.

Long-buried emotions flooded over Carla, much stronger feelings than those evoked by the scent of roasted turkey. This was her mother's apartment, all right. A different city, perhaps, but everything else was the same.

There at the windows were the frilly white curtains she remembered, their ruffles starched and ironed to crisp perfection.

The sofa cushion beneath her bore a tiny round cigarette burn in its gray looped fabric. Carla remembered when she and her girlfriend, Paulette, had smoked their first cigarette one afternoon while Sadie was at work. They had thought their lives were over when they had accidentally burned that hole in Sadie's new sofa.

But instead of beating them to a pulp as they had expected she would do, Sadie had invited, or rather insisted, that they smoke cigarette after cigarette until they were both a deathly shade of green. Neither Carla nor Paulette had touched a cigarette since.

Sadie had been a good mother. But the thought only made Carla feel worse as she looked across at the woman who had ironed her clothes, combed her hair, sewn clothes for her dolls, and dried her many tears.

Here in her mother's apartment, she could still feel that love. The room held bits and pieces of her own history: the ceramic planter she had made for Sadie on Mother's Day, the brass candleholders that had been her great-grandmother's, and the family Bible in its customary place of prominence, the center of the coffee table.

"Do you live here alone, Mama?" she asked when she found her voice.

Sadie stared down at the braided rug beneath her feet. "Of course I live alone. Who would I live with?"

Carla felt her throat constrict. "Haven't you heard anything from Daddy since—"

"I've heard the same from your father as I've heard from you in the past sixteen years, Clara. Nothing."

Carla tried to think of something to say. "I'm sorry" hardly seemed strong enough. How could she explain? How could she possibly justify having walked out on the only person who loved her?

"So, your name is Benari now," Sadie said, venturing a glance in her direction. "Did you get married?"

"No. I . . . I changed my name. I thought that Benari sounded more Italian. It's easier to get jobs if they think you're . . . Italian. So I changed it."

"Too bad you couldn't change your skin as easily."

Carla winced as the words stung her heart, leaving a painful welt of guilt. "Mama, you don't understand how hard it is—"

"How hard it is to be a black woman?" Sadie's dark eyes flashed with anger. "No, I wouldn't know anything about that. Why don't you tell me all about it, Clara? Tell me how it feels to be considered less than a human being because of the color of your skin. Tell me about prejudice and segregation and bigotry. But while you're at it, tell me about pride . . . pride in your own people. Pride in our strength, in our endurance, in our courage."

Sadie stopped and took a deep breath. "But you don't understand that side of being black, Clara. If you'd ever felt that pride, you couldn't have turned your back on your people."

Tears filled Carla's eyes as she stared at her mother . . . a darker, older image of herself. Although her warm brown eyes viewed the world with kindness, as windows of the soul, Sadie's eyes were carefully shuttered against those who might look inside and see her pain.

"But, Mama, I'm as much white as black," she pleaded. "I'm both."

"No, Clara. What's black is black. And what isn't is white. There's no in between. Your father and I tried to believe that there was a middle ground. We tried to create our own world where love erased all color. But it didn't work. Our family and friends wore us down until we realized that we had to choose. And in the end we each chose our own people."

"And now you're making me choose."

"You've already made your choice. As long as you're living as Carla Benari, my daughter, Clara Gray, is dead."

Meredith grimaced as the needle found the vein it was seeking on the inside of her elbow, but she didn't flinch. This was getting to be old hat by now.

"I know why you're doing all these blood tests, Dr. Craig," she said.

He shot her a quick glance, then returned his attention to the task at hand. "And why is that, Meredith?"

"You're using these samples that you're taking from me to restock your blood bank."

Jim Craig looked relieved as he pulled the needle from her arm. "Ah, you've found us out. Now we'll have to find a new source of blo-o-od," he said in his best Bela Lugosi imitation.

She giggled, but the smile quickly faded from her pretty face. "I do know why you're doing these tests," she said. "You don't have to hide the facts from me anymore."

"What do you mean?" Jim's pale blue eyes searched hers.

"I know that I'm dying," she said simply. "My father told me so. He didn't want me to marry Larry Wolek, and so he told me on my wedding day."

She watched the sympathetic expression on Dr. Craig's face change into anger, then back to compassion.

"I'm sorry that he told you, Merrie. We asked him specifically not to do that."

She shrugged. "Oh, well, Father never was one to follow orders, even doctors' orders. But I'm glad he told me. If I'm dying, I need to know."

Jim pulled up a stool and sat beside her. He lifted her small hand and enclosed it between his. "We're all terminal, Merrie. We're all going to die someday."

"Yes, but I know when I'm going to die," she said.

"No, you don't. This illness of yours is a tricky thing. It can progress very rapidly, or it can go on for years. The best defense we have against it is your own positive outlook. Don't give up hope, Meredith. Fight, Merrie. Fight for your life."

She sighed and pulled her hand away from his. "I'm too tired to fight, Dr. Craig," she said. "And besides, there isn't anyone or anything in my life right now that's worth fighting for."

As Larry Wolek made the file notations for his last patient of the day, he felt a bit guilty. He hadn't really given Mrs. Hanson his best this evening. He had found it difficult to listen to her long-winded tirade about her unfaithful husband, her nosy neighbors, her ungrateful children, and her poodle's psoriasis.

Larry's mind kept wandering, but never very far away. Just across town to a certain Tudor mansion and a certain lonely princess shut up in that fortress. He wanted to crash through those brick walls, sweep his lady into his arms, and ride away with her on his white charger.

There was just one little problem: Lady Meredith Lord didn't want to be rescued.

She had certainly made that clear enough when she had left town without a word on their wedding day.

He had heard through friends that she was back in Llanview; she'd been back for several weeks. But she hadn't bothered to come by the hospital to see him—not even once.

So much for fairy tales and "happily ever afters."

He postponed leaving his office for as long as possible. There was no point in hurrying home to an empty house. Maybe he could drop by Anna and Vinnie's apartment for a couple of hours. Anna was always good for a cup of coffee, a piece of pie, and a good game of Scrabble.

No, he'd been there four nights already this week, and as much as they assured him that he was welcome, there was no point in taking advantage of their hospitality.

He glanced around the office once more, and finding nothing to keep him there, he took his sports jacket from the coat tree and left the room.

As he stepped into the hall, he collided with someone who was walking, head down, not paying attention to where she was going.

"Meredith!"

"Larry, excuse me. I wasn't watching and I—"

"It's okay. I'm glad you came to see me. I was just leaving and . . ."

Something in her eyes told him that his assumption had been overly optimistic. She hadn't come to see him. She was in the hospital for some other reason, and he had simply bumped into her.

She pointed to the round, adhesive bandage on the inside of her elbow. "I was just getting some more blood tests run," she said, confirming his disappointment.

"Well, since we've run into each other, so to speak, do you think we could talk for a few minutes?" He hated himself for asking, for begging for the crumbs from her table, but he couldn't help it. Cursing himself for his weakness, he held his office door open and motioned her inside.

Once the door was closed and they were alone, the feelings were even stronger. He wanted to take her in his arms and kiss her, shake her, and demand to know why she had left him. He wanted to tell her how much he loved her and how confused he was.

But she was the first to speak. "I'm so sorry about your accident, Larry. How are you?"

Do you care, Merrie? he thought. *Do you really care? If you gave a damn, why didn't you come to see me?*

"I'm fine, Meredith. Just dandy." He saw the pain in her soft brown eyes and gentled his tone. "How are you feeling?"

She shrugged her thin shoulders. "Okay, I guess."

He noted the paleness of her skin and the dark smudges beneath her eyes. He didn't have to be a doctor to see how ill she was. But in spite of her pallor, she was the most beautiful woman he had ever seen. And he was thrilled to see her, to be alone with her, to be standing so near to her.

"I'm glad to see you, Merrie," he said softly, unable to hide the tenderness in his voice.

She looked up at him, her brown eyes wide with surprise. "You are? I didn't think you would be. I thought you hated me for . . . what I did."

"Of course I don't hate you, Merrie." He stepped closer to her and placed his hands on her shoulders. "I still love you. I always have."

"Oh, Larry." A sob caught in her throat. "I'm so sorry for running out on you like that. But I was sick and—"

"It's okay. I understand."

"You do?"

He shook his head. "No. I don't understand why you did it, but I forgive you. I'd forgive you for anything, Meredith. And I still want to marry you."

"We can't be married, Larry. Not now or ever. I'm dying. I have a terminal illness and—"

"I know."

She stared up at him in astonishment. "You do?"

"Yes. But I didn't think that you knew. How did you find out?"

She hung her head and tears dripped down her sallow cheeks. "My father told me."

"Is that why you ran away?" The light was beginning to dawn on him. Victor Lord had been at the bottom of this all along.

She nodded silently as more tears slipped down her face.

"Merrie," he whispered as he drew her to him. He held her tenderly against his chest and stroked her soft golden hair. "If I'd only known, I would have come after you. But I thought you left because you didn't love me anymore." He lifted her chin with his forefinger, forcing her to look up at him. "Do you still love me, Merrie?" he asked.

He searched her eyes for the answer, but saw only incredible hurt . . . and a battle raging inside her.

For a moment her face softened, and he felt her lean toward him. Her hand lifted as though to reach out to him.

Then she pulled away. "No. Larry, we can't. I mean, I don't." She headed toward the door, and he rushed to stop her.

"No, wait. Merrie, don't run away from me. Not again. Please!"

Her brown eyes were full of tears when she paused at the door and looked back at him. She bit her lip and took a deep breath of resolve. "I don't love you, Larry," she said. "Not anymore. I'm so sorry."

A moment later she was gone, and he was alone—again.

For the third time Larry reached for the telephone to call Anna and Vince, and for the third time he decided against it. He wouldn't wish his own company on anybody tonight, especially his brother and sister.

And he wasn't up to hearing Vince say, "I told you so," about Meredith.

He switched on the television, kicked off his shoes, and settled back with a can of cream soda. He had decided against having his customary beer. It wasn't a good idea to drink when one was depressed, and he was about as low as he'd been in a long time.

The football game was interrupted for a pickup-truck commercial. He watched over the top of his soda can as the truck did wheelies on a sparkling beach, and several bikini-clad beauties draped their sun-kissed bodies over the vehicle's contours.

What gorgeous blondes in French bikinis had to do with selling pickup trucks, he didn't know. But he watched the commercial with rapt attention, realizing that he had been too long without feminine companionship.

Maybe there was something to Vinnie's carefree, playboy attitude after all. Larry had always considered himself a one-woman man, faithful to the end. The "any port in a storm" attitude had seemed cheap and unfulfilling.

But tonight . . . tonight old One-Woman-at-a-Time Larry decided that there might be a night when loneliness could drive a man to settle for second best, if it were available.

The telephone jarred him out of his reverie. He grabbed it in the middle of its second ring.

"Hello? Oh, hi, Karen. I'm glad you called. I was just thinking about you."

"Hi, Larry. I'm so glad you could come over."

He caught his breath when he saw her standing there in the doorway, gazing up at him with her blue eyes sparkling.

Karen was a pretty woman; he had never denied that. But he'd never seen her looking so good and so sexy. Her long blond hair spilled over her shoulders and onto the filmy chiffon that covered her voluptuous figure in layers of aqua froth.

And what touched him most was the fact that she was obviously thrilled to see him. Her face shone with pleasure as she ushered him into her apartment.

After his episode with Merrie, he was feeling wounded and rejected. It felt good to be adored . . . for a change.

"You look nice, Karen," he said, accepting the glass of sparkling champagne she offered.

"Thank you," she breathed. "I'm glad you think so. Here, sit down."

He sank into the thick cushions of her couch, and she settled next to him, close enough for him to catch the exotic scent of her perfume, to feel the warmth of her body emanating through the thin chiffon.

"The lasagna's in the oven. Dinner won't be ready for a while," she said as she sipped from the crystal fluted glass. He had never noticed before how full her lips were, how they glistened with the dew of the champagne.

"I hope you aren't too hungry," she added.

He was starving, but not for lasagna. "That's okay, Karen. I can wait. It was very nice of you to invite me over. I could use some company tonight."

She blushed slightly, and for just a moment she resembled an innocent schoolgirl receiving her first compliment. For some reason, Larry found that particular look terribly attractive on her.

"I couldn't believe it when you said that you would come over, Larry," she said. "You've thrown so many invitations back at me lately."

The humiliation on her face was real, and it pricked his heart to think how many times he had yelled at her, had thrown her out of his hospital room when she had nursed him through his convalescence. He knew how much it hurt to be rejected by someone you loved. He knew far too well.

"I'm sorry I've been so rotten to you, Karen," he said, setting his champagne glass on the coffee table and taking her hand in his. "You've been a good friend to me."

"I want to be more than just a friend, Larry," she said, lifting his hand to her lips. "I could be anything you want me to be. . . ."

Her lips, soft and moist, trailed slowly over the back of his hand, sending warm tendrils of desire into every part of his body.

The sparkling champagne, the erotic scent of the incense that smoked in its brass burner, and the soft jazz playing in the background were beginning to affect him. He knew that Karen had invited him here for one reason, to seduce him. But was that so terrible? He tried to feel indignant. But Karen wanted him, badly enough to pursue him, to lure him with candlelight, incense, and champagne. And it felt wonderful to be wanted. If not by Merrie, by someone else.

He tried to think of Meredith and of how they had pledged their love to each other. Theirs was a love that was supposed to last forever. But she had broken that pledge. *She* had been the one to destroy their love, not him.

"I thought we should celebrate tonight," Karen was saying. She had moved even closer to him. Her golden hair gleamed, catching the candle's flickering light in its silky curls. He wanted to plunge his hands into that softness and feel those curls wind around his fingers.

"What are we celebrating, Karen?" he asked. He found himself whispering, although there was no one else in the room.

"Your recovery, of course." Her hand slid up the front of his sportshirt to the spot on his shoulder where he had received the skin graft several weeks before.

"Of course," he murmured.

"It *is* healing nicely, isn't it?" she asked.

"Yes." For some reason he was finding it difficult to breathe. Maybe it was the incense.

Her fingers moved over the buttons of his shirt, and in seconds they were open. Her hand slipped inside and trailed along his chest. He shivered as he felt what little control he had floating away, out of reach.

She leaned against him, filling his senses with her soft, fragrant warmth. "Let me see it, Larry," she said, sliding the shirt away from his shoulder. She gave the skin graft only a cursory examination. His bared chest received the better part of her attention as her fingertips explored the crisp light brown hair.

Larry knew when he lost the battle. He knew the exact second when his inhibitions fled, along with his thoughts of Meredith and all of his common sense.

"Oh, what the hell," he said as he filled his hands and arms with that warm softness wrapped in blue chiffon. He took the moist lips that had been so graciously offered and sipped their champagne.

Then he pressed her back into the cushions, covered her body with his, and forgot everything . . . even his loneliness.

Chapter
Six

"Oh, Mr. Riley, come in before you freeze to death. My, but it's cold out there tonight." Felicia, the Lords' housekeeper, threw open the massive oak door and ushered Joe inside with all the aplomb of welcoming royalty. She flushed slightly at the pleasure of seeing him. Joe Riley was one of her favorite visitors at Llanfair and one of her favorite men.

He flashed one of his famous smiles that made her tingle all over. "It is a bit nippy out, Felicia, but the sight of a pretty lass such as yourself would warm the heart of any man."

Felicia wasn't pretty, and she knew it. It had also been a long time since anyone had considered her a lass, but it was nice to hear such compliments from a man as handsome as Joe Riley.

She giggled and looked up into his dark

eyes that were glistening with good humor. "Aye, and you're full of the blarney," she said with an Irish accent that was slightly tinged with Spanish around the edges.

He laughed, a full-bodied, hearty laugh that echoed through the marble-tiled foyer. It was a sound seldom heard in the halls of Llanfair. "I must admit," he said, "that I've been accused of being 'full of it' before, Felicia. But this time I was totally honest. Having you greet me at the door is often the nicest part of coming to Llanfair."

He was sincere, she knew. Mr. Riley liked her; she could tell by the way he talked to her, by the way he treated her as a person and not merely as a servant. But then, Mr. Riley liked women . . . and kids . . . and other men. He just liked people, period, unless they gave him good reason not to.

The library door opened and Victoria Lord walked into the foyer, her high heels clicking on the marble. "Joe," she said, holding out her hand to him. "I thought I heard you laughing out here. I'm so glad you came."

Felicia watched a change come over Joe Riley, as it always did when he saw Victoria. His eyes softened and filled with a longing that Felicia hated to see. Not that she wanted Mr. Riley for herself; that was an impossible dream. But she did want him to be happy, and she couldn't help being angry at Victoria for her callous treatment of him.

As Felicia watched her mistress lead Joe Riley into the library and close the door behind them, she thought how lucky Victoria was to have the love of a man like that—and how foolish she was to take his love for granted.

Joe tried to slip his finger through the tiny handle of the china teacup, but finally gave up. What good was a handle if you couldn't get your darned finger through it? What good was tea, for that matter? He'd much prefer a hefty mug of rich black coffee.

Every time he came to Llanfair, Victoria offered him some sissy thing to eat or drink, usually some fluffy French thing that he couldn't pronounce or some weird health-food stuff. This time it was tea, an herbal concoction that was supposed to clean out your blood. But it looked, smelled, and tasted suspiciously like grass to him . . . and not the illegal kind either. Just plain old grass.

He lifted the cup to his lips, held his breath, and tried to down as much of it as possible in one gulp. When he set the cup back on its saucer, he looked up to see Victoria watching him, her blue eyes twinkling with suppressed laughter.

"You don't have to drink that if you hate it," she said.

"Hate it? Why would I hate it? It tastes great." *If you're a goat,* he added silently.

"Really? I think it's pretty rank myself," she said, placing her still-full cup on the coffee table.

"Then why did you sit there and make me drink it?"

She shrugged. "I don't know. Just sadistic, I guess. I'd never served it before and I had no idea that it was so bad. Would you like some coffee?"

"No." He decided not to take the risk. She would probably put brewer's yeast or something gross in it. "I'll pass, this time." He thought of Anna Wolek's great coffee and apple pie. *Oh, well.*

Victoria leaned back on the sofa, her delicate hands toying with the cameo brooch at her throat. Joe noted the gesture and wondered what was bothering her. She always fumbled with her jewelry when she was nervous.

Tonight she seemed more uptight than usual. She was still wearing the gray suit that she had worn to work. He wondered why she hadn't changed into something more comfortable. Then he realized that he had never known Victoria to wear anything comfortable. Straight-laced and uptight—that was Victoria Lord.

He wouldn't be surprised if she wore a corset under those tailored suits of hers. But then he tried not to think about what Victoria wore under her clothes; it was hard on his libido.

"I was surprised that you were willing to come over tonight," she said, "after . . . after last time. I still feel terrible about that."

He turned to face her and pulled his knee up onto the sofa, feeling slightly self-conscious about sitting on a silk-upholstered sofa in his jeans. "Forget it, Viki," he said. "You don't need to feel bad. The vase didn't hit me."

"No, but it hit the wall and broke into a thousand pieces. Father made me pay to have it repaired out of my own pocket. That's why I'm sorry. It was a terribly expensive vase."

"I see." He knew that she was trying, in her own way, to make amends for throwing him out the last time he had visited her. Like her father, Victoria Lord wasn't skilled in the art of delivering a sincere apology. But it was enough for Joe.

"I never should have talked to you the way I did, Viki," he said. "I never should have pushed you to see things that you weren't ready to accept. It was my fault."

To his surprise, she moved across the sofa to sit next to him and took his hand in hers. "But you were right to show me that postcard. You were right to confront me with your suspicions about Nicole Smith."

Her fingertips slowly stroked the back of his hand, and as always when she touched him, he wanted more. Simply holding hands wasn't enough. He wanted to take her in his arms. But then he would want to kiss her, and then . . . there would be no end.

"I've been thinking about what you said, Joe, about the postcard and all."

Her lower lip trembled slightly, and Joe had to look away to keep himself from kissing her. He knew, better than anyone, what this whole Nicole Smith thing was doing to her.

"And what have you decided?" he asked.

"I realize that I have to take this situation seriously. Nicole Smith might actually be—" Her voice broke, she swallowed hard, and then she tried again. "She might be me."

Joe was shocked that she had come so far in her thinking since the last time he had spoken to her. Moving closer to her, he put his arm around her shoulders and hugged her to him. "I believe she is, Viki," he said.

"But why would she . . . why would *I* do that?"

"Well, I'm no shrink, but I think that when you become Nicole Smith, you put aside all the inhibitions that your father imposes on you. You can be carefree and fun-loving without fear of being judged."

"But dressing up in gaudy clothes and a red wig? It sounds so . . . crazy. Did Vincent Wolek really say that Nicole looks just like me?"

"That's what he said. And I know that it's true, Viki."

She lifted her head from his shoulder and looked up at him, her bright blue eyes filled with questions. "How do you know?" she asked, as though afraid of hearing his answer.

"Because I saw Nicole Smith the other night at a bar with Vince. I met her and talked to her."

"And did she look like me?"

He could tell that her question was weighted. She was asking about more than just Nicole Smith's appearance. "I believe she *was* you, Viki. I'm sure of it. The hair and the clothes were different. But I made her angry and, even though she used words that I've never heard you use, I would recognize those blazing blue eyes of yours anywhere."

She stared at him, slowly shaking her head in disbelief. "Oh, Joe," she said. "If anyone . . . *anyone* other than you were telling me this, I'd—I'd—"

"You'd throw a Ming vase at them?" he asked, smiling at her affectionately.

She stood and walked over to the fireplace where a pine log burned, casting its warmth and golden Midas glow into the dimly lit room.

Joe followed her and stood at her side, his hands stretched out to the warmth of the flames. "It's okay, Viki. I'll never mention the vase again. I know this is a difficult time for you, with Merrie and all."

She nodded solemnly. "Yes, it's a difficult time, the worst . . ." She glanced up at the portrait of her mother, Eugenia Lord, which hung over the mantle. "No, this is *one* of the worst times I've ever lived through."

She stared at the painting for a long time, and Joe watched the series of expressions that crossed her face.

"What is it, Viki?" he asked. "What does your mother have to do with all of this?"

"I'm not sure," she said, fingering the brooch at her throat. Joe suddenly remembered her telling him that the pin had been Eugenia's. "I'm not sure, but—"

The library door opened and Victor Lord walked in, carrying the *Wall Street Journal* in one hand and his pipe in the other. When he saw Joe Riley standing before the fireplace, he scowled, then pretended to ignore both Joe and Victoria. At the bar he stopped to pour a bit of brandy into a crystal snifter.

With his paper, brandy, and pipe he settled into his favorite leather wing-back chair and lit up.

Joe watched him out of the corner of his

eye, admiring him and despising him at the same time. Not that Joe minded being ignored, he didn't. But it irked him to see that Victor hadn't bothered to acknowledge his daughter's existence. Joe was sure that this was not an oversight, but a way of life at Llanfair.

"Good evening, Mr. Lord," he said, with politeness taken to the point of sarcasm. "How nice to see you."

Victor grunted, puffed on his pipe, and unfolded his paper.

"Joe and I were having a private conversation, Father, if you don't mind," Victoria said with a tone that reminded Joe less of Viki and more of a certain redhead with whom he had recently exchanged heated words.

Even Victor was taken aback by her sudden change of attitude. He lowered his paper, his heavy silver eyebrows raised slightly over his gray eyes. "Well, pardon me," he said caustically. "Please don't let me disturb you. Go right ahead with your conversation. I'm sure I'm not interested in anything you two would have to say."

Victoria glared at him as he disappeared once more behind his paper. Joe watched her carefully; this wasn't like her at all, defying her father's authority. Could a bit of Nicole Smith be seeping into Victoria Lord's psyche?

"I think you *would* be interested, Father," she said evenly. "Very interested. Joe and I were just discussing the fact that I may have developed a split personality. And I was just about to tell him that I believe it started a long time ago—when my mother died."

When Victor lowered his paper again, Joe saw a sight he had never thought he would see. Victor Lord's face drained of all color except an ashen gray. Victoria's words had hit the spot . . . and knocked the breath out of him.

"Wh-what?" he stammered.

"You heard me. My mother's death must have been very traumatic for me, but I don't remember it. Not a single moment of it. Doesn't that seem odd to you, Father?"

As Victor laid his pipe on the smoking stand beside his chair, Joe noticed that his hand was shaking. Joe would have ventured a sizable bet that Victor Lord hadn't trembled over anything in a long time.

"Why don't I remember it, Father?" Victoria said, pressing the point. "Why can't I recall my own mother's death?"

By the time he had finished fumbling with his pipe, Victor had managed to put his poker face back on. He turned cold, expressionless eyes on his daughter. "You were only a child, Victoria. You were too young to remember."

"I wasn't that young. I was five years old, plenty old enough to remember something like that. What happened to her, Father? How did she die?"

Joe's eyes darted between the two of them. He knew that this was an important moment for both of them, and he was fascinated by this exchange. Victoria the interrogator, Victor the interrogated. That was a switch.

"Eugenia died in childbirth," he said, "just as I told you when you asked years ago. She died giving birth to Meredith."

Joe watched him closely with all the probing instincts of a top-notch reporter. He saw the muscle that twitched in Lord's square jaw, the darting of his tongue to moisten his lower lip. Joe had heard the stress in his voice, the boisterous delivery that lacked the ring of conviction. Victor Lord was lying.

"You're lying, Father," Victoria said, echoing Joe's conclusion. "You're lying through your teeth."

Victor threw his paper to the floor, stood, and stomped across the room. Pausing at the door, he whirled back toward his daughter. "You'll regret this, Victoria," he hissed. "No one calls me a liar in my own home—no one! And especially not my daughter."

The moment he slammed the door behind him, Joe felt something drain out of Victoria. Whatever it was that had given her strength seemed to vanish as quickly as it had appeared.

He put his arms around her waist and drew her to him, quietly offering his comfort. She accepted it, leaning against him and resting her cheek on his broad chest.

"I have to find out how my mother died, Joe," she whispered. "That's the key to all of this. I have to know."

"Don't worry," he said as he held her close and buried his face in the golden softness of her hair. "I'll find out for you, Viki. That's what I do best."

Standing before her dresser mirror, Victoria removed the cameo brooch and fingered it tenderly before laying it on the red velvet lining of the jewelry tray.

Her hands returned to her throat, where they slowly unfastened the pearl buttons of her blouse. For a moment, but only a short moment, she allowed herself to fantasize that it was Joe's hands which were moving over the front of her blouse. Joe's strong dark hands touching her, caressing her, making love to her.

A warm trickle of longing ran through her, and the sheer pleasure of it frightened her. Joe scared her. His masculinity and his thinly veiled desires frightened her. She was no child; she knew exactly what he wanted when he held her body tightly against his.

Joe was very fond of her, maybe even in love with her, and she was happy about that. It was wonderful having a friend like Joe to rely on, to have fun with, and to fight with. But he wanted to be more than a friend. He wanted to be her lover, and she wasn't ready to take that step.

As she slipped out of her blouse and skirt she wondered if Nicole Smith had the same problem, being afraid of men and physical closeness. Probably not. From what Joe had told her about Nicole Smith, it seemed that Niki had no inhibitions at all. Victoria envied her.

She slipped on a black lace nightgown, one that would undoubtedly shock her father . . . and please Joe. Then she slid into her big double bed which, tonight, seemed terribly empty. If Joe were there beside her—

She wasn't sure exactly what she would do, or what he would do. But whatever it was, it would be wonderful. She was sure of that.

Oh, well, she thought. *Maybe someday, when this is all over.*

Someone screamed. Victoria woke and sat upright in her bed, straining to listen. Then she realized that it had been the woman in her dream. Once again she lay back against the pillows, pulled the satin comforter up around her neck, and shivered as she stared into the darkness.

Another nightmare. She hadn't had one for nearly two weeks, and she had hoped that they were over. But this had been one of the worst.

She had dreamed that she was standing on a dark staircase. Someone was telling her to be very quiet as they tiptoed together down the steps. There were shouts and someone pulling on her wrist until she thought her hand would be torn from her arm. A woman screamed . . . and screamed again. Then there was only darkness.

Victoria lay awake for over an hour, trying to remember the details, but they seemed just out of reach, hidden in that swirling black void.

She felt a throbbing in her temples and realized that another headache was coming on. Nightmares, headaches . . . when would it all stop?

Joe Riley killed his headlights and drove his black Corvette slowly into the dark parking lot. He gave his quarry, the two guys in the Cadillac convertible, plenty of time to get out of their car and disappear into the nightclub. Then he parked, got out, and followed them inside.

The Cave, the hottest new club in town, lived up to its name. The interior walls had been covered with a stone veneer, and on small stages in the four corners, shapely cavewomen wearing the briefest of furry bikinis danced the latest craze.

On the dimly lit floor dancers writhed to the sensuous, psychedelic strains of "In-A-Gadda-Da-Vida," while waitresses with plastic bones knotted in their hair served drinks to customers seated at tables fashioned from slabs of stone.

It took Joe only a moment to locate the two men he was following. They were seated at a table in the back, joined by another guy whose pin-striped suit looked as though it had been stamped from the same mold as theirs. Their white ties glowed in the semi-darkness against their black shirts. *And they're probably wearing white patent leather belts and shoes to match,* Joe surmised. All they needed was to have the letters *MOB* tattooed across their foreheads.

He found a stool at the bar where he could keep an eye on them without being too obvious.

"What do you need, buddy?" The overweight, out-of-breath bartender rubbed his chafed hands on his apron, pulled a handkerchief from his pocket, and mopped his brow. "Hurry up, it's hopping in here, and I haven't got all night."

"A beer," Joe said, his eyes on the three who had just grown to a foursome. He recognized the newcomer as the bouncer at the Moonshadows. Joe had covered the story when the man had been sent to prison four years ago for assault and battery.

"That'll be four bits." The bartender sloshed the brew on Joe's hand as he plopped the mug in front of him.

Joe carefully took a twenty dollar bill from his pocket and laid it on the bar.

"You got nothing smaller than that?" the bartender growled.

"You can keep the change," Joe said.

The barkeep's round face grinned all the way through his three chins. "Oh, thanks, buddy. Let me know when you need a refill."

He reached out to grab the twenty, but Joe slapped his hand down on it first. "I just have a couple of questions," he said smoothly.

The bartender's grin faded. "So, ask 'em."

"See those four guys in the corner?"

He craned his short neck. "Yeah."

"Who are they?"

His eyes narrowed to slits in his pudgy face. "Who's asking?"

Joe picked up the bill and held it in front of his face. "I don't see that it matters," he said.

"Yeah? Well, it matters to me, buddy.

Give me four bits for the beer and keep your twenty."

Joe sighed, stuck the money back into his wallet, and plunked down two quarters. Obviously the hoods in the corner had at least one friend in this joint.

He lifted his beer, blew off the foam—and promptly forgot why he had even come into the Cave. His eyes were fixed on the dance floor, where his dearest and oldest friend, Vince Wolek, was snuggling up to the woman he loved—or some red-haired version of her.

Joe swallowed his heart along with a gulp of beer. Except for the red wig, this woman looked exactly like Victoria. She was even wearing the same tailored wool suit that Viki had been wearing earlier that evening. Joe recalled how Victoria had boldly accused her father, and he wondered briefly if the personalities of Nicole Smith and Victoria Lord might be merging.

But he didn't wonder about such psychological dilemmas for long; there were other things on his mind . . . like murdering Vinnie.

As Joe watched over the rim of his beer mug, Vince wrapped his arms even tighter around his date and nibbled at her neck. Joe set his beer on the bar and rose to his feet, his fists clenched at his sides.

"You rotten little . . ." he muttered as he worked his way through the crowd toward the dance floor.

But what he saw next stopped him dead in his tracks. Nicole or Victoria, or whoever she was, lifted her face to Vince's and kissed him, right there in front of everybody. It wasn't a long passionate kiss, but it was a kiss just the same. And it was a heck of a lot more than Joe had ever gotten from her.

First he felt rage, searing jealous rage that made him want to yank Vince away from his girl and beat him to a pulp.

But Joe could see that Vince was only responding the way he, himself, or any other living, breathing man would respond. Victoria was the one kissing Vince. It was she who was betraying him—and with his best friend.

His anger melted into hurt and left him feeling weak and shaken. He turned and elbowed his way through the crowd to the door.

He didn't see the second kiss Nicole gave Vince, or the third or fourth, and he didn't see the bartender squeeze out from behind the bar and go over to the corner to talk to the pinstripe-suited foursome.

Joe hurried across the dark parking lot toward his Corvette that gleamed black and sleek beneath the lot's one dim lamppost.

Damn Vinnie, he thought. *Damn them*

both. But even as the words ran through his mind, he tossed them aside.

Viki was sick. Something was terribly wrong with her, and she wasn't responsible for her behavior. And Vince? How could he fault Vinnie for falling in love with a woman whom he, himself, couldn't help loving?

But all the rationalization in the world couldn't take away the hurt, the sting of betrayal, the mental picture of Vince holding Viki, of her kissing him.

Joe took two deep breaths and reached into his pocket for his keys. That was when he heard it . . . a slight scraping sound behind him.

He spun around, but not fast enough. A shadow blotted out the streetlamp's light for a split second.

Then something heavy and hard crashed down on the back of his head. He saw, rather than felt, the pain as it coursed through his body. A glittering constellation of stars circled in the darkness, and he felt the ground rise up to strike him. He lay there, watching the stars, feeling his body spasm from the electrifying jolt of the pain.

Then the stars faded, and there was only darkness.

Chapter
Seven

Dr. Price Trainor flipped the toggle switch of the X-ray viewer and waited as the fluorescent bulbs flickered blue-gray in the dark room. Clipping Mr. Anderson's X-rays to the screen, he squinted at the discouraging details revealed there.

It didn't look good for Mr. Anderson. It didn't look good at all. He would have to get Jim Craig to examine these and give him a second opinion. Maybe he could think of some alternative to surgery.

There was a timid knock at the door before it opened a crack, letting in a shaft of light from the hallway. "May I come in?" asked a sultry feminine voice that he knew all too well.

"No, give a guy a break and get lost," he growled. But his tone wasn't nearly as harsh as his words.

Carla walked into the dark room and closed the door behind her. "I was talking to Jim, I mean—Dr. Craig," she said. "He told me that you were in here. I'd like to talk to you if you don't mind."

He quickly switched on the overhead light, not trusting himself to be in a dark room with her. "And if I do mind?" he asked.

"I'd like to talk to you anyway," she said as she glided across the room and sat on a green vinyl sofa in the corner.

When she crossed her long legs, Price tried not to notice how shapely they were, but his male interest got the best of him. Damn, she could even make that ugly couch look good.

"So, what's on your mind?" he asked, hoping that she hadn't guessed what was on his.

"I wish you'd come sit down with me," she said, patting the cushion beside her. "This is important."

"No, thank you," he said dryly as he turned his back to her and re-examined the X-rays. His pride still stung from her slap, and he had no intention of making this easy for her.

"Jim told me that you might be leaving Llanview. Is that true?"

"I might be," he replied.

She was quiet for a few moments. Then he

heard her draw a deep breath. "Am I the reason you're leaving?" she asked.

He thought that she sounded almost sorry. But he couldn't be sure without looking at her, and he didn't trust himself to do that just now.

"You might," he said. "And then, I might have other reasons that are more important than you. Did you consider that?"

She bit her lower lip. "I don't want you to leave, Price." This time there was no mistaking the sincerity in her voice.

Surprised, he turned around to face her. "Why not?" he said, trying to keep the eagerness out of his voice.

"Because . . ." She toyed with the fringed blue sash that belted the simple shift around her waist. Her long black lashes screened her eyes as she looked down, avoiding his gaze. "I'd hate to think that I chased you away, Price. This is your home, and you have a good job here. I wouldn't want you to leave all of that just because I . . . because I hurt you. I thought that I should be the one to leave. I don't have that much to lose."

Price walked over to the sofa and sat down beside her on the cracked vinyl sofa. He cleared his throat and leaned forward, resting his elbows on his knees. "Well, maybe neither of us will have to leave," he said. "Maybe we could find another solution to this problem."

When he ventured a sideways glance at her, his heart plummeted to his shoes. Why did she have to be so pretty? Why did she have to have those gorgeous brown eyes that seemed to melt every bone in his body, leaving him feeling like a puddle of warm gelatin?

"Price, do you think we could get along?" she asked. "I'd like that very much. But how? We got off to such a bad start."

"Oh, I don't know," he said and grinned in spite of himself. "It had its good moments." He thought of how she had collapsed into his arms in the laboratory and how her lips had responded to his when he had kissed her after the Christmas party.

The delicate blush on her cheeks told him that she was remembering, too. "I'd like to be your friend," she said softly.

"I'd like to be your lover." The words slipped out before he could censor them, and he nearly bit his tongue.

He heard her sharp intake of breath and half expected her to slap him again. This time he might even deserve it.

But she didn't look as though she were going to hit him. Her eyes swept over his face, lingering on his lips. He quickly decided that if she didn't stop looking at him that way in the next two seconds, he was going to kiss her. And she would *definitely* deserve it.

Her gaze moved upward at the last moment, capturing his. He moved closer to her and laid his palms along the sides of her face. His thumbs lightly caressed the delicate skin over her prominent cheekbones.

"Well?" he asked, as the pad of his right thumb slowly traced the outline of her full lower lip. "Would you ever consider having a relationship with a black man?" he asked. "A permanent relationship."

"Permanent?" she breathed.

He nodded, not trusting his voice.

Her eyes probed his, testing, weighing his intentions. "Do you mean marriage?" she asked. "Marriage to you?"

Something in her voice set him on edge. A certain tone that made him feel that she thought the whole idea ridiculous. "No, marriage to Sidney Poitier," he replied sarcastically.

She shook her head as though in disbelief. "You meant marriage to you," she said. "That *is* what you meant, isn't it?"

He stood, walked over to the viewer and ripped the X-rays down from their clips. "Yeah, that's what I meant. But forget it, I must have been crazy. I seem to go a little nuts every time I'm around you."

She quickly rose and crossed the room to stand beside him. "Price, I didn't mean to hurt your feelings, really." She placed her hand lightly on his sleeve. "I just had no idea that you were thinking—"

"I *wasn't* thinking. That's just the trouble," he said, brushing her hand away. He shoved the X-rays into a manila envelope. "I take one look at your big brown eyes and your great legs, and I forget that you're a bigot."

He saw the hurt in her eyes, but he tried to not let it get to him. She deserved it. If the truth hurt, so be it.

"See what I mean about leaving Llanview, Miss Benari?" he said, tucking the envelope under his arm and heading for the door. "I'm not sure this town is big enough for the two of us." He yanked open the door and saw an orderly standing there with his hand raised to knock.

"Oh, Dr. Trainor, I was just coming to get you. Dr. Craig needs you in emergency. That reporter, Joe Riley, has just been brought in. He's been beaten, and he's in really bad shape."

Meredith knocked again at Victoria's bedroom door, then eased it open. "Viki," she said softly. "Viki, wake up."

Victoria stirred in her bed and reached for the lamp switch. Shielding her eyes from the light with the back of her hand, she sat up on the bed. "What is it, Merrie?"

Meredith was surprised to see that Viki was wearing a leopard-print bra and panties, not a nightgown as she usually did. "I thought I should wake you," she said. "Larry just called from the hospital."

Victoria looked over at the clock on her nightstand . . . three-thirty. "Why would he call at this time of night? What's wrong?"

"It's Joe, Viki. He's been hurt."

"In an accident?"

Meredith hesitated. "No, it was no accident. He was beaten."

"Larry, how is Joe?" Victoria charged into the emergency room with Meredith following close behind. She glanced frantically around the ward at the four empty beds and the vacant waiting area. "Where is he?"

"He's upstairs getting some X-rays taken of his skull. We'll know more after we have a look at them. He has some bad contusions, possibly some broken ribs."

"Oh, God." Victoria covered her face with her hands and burst into tears. Meredith stepped forward to put her arms around her sister, but Larry had already done so.

"There, there," Larry said, smoothing Viki's hair with his palm.

"He's not going to die, is he?" she sobbed.

"I don't think so," he replied with less conviction than Meredith wanted to hear.

She loved Joe, too, though not in the same way that Viki did. Everybody loved handsome, charming Joe. Everybody except Victor. And, apparently, someone else didn't love him, the person or people who had done this terrible thing to him.

As Meredith watched Larry cradle Victoria in his arms, she remembered when he had held her that way and how wonderful it had felt to be enfolded in his embrace.

Finally Victoria pulled away from him and sank onto one of the metal folding chairs lined up against the wall. "How did this happen?" she asked.

Larry shook his head. "We don't know who did it. He was found lying unconscious in the parking lot of a local bar."

"A local bar?" Victoria sprang to her feet, and Meredith wondered at the startled expression on her face. "Which bar?"

"I'm not sure," Larry said. "I believe it was that new club down by the waterfront."

"The Cave?" Viki's eyes were wide with alarm. "Why would Joe go there?"

"Well, I don't know, Viki," Larry replied quizzically. "Does it matter?"

"No." She sat down quickly, as though her legs would no longer support her. "No, of course not."

"Merrie, I can't stand this waiting," Victoria said as she paced the threadbare shag carpet of the waiting room for the hundredth time. "I can't stand not knowing . . ."

"I understand, Viki," Meredith replied, and she did understand. Victoria, like her father, couldn't bear to be in a helpless situation, couldn't stand having to rely on other people to remedy a problem for her, even if they were highly skilled physicians.

"Come, sit down before you wear out the rug. It's on its last threads as it is." Meredith patted the seat of the chair beside her.

As Victoria sat down next to Meredith, she noticed her sister's paleness and the fatigue that dulled her brown eyes.

"Why don't you go on home, Merrie," she said. "You shouldn't be here. You need your rest."

"I'm all right, and I'm staying here with you until we get some word on Joe."

Victoria put on her authoritative face and voice. "Now, Meredith, I must insist. You should—"

"Viki, stop sounding like Father. I'll do as I please, and I please to stay here with you."

"But, Merrie, you don't know how important it is that you get your rest," she said gently.

Meredith drew a deep breath, marshaling her strength. "Yes, I do know, Viki. I know all about my . . . condition."

"You—you do?"

Meredith dropped her eyes to shield them

from Victoria's probing gaze. "Yes. I know that I'm going to die."

Viki was silent for a long moment. Then she took Meredith's hands in hers. "How did you find out?"

"Father told me, the day that I was going to marry Larry."

"Father?" Stunned, Victoria dropped Meredith's hands and shook her head in disbelief. "Father told you himself?"

"Yes."

"I . . . I can't believe it," she sputtered, her anger growing as Meredith's words sank in. "He told you a thing like that and jeopardized your health to keep you from marrying someone he didn't approve of?"

Merrie nodded silently.

Uttering a vehement curse, Victoria sprang to her feet. Meredith looked up at her in surprise and saw a stranger. Cool, collected Victoria was gone, and in her place was a passionate, enraged woman with fury in her blue eyes. "I'll kill him. I'll murder that dirty—"

"Excuse me, Viki," Larry said from the doorway. He was staring at her with amazement and apprehension. "I don't mean to interrupt you, but Joe is semiconscious now, and he's asking for you."

Chapter
Eight

Anna Wolek flew into her little brother's outstretched arms, her little brother who stood over a foot taller than her own five feet two inches. "Oh, Larry, how is he? How is Joe?"

"Better," he said, unwinding her strangling grip from around his neck. "He's stable now, and the x-rays don't show any fracture of the skull."

Anna crossed herself and whispered a quick prayer of thanks.

Behind her stood Sadie Gray, her dark face glowing with relief at the good news.

"Praise the Lord," she said. "I knew that nothing too bad would happen to such a fine young man as Joseph Riley."

"Where is he?" Anna asked. "I want to see him."

Larry shook his head and patted her

shoulder sympathetically. He was one of the few people who knew that Anna was in love with Joe. "I'm sorry, Anna," he said, "but Joe isn't strong enough for visitors yet. He's barely even conscious."

"But, but I saw Victoria Lord go in there just a minute ago," she argued, knowing that her pleas were in vain.

"Joe asked for Victoria," Larry said gently. "That's the only reason I allowed her to go in."

Anna nodded and slowly turned away. "I see," she said. And she did. She didn't need to be reminded of where she stood with Joe Riley, or where Victoria Lord stood with him.

She walked over to a chair in the waiting room and sat down, her back straight, her head high. "May I wait here until . . . for a while?" she asked.

"Of course. Wait as long as you like," he said. "I'll try to keep you posted as often as I can."

"Don't worry about me, Larry," she said, taking a tissue from her pocket and dabbing at her eyes. "You just take good care of Joe."

As Larry left the waiting room, Sadie walked to a coffee machine in the corner and inserted two nickels. She uttered a quaint almost-profanity as the confused machine spewed the hot liquid, then dropped the cup.

"I'll go down to the cafeteria and get us

some coffee," she said to Anna. "You look like you could use some."

"Thank you, Sadie. You're a dear."

As Anna watched her friend leave, she thought how lucky she was to have someone to wait this out with, someone who cared about her and about Joe.

Where was Vinnie? she wondered. He had already gone to work when she had gotten the call from Larry. But she had left a message with Barney at the warehouse. Surely he had gotten it by now.

She watched the double swinging doors of the Intensive Care Ward and jumped every time someone came through them. What was going on in there?

And why had Joe asked for Victoria instead of her? That question wasn't difficult to answer. Joe was in love with Victoria. And Anna was just his good buddy, like Larry and Vinnie.

Good old Anna Wolek, she thought. *Just one of the boys.*

Sadie's mind and heart were with Anna as she left the waiting room and headed toward the cafeteria where a few members of the white-smocked hospital staff were catching an early breakfast. What a shame it was that Joseph couldn't see what a fine woman Anna was and how much she loved him. Sadie didn't know Victoria Lord, but she couldn't imagine that any woman would be better suited for Joe than dear, sweet Anna Wolek.

A lone figure seated at a table in the corner made Sadie temporarily forget all about Anna and Joe. This person was the only one, besides herself, who wasn't wearing a white smock.

She walked slowly over to the table, fighting her inclination to turn and run without speaking. "Hello, Clara," she said. When the young woman looked up with a startled expression, Sadie amended her salutation. "Excuse me, I mean *Carla.*"

Carla cast a nervous glance around the cafeteria. "Good morning, Mama. Won't you join me?" She waved a hand toward the empty chair across from her.

"Just for a minute," Sadie replied, settling into the chair. "I just came down to get a cup of coffee for Anna. I thought she needed one. She's so upset."

"Anna's upset? What's wrong?"

"That young reporter that she's so fond of, Joe Riley, got the tar beat out of him last night."

"Oh, no. Is he going to be all right?"

Sadie noted the genuine concern on her daughter's face with satisfaction. At least Clara had grown into a woman who cared about her friends.

"Dr. Wolek says he'll be okay."

"Oh, that's good. I'm glad."

Sadie leaned forward and peered into her face. "Well, you don't look very glad. What's the matter with you, girl?"

"The matter? Nothing really."

"Then why is your forehead all wrinkled up like that? What if you got paralyzed at this moment and had to stay all crinkled up for the rest of your life?"

Carla laughed, and the frown temporarily disappeared. "Oh, Mama. You always used to tell me that, and it's so silly."

Sadie leaned back in her chair and grinned broadly. "Well, you didn't used to think it was so silly. I kept you from crossing your eyes by telling you that."

"That's true."

"So, what's wrong?"

"I'm just worried . . . about a man."

"You've grown up, Cla—Carla. You used to only worry about boys."

"I know. Life was easier then. Boys don't propose to you, or if they do, they don't mean it."

Sadie's face lit up with maternal interest. "Someone proposed to you? Who?"

"I don't think you know him. Dr. Price Trainor."

"Well, did you tell him yes or no?"

"Neither. We had a fight, as usual, and that was the end of it. Every time he gets mad at me, he calls me a bigot. Can you imagine that?"

Sadie bit her bottom lip, but not her tongue. "Yes, I can imagine that," she said bitterly.

Carla's temper flared. Her wound was sore enough without having her mother dig at it. "I am *not* a bigot, and I resent you and Price for calling me that. So, I have problems dealing with my feelings about my own heritage, but I have no problem with other people. I just can't rush into a relationship with a man without telling him the—" She glanced around the room and lowered her voice. "Without telling him the truth about myself."

Sadie shook her head and clucked her tongue. "Sounds like you've woven yourself one of those tangled webs I always warned you about when you were little."

"Well, it's my web, isn't it?" Carla said, her volume rising again. "And if I'm caught in it, I'll get out on my own."

"Clara, sooner or later you're going to have to tell these people about yourself. You realize that, don't you?"

"I realize that you don't understand my situation. You've never understood."

"Good morning." Dr. Jim Craig stood beside their table, his breakfast tray in hand. From the sunny smile on his face, they both surmised that he hadn't overheard their heated discussion. "And how are you lovely ladies this morning?"

"Fine," they mumbled in unison.

"I didn't realize that you two were acquainted," he said. "How long have you known each other?"

Sadie looked across the table at her daughter, and their eyes met. Sadie said nothing, leaving the situation in Carla's hands. But she steeled herself against the pain she would feel if her only daughter denied her.

Carla's wide brown eyes reflected the indecision and the fear she felt. Then Sadie saw a flicker of pride in those amber depths before Carla turned back to Jim.

"We've known each other forever," she said. "Dr. Craig, this lady is my mother."

Victoria had tried to brace herself for the shock of seeing Joe battered and bruised, but nothing could have prepared her for this. The right side of his face was discolored, puffy, and distorted. His right eye was badly swollen with a long, sutured gash through his eyebrow.

But the thing that struck her as unusual wasn't the swelling, the cuts, or the bruises. It was the terrible blankness, the total lack of animation about his face as he lay there, his swarthy skin nearly as white as the bandaging around his head. She had never seen Joe without a smile on his face, or a scowl, or without that wicked gleam in his dark eyes that told her how much he wanted her.

"You said that he was conscious." She looked questioningly at Larry, who stood beside her, his head down, his hands thrust into the pockets of his smock.

"He was. He must have slipped under again." Larry walked to the door and turned back to her, studying his patient thoughtfully. "Why don't you stay with him for a while, Viki? Talk to him. Maybe he'll come around again."

Larry closed the door behind him, and Viki saw Joe stir slightly at the sound. "Joe," she said, taking his hand. She winced when she saw the I.V. taped to his arm. "Joe, it's me, Victoria. Wake up."

His eyes fluttered open, and he stared at her without comprehension. She squeezed his hand as hard as she dared and leaned over him.

"It's Viki, Joe," she repeated, her face only inches from his. "Can you speak to me?"

He moved his swollen lips and grimaced. "No," he mumbled.

"No? You can't speak? Why not?"

He closed his eyes for a moment as though gathering strength. "Because . . . it hurts, dummy," he whispered.

"Oh, of course it does. I'll bet it even hurts to breathe with those fractured ribs."

He nodded. "Breathing . . . hurts, yes. I'll try . . . not to."

Victoria smiled, reassured. They might have knocked the stuffing out of him, but his sense of humor was still intact. "You're going to be all right, Joe," she said, patting his hand soothingly.

"Going . . . to live?" he gasped.

"Most certainly."

He sighed and closed his eyes. "Damn."

"Oh, Joe, it can't be that bad," she said.

"Wanna bet?"

She reached out and stroked his cheek, finding an unbruised area on the left side. "So, don't talk," she said. "Just lie still and rest."

"Viki . . ." She felt him squeeze her hand and was surprised at his strength.

"Yes, Joe, what is it?"

"Don't go. Have to tell you—"

"I'm not going anywhere, Joe. What do you want to tell me?" His sudden intensity frightened her deeply, and she wasn't sure why.

"I saw you . . . or Nicole . . . kiss Vinnie," he said.

Her heart leapt in her chest, and she could hear her pulse booming in her ears. A pain in her temples began throbbing in rhythm with her rampant heartbeat. "What do you mean, Joe? I don't know what you're talking about."

She thought she saw a softening like compassion in his eyes just before he closed them wearily. "It's . . . okay, Viki. I forgive you . . . and Vinnie."

The pounding in her head intensified, and she thought of the headache last evening. She thought of how she had gone to bed wearing a nightgown and wakened to find herself in leopard-print underwear.

She had no idea what had happened during the night but, for some terrible reason, she felt responsible for Joe's injuries. Somehow it was her fault, hers and Vince Wolek's.

"Joe, I'm so sorry," she whispered.

He shook his head slowly from side to side. She could sense a sudden agitation in him. "Don't be," he murmured. "Don't be sorry. I understand now . . . died from head injury."

Viki looked up and saw that Larry had come back into the room. "No, Joe," she said, leaning over him. "You aren't going to die of your head injury. You're going to be okay."

He shook his head again. "Not me, your mother, Viki. I checked records. Subdural —hematoma."

Larry stepped up to the bed. "He's hallucinating, Victoria," he said. "He must have heard us discussing his condition."

"It's not a hallucination," she told him flatly. "Joe's been investigating something . . . for me."

Her eyes blazed as she turned back to Joe.

She bent down and placed her lips against his ear. "I love you, Joe," she whispered so that only he could hear. "Nicole may have kissed Vince Wolek, but I'm in love with you."

His eyes opened, and the wonder that she saw there melted her heart. "Really?" he asked.

In answer she pressed her lips gently to his. He moaned, and she knew that it was more from pleasure than pain.

His left hand burrowed through her hair and held her firmly, prolonging the kiss. Swollen lips, battered skull, cracked ribs or not, Joe Riley wasn't going to let this opportunity pass by without making the most of it.

When he finally released her, she had been thoroughly, passionately kissed.

"He's fine," she pronounced to a slightly embarrassed Dr. Wolek. She sighed and added, "In fact, he's excellent. Which is more than I can say for you, Larry Wolek."

He raised one eyebrow in surprise at her brusque tone. "I beg your pardon?"

"Beg *Merrie's* pardon, not mine. She's the one who's pining over you. She's the one who still loves you and wants to marry you, even if she won't admit it. If you let her go you're a fool."

With her nose in the air, she stomped across the room to the door. "Let Merrie know that you still love her, Larry," she said. "Don't be such a jerk."

Larry's mouth dropped open as he watched her walk away down the hall. He was astonished at the change in her attitude, her language, even her posture. It was almost as though . . . she were another person.

"Hand me that phone, and be quick about it."

Karen Martin stared across the nurses' counter at a Victoria Lord she had never seen before. Victoria was assertive and headstrong like her father, but she was always courteous—or at least, she had been in the past. But without preamble she had marched up to the nurses' station and demanded the use of their telephone.

"Well, I . . ." Karen hesitated; the phone was to be used only by hospital staff.

"Just hand me the damned phone." Victoria thrust out her hand, and something in her blue eyes caused Karen to think twice about refusing her.

"Sure, anything you say," she replied haughtily, handing over the desk phone.

Boy, these high and mighty Lords think they own the world, Karen thought as she occupied herself with "busy" work so that she would be inconspicuous if she stayed in the area. She wanted to overhear this telephone conversation that was so all-fired important.

She watched out of her peripheral vision as Victoria dialed a number and stood, tapping her high heel impatiently as she waited for someone to answer.

"Yes, hello. Victor Lord, please. Just tell him that Nicole Smith would like a word with him."

Nicole Smith? Karen's ears perked up like a beagle's. What kind of game was Victoria playing?

"Mr. Lord, this is Niki Smith. You don't remember me? Well, I'm not surprised . . . it's been a long time. And I wouldn't be calling you now except that I've been hearing things about you that, quite frankly, have upset me a great deal."

Karen turned her back to Victoria and jotted some worthless notes in a file. If only she could hear the other side of the conversation. Was it as crazy as this half?

"That's right," Victoria continued. "It's one thing for you to meddle in your daughter's affairs, but to risk her life! That's low, even for you, Victor Lord.

"This is not Victoria—I told you that my name is Nicole Smith. You know me, Victor. We met years ago, the night that Eugenia died."

Karen turned and stared at Victoria, her mouth agape. If Victoria was playing a joke on her father, it was a sick joke. But Viki didn't look as though she were playing at anything. She looked deadly serious.

"Victoria doesn't know how her mother died," she said with an ominous tone, "but *I* do. I was there, remember? Your time is up, Mr. Lord. You're going to pay for all the pain you've caused over the years. I'm going to tell the world how your wife *really* died."

Chapter
Nine

"Are you shocked?"

Carla's dark eyes searched Jim Craig's from across the narrow cafeteria table. Looking for signs of rejection, she found only mild surprise on his kindly face.

"Well, are you shocked to discover that I'm a mulatto instead of a European aristocrat?" she asked again.

"Shocked?" He thought carefully for a moment, then shook his head. "No, not at all. I just don't know what to say."

"Say whatever you feel, Jim. I want to know what you think of me."

Jim Craig lifted his cup of coffee to his lips and blew across the steaming brew, obviously stalling for time. When he finally set the cup down and looked across at her, his pale blue eyes shone with genuine affection.

"I believe you know what I think of you,

Carla," he said. "I'm fond of you. In fact . . ." He cleared his throat before continuing. "I've *very* fond of you, and I'd like to pursue a relationship with you. A *close* relationship."

Carla had known all along that Jim's interest in her was of a romantic nature, but he had never said as much. She was surprised that he had chosen this particular moment to state his feelings.

"And knowing that I'm half black doesn't change your mind?" she asked.

A puzzled look creased his brow. "No. Why should it? You're a beautiful, intelligent woman, and I enjoy your company. Why should your parentage matter, especially when your mother is a fine woman like Sadie Gray?"

Yes, why should it matter? she wondered. Why was it the focal issue in her life when it didn't seem to matter to those around her?

"So, what do you say, Carla?" he asked. "How do you feel about the fact that I'm . . . interested in you?"

She could hear the little-boy vulnerability in his voice, and it went straight to her heart. "I'm terribly flattered, Jim," she replied honestly. "And any other time I would probably return your interest except—"

"Except for what? Or should I say whom?"

He knew. She could see it in his eyes.

"Whom," she replied. "I'm interested in someone else at the moment, Jim."

"I see." He sipped at his cooled coffee, staring at the cup to avoid her eyes. "And would this someone happen to be Price Trainor?"

"Yes. I'm sorry," she said.

He quickly donned a benevolent smile that she had seen him wear for his patients. "Don't be sorry, Carla. I understand. Price is a fine man, one of the best I've ever known. And I strongly suspect that he returns your interest."

Carla sat quietly, watching Jim drink his coffee. Beneath his facade of indifference, she could see that he was deeply disappointed. Was she making a terrible mistake, turning down this man's love for that of someone she couldn't be around for five minutes without fighting? A relationship with Jim Craig would be so easy, so comfortable . . . too comfortable. The chemistry just wasn't there.

"Have you told him, Carla?" he asked, his gentle voice breaking through her introspection. "Have you told Price that you're half black?"

"No."

"Why not?"

She shrugged. "You said yourself that it doesn't matter."

"It doesn't . . . to me."

"And you think it will to Price?" she asked fearfully, knowing the answer even better than he.

"It'll matter."

"Are you saying that Price is prejudiced against white people?"

"Not that I've ever noticed," he said. "But I can tell you one thing, Carla. Price Trainor is fiercely proud of being black . . . and he'll expect you to be, too."

"Hey, Larry, wait up."

As Larry turned and saw Karen running down the hall after him, it occurred to him that she had been chasing him for weeks, ever since that night when he had been stupid enough to have dinner with her. Actually, having dinner with her hadn't been his biggest mistake; it had been going to bed with her.

Now, looking back on that night, he couldn't remember why he had been so foolish. He knew that it wasn't gentlemanly to avoid her this way, after having been intimate with her. But on the other hand, it wasn't fair to either of them to prolong this pointless relationship.

"Yes, Karen. What is it?" He heard the harshness in his voice and tried to temper it. "What can I do for you?"

"I just want to talk to you for a minute, Larry," she said, her full lower lip protruding in what was undoubtedly supposed to be an adorable pout. For some reason, he didn't find it all that appealing. "You can take a minute, can't you? For *me?*"

"I'm rather busy right now, Karen," he said. "I have Joe Riley in Intensive Care and—"

"I know. I just heard Victoria Lord on the phone talking to her father, and wow—was she ever strung out. You should have heard her."

"Victoria's worried about Joe," he said curtly, continuing down the hall toward the Intensive Care Unit.

She followed at his heels, tripping along like an adoring cocker spaniel. "I just wanted to ask you if you'd like to go to the hospital Valentine's Dance with me. I thought it might be fun."

She reached out and grabbed the sleeve of his smock, yanking him to a stop.

"Karen, I don't know." He fought down his irritation. After all, she was just trying to be nice, but she was driving him crazy with all these invitations. Couldn't she take a hint?

"Come on, Larry," she wheedled. "We'd have such a good time at the dance—*and* afterward at my apartment."

She stood with her hands on her waist, her ample bosom thrust forth provocatively. *Subtle, Karen,* he thought. *Really subtle.*

"I appreciate your asking me, Karen," he said, resisting the childish urge to cross his fingers and negate the lie. "But I'm afraid not."

She dropped the plaintive tone as quickly as she had assumed it. "Well, thanks a lot for nothing," she snapped. "I don't know how you can do this to me, Larry Wolek."

"Do what?"

"Drop me like a hot potato, after all we shared together!"

Larry sighed and ran his fingers through his hair. He should have seen that one coming. He reached out and put his hands on her shoulders, reminding himself to be gentle and not shake her until her teeth rattled. "Karen, what we *shared* that night was very nice, and I'll always remember it fondly," he added, embroidering the facts. "But it was a mistake, and it must never happen again."

"A mistake! You call what we did a mistake?"

He glanced quickly down the hall toward the nurses' station. "Sh-h-h . . ."

"Don't you shush me, Larry Wolek. You just don't want people to know how you took advantage of me. You only used me to get what you wanted, and now you think you can dump me like yesterday's trash. Well, I won't have it, Dr. Lawrence C. Wolek. You haven't heard the last of this yet."

With that she spun on her heel and stomped down the hall.

As Larry watched her retreat, he muttered three curses; one for her, one for himself, and one for his momentary lapse of sexual discretion.

Instead of waiting for the elevator, Vincent Wolek charged up the stairs to the fourth floor and the Intensive Care Ward.

His face was a variegated shade of red and purple when he threw open the door and rushed inside.

"Vinnie!" Larry lifted the stethoscope from Joe Riley's chest. "You can't come in here!"

Vince ignored his younger brother and hurried straight to his friend's bedside. "Joe, are you all right, buddy? I just heard. God almighty, they must've dragged you around on your face."

But Joe didn't answer or even open his blackened eyes.

"Vinnie . . ." Larry walked around the side of the bed and grasped his brother by the arm. "You have to leave. I don't want you upsetting Joe."

Vince tried to shrug Larry's hand away, but his grip was firm, and so was his manner. Larry usually submitted to his boisterous older brother, but not where his patients' welfare was concerned. In the hospital Vince was on Larry's turf.

"Out. Now," Larry said, tightening his grip.

"But . . . but . . ."

"No *buts*. Come on, we'll talk outside."

In a fleeting moment of compliance, Vince allowed himself to be led into the hall.

"I gotta talk to Joe," he argued, close to tears. "He's the best friend I've got in the world, and he's layin' there all busted up."

"So do Joe a favor, Vinnie, and let him rest. He knows you care about him. When he wakes up I'll tell him that you're here, and maybe you can talk to him for a minute. Okay?"

"As soon as he wakes up?"

"Yes, I promise. Why don't you go downstairs to the cafeteria and have a cup of coffee? I think Anna and Sadie are down there, and I know that Anna could use some support from you right now."

Vince cast one more haunted look toward the door, then nodded and walked away down the hall.

That was exactly what Vince wanted to hear, that Anna needed him, needed him to be strong for her. He wanted to think that there was something he could do for somebody, since he couldn't help Joe. Every time he thought about Joe being hurt, Vince felt horribly guilty. He wasn't exactly sure why, but he was pretty sure that God had let Joe get beaten up to punish Vince for trying to steal his best friend's girl.

It just don't pay to mess up, he thought. *God'll get you in the end. One way or the other, he'll get you.*

He punched the elevator button with his thumb and waited, shifting nervously from foot to foot.

"Let Joe be all right, God," he whispered, closing his eyes and crossing himself reverently. "If you do, I promise that I won't ever try to steal his or anybody else's girlfriend ever again."

He opened his eyes and looked around to see if anybody had seen him, but the hallway was empty. It was only him . . . and God.

Somehow his prayer didn't sound sincere enough to his own ear. It probably wouldn't hold much weight with God either, if he was mad enough to let Joe get beaten up.

"And I'll cut back on my Saturday-night drinkin', too," he added.

He breathed a sigh of relief. Surely God would take him up on that deal; especially since he had thrown in the bit about the drinking. Temperance was the biggest penance he could think of, and he had heard that God was big on paying penance.

But the instant the elevator doors opened, he forgot all about his bargain with the

Almighty. There she was, looking as pretty as a picture, wearing that same pink blouse that she had been wearing last night. He could still remember how silky it had felt when they had danced.

"Niki! What are you doin' here, honey-bunch?" he asked, getting into the elevator with her and pushing the CLOSE DOOR button.

"I was here to see Joe Riley," she said in an uncharacteristically subdued tone. The customary sparkle was absent from her blue eyes.

"Joe Riley?" He studied her suspiciously. "Why would you wanna see Joe? He ain't no friend of yours. You only met him that once."

"He's Victoria Lord's friend," she said, as though that explained everything.

"So, you got to see him?"

"For a few minutes, yes."

"Umph," he sniffed. "Larry wouldn't let me in there. Threw me out. How come he let you in?"

She looked up at the flashing numbers over the elevator door. "Joe asked to see Victoria," she replied curtly.

Vinnie didn't like this a bit. His Nicole was acting a lot like Victoria Lord, and that just wouldn't do at all. "What's the matter with you, Niki?" he asked. "You're actin' funny."

For the first time since he had stepped into

the elevator, she turned her full attention to him. "What?" she said, staring at him blankly. "Oh, I'm sorry, Vince. I just have a lot on my mind."

The elevator came to a halt on the main floor, and Vince felt his belly do a double flip-flop, the way it always did in elevators. But this time his stomach's disturbance had something to do with the way that Nicole was behaving.

"I get off on this floor, Vince," she said, stepping out of the elevator. "I'd stay and visit with you for a while, but there's someone I have to see. There's an old score that I have to settle, and now is as good a time as any."

"An old score?" he asked. He didn't like that look in her eye.

"Yes. There's a certain king whose head is going to roll."

Chapter
Ten

Larry swore and kicked the coffee machine in its already multidented side, expending what little strength he had left. First the coffeepot in the doctors' lounge had been empty, and now this blasted machine had robbed him of his dime by giving him a cup with cream and sugar, but no coffee.

This was going to be one of those days. He could tell already.

Oh, stop feeling sorry for yourself, he thought. *If your life is the pits, it's your own doing. You're a stubborn jackass, just like Victoria said.*

"Larry, have you seen Viki?"

The soft voice washed over him with a flood of tender feelings. He turned and saw her standing there in the door of the waiting room.

In her yellow eyelet dress she looked like a daffodil, a delicate spring blossom, pushing its way up through an icy blanket of winter snow. Seeing her, no one could ever guess . . .

"Merrie." When he whispered her name, his frustration and weariness flowed away. He walked across the room and took her hand between both of his. "No, I haven't seen Viki for quite a while. She visited Joe, and then she made a phone call. Someone said she left the hospital."

"She left? I can't imagine her leaving while Joe is still critical."

"He isn't critical anymore, Merrie. He's stable and out of danger. Why don't you go home, too, and get some rest?"

She nodded and withdrew her hand from his. "If you're sure that Joe will be okay?"

"He'll be fine. It'll take more than that to knock a hole in his thick skull."

"Okay. Thanks, Larry."

He wondered what she was thinking as she stood there, gazing up at him with those big brown eyes. Then she added, "I'm glad I got to see you again."

"Me, too," he said softly.

As she began to back away from him, he thought of what Victoria had said. Could it be true? Did Meredith still love him, still want him?

"Merrie, wait." He closed the space between them with two long strides. "Could we talk? I mean, could I come to Llanview tonight? Please. We should at least discuss . . . our situation. Don't you think so?"

He waited breathlessly for her reply. He saw the emotions battling on her face and wondered what it meant. Was she just too softhearted to tell him that she didn't love him anymore?

"Okay," she agreed, although she didn't look very happy about it. In fact, she looked miserable. Was this a mistake? Should he just leave her alone? "Why don't you come for dinner?" she added.

"Are you sure?" he asked, offering her a way out.

"No. I'm not sure," she said. "I'm not sure about anything anymore, Larry. Except that I want to see you, and that I want to be with you tonight."

As she turned and walked away, Larry felt the heavy burden on his heart shift ever so slightly, easing just a bit. Llanfair tonight . . . and Merrie. Maybe this wasn't going to be such a terrible day after all.

"Hi, Mickey. How's my favorite lab tech tonight?" Karen leaned through the opened top half of the laboratory's door and batted her long lashes at the young technician who was rinsing test tubes at the sink.

His freckled face lit up with delight. "Oh,

hi there, Karen. I ran that test for your friend." His eyes strayed down to her shapely body. "Is your friend going to come pick up the results herself?"

"No, she's a bit nervous about the whole thing. She asked me to stop by for her. Besides, I wanted to touch base with you again," she said in her most seductive tone.

"Touch base, huh?" His gaze slid down for a split second, then bounced back up. "Sounds like fun."

"Mickey, you're a dirty old man," she chided.

"Really?" Mick was flattered beyond words. He'd never thought of himself as even flirty. He took an envelope from the table and handed it to her. "Here's your friend's results. Just don't tell anybody that I ran this for you. We're not supposed to do tests without a doctor's order."

She took the envelope and gave him a coquettish smile. "I won't tell a soul, Mickey. It'll just be our little secret."

"So, what do I get in return?" he asked, emboldened by his new status as a masher.

"What did you have in mind?" she said, running her tongue over her lower lip.

He watched the movement, mesmerized. "How about a kiss?" he asked breathlessly.

"Okay." She leaned farther through the door, making herself more available.

Mickey couldn't believe his luck—kissing

Karen Martin! It was the stuff fantasies were made of; at least, most of *his* fantasies. He closed his eyes and puckered up. This was going to be good.

But when he made contact, he realized that something wasn't quite right. He seemed to have missed her lips and landed on her cheek. His aim must have been off, or she had turned her head at the last moment. In the end he had to settle for a peck.

"Thanks a lot, Mickey," she said as she sauntered away, envelope in hand.

"Sure, anytime, Karen. Anytime at all." Mickey sighed. Oh, well. He hadn't gotten a kiss, not a real one anyway. But he had new fantasy material for the next three weeks.

Karen waited until she was around the corner before ripping the envelope open. Her hand shook so hard that she could barely read the typed form.

PREGNANCY TEST
for
LINDA BRAY
Results: POSITIVE

So, good ol' Linda was pregnant. . . .

Karen clutched the paper to her breast and leaned back against the wall. She closed her eyes as though savoring the moment. Then she laughed. She laughed until tears rolled down her cheeks and dripped onto the form.

Linda Bray . . . pregnant.

Of course, there was no friend named Linda. The specimen had been her own. The test results were hers.

Karen's hand slid down to her abdomen and lingered there. The results were hers and the baby was hers—hers and Larry's.

"There you go, young man," Dr. Price Trainor said as he clipped and removed the last stitch in the boy's finger. "That healed up very nicely, if I do say so myself."

"Can I leave off the bandage now?" the child asked, studying the red scar on his pinky.

"Yep. You can show it to all your friends at school. Just be sure to charge them a quarter for looking at it."

The boy grinned up at the doctor, wrinkling his nose. "Ah, they won't pay a whole quarter to see a little boo-boo like that."

"They will if you tell them that a bear bit it," he said, ruffling the child's sandy curls.

"Hey, yeah!" The boy surveyed the injured finger with renewed respect.

"Just don't ever put a firecracker in a pop bottle again, okay?" Trainor said firmly.

The child nodded. "I promise."

Price smiled and turned to leave the room, but he stopped in midstride when he saw the object of his dreams, and his most recent nightmares, standing in the doorway. As usual, when seeing her, he felt as though his equilibrium had been knocked out of kilter. She was smiling that slow, easy smile that he hadn't seen nearly often enough. Her big brown eyes were soft, almost tender.

"May I have a word with you, Dr. Trainor?" she asked.

He felt his protective wall slide up between them, and he almost resented its presence. He wanted to get close to her, and yet, when he got too close to that alluring flame, his wings were singed every time. Better to keep one's distance.

He walked past her and out into the hall. She followed at his side, taking two steps to his one. "You and I have already had words, Miss Benari," he said, hating the bitterness in his own voice. "Several, if I remember correctly."

"Price, wait a minute, please."

Her hand resting lightly on his arm was enough to bring him to a halt. It didn't take much where she was concerned, he noted wryly.

"What?" he snapped.

She looked up and down the busy hallway full of cleaning carts, and patients on gurneys and in wheelchairs. "Could we go somewhere . . . private?"

What was it about the word *private* that

made his blood pressure rise several notches? He studied her face, trying to read her intentions. Was she just going to pick another fight with him? Or had he been the instigator of their quarrels? With Carla staring up at him that way, he couldn't be sure of anything.

Was that a warm light glowing in her amber eyes? It looked like—no, it couldn't be. Surely she hadn't had a change of heart.

"So, you want to be alone with me, huh?" he asked pointedly. "That *is* what you said, isn't it?"

She nodded.

Okay, she was asking for it, and he knew just the spot. "Come along, Miss Benari. I know the perfect place where you and I can be alone."

Carla caught her breath. "Price, this is lovely," she said as she looked around the solarium. Moonbeams streamed through the overhead glass, bathing the room in silver splendor. Ferns, philodendrons, and creeping Charlies surrendered their rich verdant coloring to the muted pastel of the moonlight.

"Haven't you ever been here before?" he asked, leading her to the glass wall that offered a panoramic view of the town and the glistening ribbon of river that twisted and turned through its center.

"I was here once, in the daytime. But it's beautiful at night."

"You wanted . . . privacy," he said.

His voice was deep and husky, sending a chill over her. He was acting strangely, looking at her with an intensity that frightened and thrilled her at the same time.

Carla had known more than her share of men; an entertainer's life was hardly a sheltered one. But she had never met a man who affected her the way that Price Trainor did.

He stepped even closer to her, filling her senses with his masculine presence. "So, now that you have me all to yourself," he murmured, "what are you going to do with me?"

What indeed? she wondered. She had the distinct feeling that with Price Trainor she was taking on more than she could handle. The very thought of handling this man made her weak all over.

She still burned from the heat of that one kiss he had given her after the Christmas party. Did she dare risk stirring those embers again?

She remembered something that Sadie had told her once, a quote from the Bible about taking fire to your bosom and being burned by it.

His hand reached up, and he lightly fingered the golden loop of her earring. "What do you want from me, Carla?" he asked, the moonlight reflected in his dark eyes. "Do you even know yourself?"

Oh, yes, she knew. She wanted to embrace that forbidden fire and let it melt away the ice that had encased her heart for so long.

His fingertips trailed down her neck and along the delicate gold chain around her throat. She could feel the tension radiating from him as he kept his emotions and desires tightly reined. What if he let go of those restraints?

"Price, I'm afraid," she whispered.

"Afraid? What are you afraid of, Carla?"

His fingers glided along her cheek and down to her chin. She wondered if he could feel her trembling.

"You're not afraid of me, are you?" he asked gently. When she didn't reply, he gathered her into his arms. His hands moved restlessly over the back of her fluffy sweater. His lips were close to her ear. "Don't be afraid of me, Carla. Don't ever be afraid of me."

Softly his lips grazed her cheek, then lingered there for a kiss.

She allowed her hands to roam across his broad shoulders, feeling the hardness of his rounded muscles. The heat from his body filtered through the crisp cotton of his shirt, warming her palm.

At her response, he pressed her body even more tightly against his. "What are we going to do, Carla?" he said, his moist breath fanning her cheek.

She pulled back slightly until she could look up into his face. His lips were so full and sensuous . . . and so near to hers.

"Why don't you kiss me?" she breathed. "And we'll take it from there."

He didn't wait to be asked twice. In a heartbeat his mouth had covered hers, taken hers with all the passion she had anticipated. She floated away, lost in the kiss she had dreamed about but never experienced.

She felt herself melting into him, melding her own desires with his and feeling them multiply tenfold.

When he finally broke the kiss, he buried his face in her hair and sighed. "I'm scared, too, Carla," he said, still holding her tightly against him.

"You? But why?" she asked.

"Because I've never been in love with a white woman before. I've been attracted to a few, but I always thought that life was complicated enough without borrowing trouble." She felt him draw a deep, shuddering breath. "But the first time I saw you, Carla, the first time I touched you . . ."

"I know," she said. "Me, too."

His hands slid up her back to her shoulders. He grasped her firmly, looking intently into her eyes. "But I don't care," he said. "Black or white—it doesn't matter to me.

Tell me that it doesn't matter to you, either, Carla. I need to hear you say it."

"It doesn't," she said, returning his steady gaze. "Not at all."

He kissed her again, but this time she couldn't respond fully. How could she when this lie was still between them?

"What's wrong, Carla?"

She wrapped her arms around his waist. Maybe if she just held him tight enough . . .

"There's something I have to tell you, Price," she said. "My name isn't Benari. It's Gray."

He shrugged and looked down at her quizzically. "So? You have a stage name. What's the big deal?"

"I'm not Italian, Price. My father was white, and my mother is black. I'm mulatto."

She watched helplessly as he wrestled with her words, trying to comprehend them.

"You're . . . you're black?" He pulled away from her; her grip hadn't been tight enough after all. "Do you mean that all this time you let me think that you hated me because I'm black, you were—"

"Yes. Don't you see? It isn't *your* color that I have a problem with. It's my feelings about my own color that I've never resolved."

He nodded as though understanding at last. "I see. You're ashamed of being black."

"No, not ashamed. Confused. I've never felt a part of either world. Please understand, Price."

"I understand." His dark eyes flashed with anger in the moonlight. "You're some kind of chameleon who changes color when it suits you."

Her own temper flared, and she felt her face grow hot. "How dare you judge me!" she exclaimed. "You're black. I'm black *and* white. I'm both . . . but I'm neither."

She tried to swallow her tears, but they wouldn't be held back. "You can't possibly know my pain, or understand how I feel."

He didn't speak for a long time, and when he did, his voice was tempered with compassion. "That's true. I can't understand. I could never pretend to be Italian; anyone who looks at me knows that I'm black. But even if I could change the color of my skin, I wouldn't. I'm black, and I'm damned proud of it."

When she blinked away her tears and looked up at him, she saw the dignity shining in his eyes, the determination in his stance. Everything about Price Trainor spoke of his pride in his heritage, his confidence in himself.

"I envy you," she said.

"Carla . . ." He reached out and tenderly brushed the tears away from her cheeks. "If you want to be white, be white. If you want to be black, be black. Or be mulatto. But don't try to be something that you aren't. If you keep lying to yourself and to everyone else, someday you'll look in the mirror, and you won't know who the hell you are."

He turned and walked away, leaving her standing there, alone in the moonlight.

She felt the tears welling up again, and this time she allowed them to fall freely.

"You're wrong, Price Trainor," she whispered to the empty room. "How could I forget who I am . . . when I've never known?"

Victor Lord lifted the heavy French dueling pistol, took careful aim, and pulled the trigger. A sadistic smile crossed his handsome face, accentuating the deep lines on either side of his mouth. "You're dead, you bloody devil," he said as he lowered the pistol.

The Bengal tiger didn't even flinch; he just stared back at his nemesis with golden eyes glimmering and fangs bared in a perpetual snarl.

The tiger and the other mounted trophies that lined the walls of Victor Lord's study had long passed the point of fighting back. Few of them had ever seen the Great White Hunter who had slain them. One minute they had been roaming the plains of the Serengeti or the jungles of Peru, and the next they had been in the hands of Lord's favorite taxidermist.

Victor settled back in his leather chair and resumed cleaning the antique pistol. This specimen was one of the treasures of his collection, and no one was allowed to touch it besides himself. With a reverence that he seldom displayed with anyone or anything else, he carefully polished the gold inlaid sideplates and the ivory handle. His long slender fingers caressed the ten-inch engraved barrel with a tenderness never shown to a woman.

Beautiful, ornate, and deadly, the pistol was Victor Lord's idea of perfection.

He heard the front door close, and he wondered briefly who it was. Surely Victoria wouldn't dare to show her face after that ridiculous phone call. What had gotten into that child lately? She had always been so obedient, so pliable. He was going to have to take a firm hand with her.

Never let a woman, a child, or an animal get the upper hand, his father had always told him. *Once you lose control over an inferior, it's much more difficult to keep them in line.*

And Victor Lord had always found that to be solid advice. He had never given an inch, and he had never regretted it. He was older and wiser than his daughters, and he knew what was best for them. Victoria had better remember that, or he would certainly remind her.

He watched the doorway of his study, which, like the library, opened onto the foyer. He always left the door ajar, so that he could keep track of his daughters' comings and goings.

When Victoria appeared in the doorway, he was mildly surprised.

"So, it *is* you," he said, returning his attention to the pistol. "You have a lot of nerve, showing yourself around here."

She walked directly into the study without waiting to be invited—another departure from a lifelong habit. "I thought we should continue our little conversation, Victor," she said, her hands on her hips and her feet splayed in an entirely unladylike posture.

His heavy brows knit together over gray eyes that flickered with indignation. "How dare you address me by my given name, young lady. I am your father, and you'd do well to remember that."

She cocked her head to one side and studied him intently. "I'm not your daughter," she said. "My name is Nicole Smith. You remember me, Victor. I'm a ghost from your past . . . long past."

He laid the pistol carefully in its velvet-lined case and set the polishing cloth aside. "Victoria, I have had quite enough of this. I don't know what kind of game you're playing here, but—"

"Don't call me Victoria!" she screamed, her face flushing bright red. Her fists were clenched tightly at her sides, her blue eyes blazing.

Victor stared at her wordlessly. What the devil was wrong with her? He had never seen her like this before. She had never dared to raise her voice to him, let alone screech like a banshee.

He rose slowly and crossed the room to stand a safe five feet away from her. "Victo—" He bit his tongue and tried again. "What is wrong with you?" he asked, unable to keep the distress out of his voice. "Have you gone mad?"

She laughed, but it wasn't Viki's soft, gentle laughter. It was a coarse, harsh sound that grated on his already strained nerves. "That's your answer to everyone who defies you, isn't it, Victor Lord? Anytime anyone goes against your wishes, you accuse them of being mentally unbalanced. Well, maybe it's time that someone stood up to you and showed a bit of sanity for a change."

As he took a step closer to her, he entertained the thought of slapping or shaking her. But something in this young woman's blue eyes told him that she would never allow him to lay a hand on her. And he wasn't ready to have a full-blown altercation with his grown daughter . . . not just yet.

"Victoria, if you continue speaking to me in this manner, I will seriously consider having you . . . looked at by a professional."

"Do you mean a shrink, Victor? I thought you hated psychiatrists, called them quacks and charlatans, if I remember correctly."

Lord recalled having expressed that opinion not long ago to Victoria when she had asked to see a counselor. Maybe he should have considered her request more seriously. If this was what it had led to . . .

"Victoria, I—"

"I told you not to call me that!" she cried, her shrill voice bouncing off the paneled walls of the study. Her eyes were wild, insane.

Victor recoiled from this stranger who had taken possession of his daughter's body; he had always had an inherent fear of the insane. They couldn't be reasoned with, couldn't be controlled.

"You must calm yourself," he said as gently as possible. "I promise not to call you—that name again, if you will only try to get hold of yourself. If you don't I'll be forced to call for medical assistance. And I'm sure that you wouldn't want to find yourself committed."

"You wouldn't dare," she said through clenched teeth. "Because if you commit me,

Victor Lord, I'll tell the world your nasty little secret. I'll tell them all how you killed your wife!"

Meredith heard them the moment she opened the front door and stepped into the foyer. Their angry voices echoed through the mansion, disturbing its gracious tranquility.

She had heard her father's voice raised in anger many times, but she had never heard her sister like this. Victoria's voice frightened her, chilled her with its shrill note of hysteria. What on earth was happening?

After tossing her purse onto a small table beside the door, she hurried to the opened door of her father's study and looked inside.

They stood, facing each other, eye to eye and toe to toe like a couple of heavyweights squaring off for a championship bout.

That was when she heard it—that one sentence which sent her world spinning out of its orbit.

"What did you say?" she asked, her voice trembling, the rush of adrenaline already hitting her system.

They both turned to stare at her. Her father's face was a deathly shade of white, her sister's bright red.

"Meredith," he said, "something is terribly wrong with Victoria. Go call Dr. Polk immediately."

Meredith looked from Victoria to her father and back again. "What did you mean, Viki?" she asked. "Why did you say that he killed our mother?"

"Ask him," Victoria said, glaring at Victor. "Ask him to tell you the truth about the night she died. Ask him why he even married Eugenia in the first place."

Meredith stepped into the room, her eyes on Lord. "What is she talking about, Father? Why did you marry Mother?"

When Lord didn't reply, Victoria answered for him. "He married her for her money. He didn't love her; he never did."

"Shut up, Victoria," he snapped. But she ignored him.

"Eugenia was a lonely, miserable woman, Meredith," she continued. "She had to find love outside her marriage, didn't she, Victor?"

The room was heavy with silence broken only by Victor's labored breathing. Meredith watched as a muscle twitched in his square jaw and his eyes narrowed with barely suppressed rage.

Victoria was studying him with her head tilted sideways and one delicate eyebrow cocked. "You still can't bear to think about it, can you, Victor?" she chided him. *"Your* wife in the arms of another man. Carrying another man's child."

Meredith felt the floor sway beneath her

feet. "Another man's child? What are you talking about?"

"I'm talking about you, Meredith," Victoria replied with a self-satisfied smile. "At least you can take comfort in the fact that this coldhearted creature isn't really your father."

"Not my father?" Meredith's eyes sought Victor's, but for the first time in her life, he wouldn't meet her gaze. "What do you mean . . . not my father?"

Victoria walked over to Meredith and laid her hand on her shoulder. "Don't feel too bad, Meredith. Eugenia loved your father deeply. In fact, she was trying to run to him when *he* killed her."

She pointed an accusing finger at Lord. "Eugenia was pregnant with you, and she was trying to run away with the man she loved, your father. But Victor caught her sneaking down the staircase with her suitcase and Victoria."

"That's enough," Victor roared. "Meredith, go call the doctor. You can see that your sister is insane."

Yes, she did look insane. And the things Viki was saying—talking about herself as though she were a third person. But Meredith couldn't run away; she had to hear the rest. "How did she die?" she asked. "How did my mother really die?"

Viki cast a triumphant look at Lord. "He struggled with her there on the staircase, pulling on Victoria's hand, a sort of tug-of-war with a child instead of a rope. Victoria was scared out of her mind. That was when I, Nicole, had to take over. While they were fighting Eugenia lost her balance. She fell down the staircase and hit her head."

"But the baby?" Meredith gasped. "She was pregnant . . ."

"She went into premature labor that night because of the fall, and she had you. But she didn't die in childbirth the way he told you. She died because of the injury to her head—a subdural hematoma."

Meredith shook her head, refusing to believe what she had heard. It was too much —too much to hear, too much to believe all at once. "No. It can't be true."

"It isn't true!" Victor shouted. "She's lying. Can't you see that?"

Meredith could see that something was wrong with Victoria, very wrong. But it was Victor's face that told her he was the one who was lying. She had never seen her father frightened before, and he was terrified.

It was true. Everything Victoria had said was true.

Meredith felt something crumble inside her. The image of who she was, who her mother had been, was gone. And this man who stood before her, this man who had bullied her, tormented her, and provided every luxury for her . . . even he wasn't who she had thought he was. Victor Lord wasn't her father.

It was all too much.

She covered her face with her hands and ran blindly into the foyer, into Larry Wolek's arms.

"Merrie, I just got here. What is it, honey?" he said, holding her trembling body against his.

"Larry, something's wrong with Viki, and Father—Oh, God—he isn't my father."

Larry placed his hands on either side of her face. "What are you talking about?" he asked. "What's going on here?"

"In there"—she pointed toward the study door—"Viki and Victor, they were fighting and—"

A blast ripped through the mansion, shaking it to its very foundations. Meredith screamed and clung to Larry.

"What the hell?" he exclaimed as the reverberations echoed through the house.

He pushed Meredith away from him and ran to the study door. The pungent smell of gunpowder filled the room.

Merrie joined him in the doorway and screamed again.

Lying on the floor was Victor Lord, a dark ugly hole in the side of his head. Blood poured from the wound onto the oriental rug beneath him, staining its hand-knotted, white threads a dark red.

Victoria stood over him, an antique French dueling pistol in her hand. Smoke curled from its ten-inch engraved barrel.

She stared at them uncomprehendingly, then down at her father and the pistol in her hand. "Oh, no," she whispered. "What happened? What's wrong with Father?"

LLANVIEW

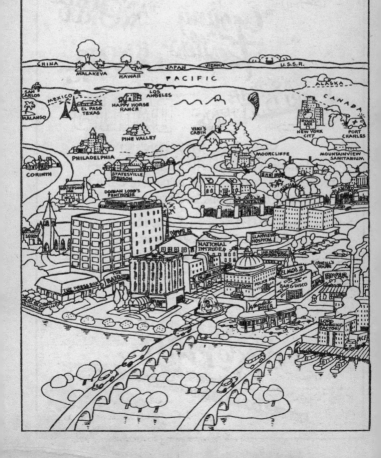

Don't miss the next
— SOAPS & SERIALS® —
novelizations of:

Guiding Light

DAYS OF OUR LIVES

The Young and the Restless

ANOTHER WORLD

KNOTS LANDING™

AS THE WORLD TURNS

DALLAS™

SPECIAL MOMENTS!
Follow your favorite characters from
month to month as they experience the trials
and tribulations of love and life.

HIDDEN SECRETS!
Discover the past—how it all
began when your favorite soap opera started.

KEEPSAKES!
Collect the entire series!

Soaps & Serials®

Exclusively from
PIONEER COMMUNICATIONS NETWORK, INC.

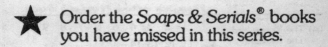

You can now order previous titles
of *Soaps & Serials*® Books by Mail!

Just complete the order form, detach, and send together
with your check or money order payable to:

Soaps & Serials®
120 Brighton Road, Box 5201, Clifton, NJ 07015-5201

Please circle the book #'s you wish to order:

(A) The Young and The Restless	1 2 3 4 5 6 7 8 9 10 11 12 13 14
(B) Days of Our Lives	1 2 3 4 5 6 7 8 9 10 11 12 13 14
(C) Guiding Light	1 2 3 4 5 6 7 8 9 10 11 12 13 14
(D) Another World	1 2 3 4 5 6 7 8 9 10 11 12 13 14
(E) As The World Turns	1 2 3 4 5 6 7 8 9 10 11 12 13 14
(F) Dallas™	1 2 3 4 5 6 7 8 9 10 11 12 13 14
(G) Knots Landing™	1 2 3 4 5 6 7 8 9 10 11 12 13 14

Each book is $2.50 ($3.50 in Canada).
Total number of books
circled_____ × price above = $ _____

Sales tax (CT and NY residents only) $ _____

Shipping and Handling $ _____ .95

Total payment enclosed $ _____
(check or money orders only)

Name_____

Address _____ Apt# _____

City _____ State _____ Zip _____

Telephone (_____)_____
     AREA CODE

'We think you're special'

ABC wants to get better acquainted with you.

If you would like to be on our preferred mailing list, please send the following information on a postcard or fill out the coupon below and send to:

 ABC AUDIENCE INFORMATION—SOAPS
1330 Avenue of the Americas
New York, New York 10019

✄ -

Name _____

Street _____ Apt. No. _____

City _____ State _____ Zip _____

Telephone (   ) _____

Circle the ABC Daytime Dramas you regularly watch:

☐ LOVING   ☐ ONE LIFE TO LIVE
☐ RYAN'S HOPE   ☐ GENERAL HOSPITAL
☐ ALL MY CHILDREN